BAD

Romance

Compiled & Edited by
Ben Thomas & D Kershaw

Also available from Black Hare Press

DARK DRABBLES ANTHOLOGIES

WORLDS
ANGELS
MONSTERS
BEYOND
UNRAVEL
APOCALYPSE
LOVE
HATE
OCEANS
ANCIENTS

BHP WRITERS' GROUP SPECIAL EDITIONS

STORMING AREA 51
EERIE CHRISTMAS
BAD ROMANCE

OTHER VOLUMES

DEEP SEA
WHAT IF?
KEY TO THE KINGDOM
BEYOND THE REALM

Twitter: @BlackHarePress
Facebook: BlackHarePress
Website: www.BlackHarePress.com

Bad Romance Anthology title is
Copyright © 2020 Black Hare Press
First published in Australia in January 2020 by Black Hare Press

The authors of the individual stories retain the copyright of the works featured in this anthology.

All characters and events in this publication, other than those clearly in the public domain, are fictitious and any resemblance to real persons, living or dead, is purely coincidental.

All rights reserved. No part of this production may be reproduced, stored in a retrieval system, or transmitted, in any form or by any means, electronic, mechanical, photocopying, recording or otherwise, without the prior permission of the publisher and copyright owner.

Paperback : ISBN 978-1-925809-45-9
Hardcover : ISBN 978-1-925809-46-6

Cover Design by Dawn Burdett
Book Formatting by Ben Thomas

(W)ere you but lying cold and dead,
And lights were paling out of the West,
You would come hither, and bend your head,
And I would lay my head on your breast;
And you would murmur tender words,
Forgiving me, because you were dead:
Nor would you rise and hasten away,
Though you have the will of wild birds,
But know your hair was bound and wound
About the stars and moon and sun:
O would, beloved, that you lay
Under the dock-leaves in the ground,
While lights were paling one by one.

He Wishes His Beloved Were Dead **by William Butler Yeats, 1899**

Table of Contents

Foreword

We've all heard the beautiful romance stories with the 'fairytale endings,' the ones where 'true love was here all along,' the 'they lived happily ever after' yarns.

The stories in this collection aren't those stories.

These stories are toxic, vengeful, chaotic, twisted…and often bloody.

Maybe a text to end a relationship goes south. Maybe you're slowly beginning to fall in love, but you're being manipulated without you even noticing. Maybe you are in love with someone who enjoys the pain as much as you.

So, sit back, get comfortable, and remember: some love is nothing more than bad romance.

C.L. Williams

Beneath the Blue Irises

by J.M. Ames

I've written you more times than I can count, every letter crumpled and tossed in the general direction of the wastebasket in the corner. There's no point in sending them when they all boil down to "I'm sorry, I miss you." If reading those words gouges holes in your heart anywhere near as deep as the wounds writing them ripped into mine, sending these letters would be just another selfish act on my part. I think you've had enough of those.

Reminders of you are everywhere, eviscerating me when I least expect it—your smiling freckled face framed by bright-red curls greeting me from my phone;

the Azure Bearded Irises sprouting in the garden, their petals as enchanting as the deep-blue irises of your eyes and the beautiful mind that lies beneath them. Our song "Bad Romance" comes on the radio, and immediately there is a lump of hot coal in my throat that somehow manages to blur my vision. I still want your drama and the touch of your hand. I still want your love.

Every night I dream that you are still here, and it takes a few moments after I wake up for the agonizing reality to set in. My arms aren't wrapped around you, protecting you from the thunder outside; they're wrapped around a pillow.

I'll never be able to hug you like that again. To hold you tight and kiss the top of your head, breathe in your sweet scent, feel the soft kisses of your full lips on my skin. You're gone. Now I have to live with the horrible knowledge that I am the one who made this so. All because I momentarily thought that maybe I could have happiness once again.

I am not at all the person you think—or at least thought—I am. It's become clear to me that I am a horrible man—really not a man at all. Years of dark emptiness have ravaged my soul. I'd forgotten what love felt like, both in giving and receiving. I didn't recognise its presence until I was completely engulfed in its fire, and by then there was no stopping the flames. Now the cinders smoulder away, eternally burning up every last bit of me from the inside, with none of your oxygen left to fan the blaze.

You don't deserve what I did to you. You've had more than enough pain in your life without my contribution. Don't you see? You made me happier than I had been in a long time. You deserve to be someone's everything, their queen. More than you'll ever know, I wish you could've been mine. But I can't give you what you want, need, and deserve.

So, now I sit here on the back porch, sipping my coffee, watching the sunrise and listening to the birds sing their morning chorus. A young rabbit that lives in the Jasmine along the wall scurries across the untended lawn in the direction of the overgrown flower garden. The cat is curled up on my lap, purring softly as I absent-mindedly stroke her fur. I wonder what you would be doing right now. Would you be in as much agony as I? I hope not, but it doesn't matter now, does it? I know I shattered your heart and mind, and in doing so, myself. I wish I could have helped you put the pieces back together, but with me around, they never would have stuck. I don't even know how to repair myself.

"Daddy, can I come sit with you?"

"Sure, *jefe*. I didn't even know you were up." I force a smile and make room on the bench for the precocious six-year-old boy I am lucky to call Son—*Hijo*.

"Why do you look sad, Daddy? Is it 'cause of auntie's blood cancer? Mommy says we can go see her next weekend. Can you come this time?"

"Yup, just thinking of your *tia*." I lie, clapping Carlos on the shoulder. "Sure I can go with you guys. Hey, your old papa needs *más café*. Take Sue. Want me to bring you back some juice?"

I put the cat on his lap and stand up, stretching.

"Grapefruit, please," he says with a grin too big for his face.

I tousle his oak-brown hair. "You are one *niño extraño*, you know that? I'll only be a second."

In the kitchen, I pour myself another mug of ebony lifeblood, savouring the rich earthy aroma that rises with the steam. I open the fridge and retrieve the juice. When I close the door, I'm greeted by an all-too-familiar pair of cold, blue-steel eyes above a slightly down-turned thin-lipped mouth.

"You left the couch a mess," she says.

"Yeah, I just got up. I'll get it in a bit."

The plastic cup comes down hard on the counter,

visibly startling her. With a deep, measured breath, I pour the juice, all too aware of her scowling gaze. My jaw tightens.

"What is your issue lately?" Her arms are crossed, her right index finger tapping her left elbow as it always does when the bomb is about to explode.

"Do I need to state the obvious, just so you can keep ignoring it? You know our issues; you just refuse to acknowledge them. You always have. I'm done fighting a one-way battle."

The juice goes back in the fridge with more force than required. My eyes close, and I take another deep breath.

"Carlos wants me to come with you guys to see your sister. I'm going."

"I think she would like that. Thank you."

The sharp edge of her iciness melts a little, and she tucks her straight black hair behind her ear.

I nod and step onto the back porch. The iris patch glows cerulean in the morning sun. It seems to be thriving since I planted it over your broken and bloody body that night—the night you showed up at our door with that shotgun and tried to remove what you perceived as the barriers between us. Perhaps those flowers bring you the peace I never could. At least I still have you close to me.

I hand Carlos his juice and settle on the bench next to him. Sue stands up, stretches, yawns, then collapses onto her side and curls into a ball, eyes tight, front paws opening and closing. Her throat rumbles like a distant engine. I wonder at such a carefree existence.

My arm slides around Carlos's shoulders, pulling him closer. At least I've still got him, the most important person in my life. The one and only being I would do anything for.

Even this.

Love Potion

by Joel R. Hunt

He stormed into the witch's cottage, hurling an empty flask onto the floor.

"You killed her!" he screamed.

"You knew what my potion would do when you bought it," said the witch.

"You told me it was a love potion! You said it would make her—"

"Love you and only you," finished the witch, "It worked, didn't it? She couldn't bring herself to love any other human for the rest of her life."

The man fell to his knees and stared at the hands that had taken down her hanging body only hours before.

"Not even herself," he whispered.

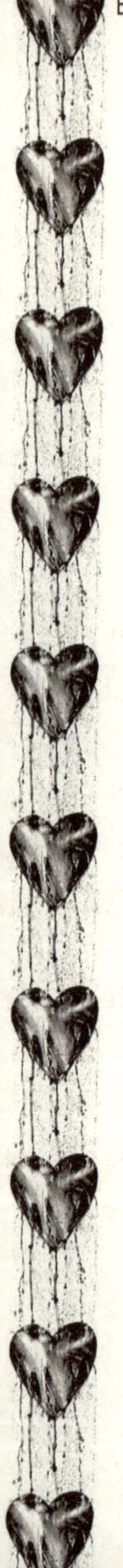

Hillbilly Necromancer: A Love Story

By Shelly Jarvis

Johnny P. Nash was waist deep in grave dirt for the second time in a week. He leaned over his shovel and took a deep, unsteady breath. The misty air was cold, burning his lungs as he gulped it in.

He felt old. In truth, he was only in his early forties; but the years were long, many of them unkind, and forty-three was feeling like a ripe old age to his bones. He was certainly too old to be digging up bodies in the middle of the night.

Johnny took a swig of piss-whiskey—moonshine made by the finest distiller in Logan County—and coughed until he hacked up a thick wet loogey. He sighed and dipped his shovel into the dirt again.

Hasn't always been like this, he thought.

And it hadn't. Once he had owned the largest Necromancy centre in all of southern West Virginia. Clients as far as Morgantown, down past Pikeville, and even the fancy coal barons living like kings in Charleston, had sought his help.

Now, though, he served the eccentric widow or grieving father for pennies on the dollars he used to make. He took his pay in homemade biscuits or pepperoni rolls, a ride to town when his truck broke down, an invitation to hear some down-home Bluegrass at the park.

Johnny spat, puckering up his lips. He always felt sour when he was digging up the dead. Maybe that was the only way you could feel.

His shovel clanged against something below. He scraped against the dirt, freeing up the edge of the coffin. Johnny dropped to his knees and began scooting the dirt away from the opening. When it was clear, he opened the casket and stared down at the young man within.

Most of him was still there, certainly enough to revive for a night out on the town. But in all fairness, Johnny could bring them back with only a bag of bones. He was good—damn good—and no dead body was going to best him.

He stood up, stretched his aching muscles, and pulled his toolbox towards the hole. Johnny withdrew his tools: two bottles with liquids in them, an eyedropper, a Ziploc baggie full of shiny black powder, and a spray can of axe body spray. Many a client had trouble with the smell of a decomposing body, so Johnny had taken to bringing the spray along to help mask the decay with something only slight less offensive.

He lined his items in a neat row along the side of the grave (he'd always believed that ninety percent of being a good Necromancer was organisation) and proceeded to voodoo the life back into—he looked up at the tombstone, then confirmed the name written in sharpie on his dirty left hand—Mikey Bowyer. Johnny smiled. At least the names matched this time.

He waited.

Sometimes the dead weren't too happy about being brought back to life, so Johnny always stayed until he saw that they were behaving. His will over them would hold for a while, at least a few days, but he liked to tell his customers it was a one night only affair. It helped them let their loved ones go a little easier or left those wanting to see them longer more willing to pay for the extra time.

The Bowyer boy twitched. About time. Johnny hoped to get a few hours' sleep before the sun came up. The body began to move in the coffin and after a moment he sat up.

"Howdy kid, I'm Johnny P. Nash. I just raised you from the dead, and I'm your master. Any questions?"

"Braaaaaaains," the boy said.

Johnny took a step back. Well, that was odd. He hadn't turned someone into a zombie since that little boy in '94. What a fucking mess that was.

"BRAAAAAAAINS," Mikey said, climbing up from the casket and reaching towards Johnny.

"Guess I'll be sending you back then. No zombies on my watch."

The boy's arms dropped, and he stopped his forward motion. "Oh gosh, Mr. Nash, don't send me back yet. I'd like to visit Maw before I'm dead again."

"Well, what's with all the 'braaaains' bullshit?" Johnny asked, raising his hands to imitate the boy.

Mikey shrugged. "I just thought it'd be funny. Like a movie, you know?"

Johnny shook his head with a sigh. "Don't pull a stunt like that when you're in town or people gonna fuck you up worse."

"I'm dead," the boy said. "How can I get worse?"

Johnny scoffed. "You're dead, but you ain't *dead*. Trust me, you don't wanna find out the difference. Now go on, scramble over to ya maw's house. She'll be expecting you for breakfast."

The boy climbed up the pile of dirt and trudged away. Johnny sat down on the edge of the grave, swinging his legs back and forth as he took a drag off his cigarette. Fucking kids with their zombie movies. Necromancers get no respect these days.

When Johnny's phone rang on Thursday morning, he didn't answer. He was tired. Too tired to deal with the annoying little shit he'd taken on as his apprentice Necromancer.

The phone chirped from the nightstand. He silenced it.

It rang a third time. Johnny huffed and shook his head. He probably hadn't taught the kid enough to cause too much trouble if he fired him now.

Johnny flipped his phone open and asked, "What now?"

"S-sorry to bother you, Mr. Nash, but there's a lady here to see you."

Johnny sighed. "I don't have any clients today, Eric. And I'm not taking any."

"Yes sir, I told her that."

"And?"

"And she still won't leave. She said she's an old friend of yours and she can't go without seeing you."

Johnny furled his brows. He didn't have any friends, old or new, and he shouldn't have a client until tomorrow. "What's 'er name?"

Eric mumbled to the lady for a few seconds, then said, "Trixie West."

Johnny dropped the phone.

He hurriedly picked it up and said, "Tell her I'll be right there."

Johnny stood in front of the bathroom mirror, trying to force his moustache to stay down. His mind raced with questions. Why was she here, today? What did she remember? Where had she been since he'd last seen her?

It did no good to speculate. He'd find out soon enough.

He threw his underwear in the corner and pulled out some almost-clean ones from the pile of clothes in front of the chest of drawers. Rifling through the pile, he found a tank top and his best cut-off jeans. Johnny considered wearing them, but no, Trixie's visit was far too important. He wanted to look nice for her.

He turned to the closet and pulled the broken chain, sending the bulb above swinging light and shadows through the tiny space. He reached into the far corner and withdrew his lone button up. Black, of course, in remembrance of the greatest man to ever live—Johnny Cash. He put it on over his faded black Levi's while he toyed with the idea of a bolo.

"Too fancy," he mumbled.

Johnny picked up the raggedy Stetson from the top shelf. His papaw left him that hat, but dust and moths had taken a liking to it and left it worse for wear. Shaking his head, he swapped his Stetson for his lucky Sunoco hat and headed outside.

He glanced at the tarp in the yard that covered his '83 Camaro. He'd give his left nut to be able to get that baby restored. But his nuts didn't seem to be worth much these days, so the old pickup would have to do.

Johnny climbed into his truck and headed towards town. His mind wandered back to the times when he had a handful of vehicles to get around in. In the beginning, there was a surprising amount of money to be had in necromancy, if you knew where to look.

And Johnny did know where to look: Logan County, West Virginia. He'd lived there all his life and understood the way people thought. His mama always said people were people no matter where you went, but Johnny didn't bother going. He figured if people were the same everywhere, he might as well stay where he was.

Johnny flicked his cigarette out the window just as he passed the entrance to Midelburg. He'd had a fine house in the rich part of town, neighbours who feared him and left him alone, and a steady income from *Nash's Necromancy.*

It had been a curiosity in the community, and a bit of a joke, for the first few months. Johnny hung posters and went door-to-door offering his services; he was asked to leave countless funerals, though he was volunteering his amenities pro bono to get the word out. No matter what he did, no one seemed to take him seriously.

That is, until he had his first customer. She was a young widow, just a wisp of a girl, and she wanted to see her dead husband. Johnny eagerly called the dead man's spirit up for the girl, and she eagerly cussed the spirit until Johnny's nose was bleeding from the effort of holding the girl back.

After the young woman told everyone she knew about getting her peace from *Nash's Necromancy*, Johnny couldn't walk down the street without someone asking him to call up a long-dead relative. He'd gone from scraps for dinner—when there was dinner—to country-fried steak as often as he wanted.

Then the lawsuits came. People upset about Johnny disturbing the natural order of things. He'd found comfort in drink, in trying to turn his fortune through the crank slots at Betty's Place. The big money dried up, leaving Johnny to feast on spam and saltines.

He climbed down from his truck and stood in front of the shop window. It was a great location—centre of town, right on the corner—and the owner was kind enough to let him use a booth for business so long as he bought a cup of coffee. Expensive shit, café o'lay or some dumb name, but it was worth it to keep a little money in his pocket.

Trixie stood in Hot Cup with her back to him, but

even now he could feel butterflies tumbling in his belly at the sight of her. He remembered the first time he'd seen her on the playground when they were in the third grade. She was the prettiest thing he'd ever laid eyes on. Granted, he was only nine and his eyes hadn't seen much, but he knew what he knew—and what he knew was he was in love with Trixie West.

That day on the playground, he'd decided to find a way to impress her, and he knew exactly what to do: he was gonna show her how far he could spit. She was not impressed. Johnny was sure she would've been, if only the wind hadn't caught his loogey and blew it right into her hair.

He went through all the best tactics in the next few years, but no matter what he did, she seemed immune to his charms. He tried making her mud pies, showing her his new frog, bringing her flowers from Mrs. Pomeroy's front yard, and making her a friendship bracelet with a little cross charm. She would smile and thank him, all sweetness and civility, but nothing more.

The day came when Johnny couldn't take it anymore. He was going to tell her straight out that he loved her. He went to her mom's trailer and knocked. Mrs. West called Trixie for him. When she waddled towards the door, Johnny felt his jaw drop. He knew she hadn't been at school for a while, and now he could see why. She couldn't hide that baby if she wanted to.

"I was worried since I ain't seen ya for a bit," he said, staring at her fine round belly. "And I wanted you to know that I missed you. Cause you know, I love you."

"You're sweet," she said, but her smile was sad. "You always were, Johnny Nash. I should've picked you."

Even in Johnny's memory, the door closing in his face was painful. It was the end of the future he had envisioned with Trixie, though the love he carried for her never stopped. When he opened the door to the coffee shop, he felt like that little boy on the playground, seeing her for the first time.

"Hey, Trixie," he said, pulling the hat from his head.

She smiled, sending those damn butterflies dancing through him. "Hiya, Johnny. You look good."

"You too," he said. He ran his hand over his own hair and said, "I like your hair like that."

She dipped her head in thanks before saying, "I was hoping to talk to you privately. About business."

Johnny looked around. Eric the apprentice was staring at the interaction, incapable of disguising his interest in the conversation. Johnny hooked his thumb over his shoulder and said, "Beat it, kid."

Eric scurried from their regular booth and Johnny motioned for Trixie to take his place. He pressed his lips together, trying to smile, but trying not to look like he was trying to smile. Johnny opened his mouth to speak, but the words didn't feel right. He'd been reading people for years with his business, learning from the tics each displayed, and he could easily see she was nervous. Better to wait for her to explain than say something stupid.

He ordered them each a cup of coffee (eight damn dollars!). She didn't drink it, but seemed grateful for something to fill her hands. When she sat the cup down, Johnny knew his cue to get down to business.

"What brings you in today, Miss West?"

She smiled. "You're not going to get formal on me, are you? We've known each other since we were kids."

Johnny nodded. "But you're here on business."

She cringed. Johnny could see she didn't like being there, didn't like what he did. She was there because she was desperate.

"Who died?" he asked, though he already knew. He'd seen it in the paper the day it happened. Broke his heart.

She watched her coffee, her lips slightly parted.

Johnny had seen it many times. She'd made it that far, but wasn't sure if she should continue. But he knew she would. People were people.

"My daughter, Josie."

She looked up at him then, her eyes asking what she couldn't.

"You want to talk to her? No problem."

Trixie placed her hand on his, her smile broadening. "That's great, Johnny. Real sweet of ya. But I was hopin' you could bring her back. Something…permanent."

Johnny inhaled sharply. The room felt tight around him.

"Trixie, I can't—" he said, pulling his hand away.

"Now don't you lie to me, Johnny P. Nash," she interrupted, all softness gone. "My cousin Rachel said you brought back her friend Bobbi Jean's baby when he died twelve years ago. I know you can do it."

Johnny swallowed. "Did she tell you what happened to the boy? To his mother?"

Trixie shook her head.

"Hell, your cousin might not've heard. I kept it pretty quiet. Most folks think they just moved away."

"Heard what?"

"The kid was okay at first, or at least we thought he

was. I kept tabs on him, just to make sure, you know?"

"Then what's the problem?"

Johnny's face scrunched up and he thought about not telling her, but she nodded her head for him to continue. "Bobbi Jean went in to feed him one day. She didn't need to, an' I told her that. Dead things don't eat. But she tried anyway. I guess the little bastard was done suckin' milk out of her tit and decided to try bitin' through it instead."

"Holy shit, Johnny."

He nodded. "Fucker wouldn't let go. She was trying so hard not to hurt him that she didn't pay attention to what he was doin' to her. She passed out from blood loss and the little shit ate her brains right out. And it was my fault."

"You don't know that for sure. Maybe there was just a problem with that one kid."

"Yes, I do know." Johnny bit his lip, trying to decide if he should tell her the thing he'd kept secret so many years. After a moment, he took a deep breath and said, "He wasn't the first."

"What are you talking about?"

"I brought back another kid, a few years before that boy. Same thing."

Trixie couldn't stop the tears. Johnny had been her

only chance.

"I can let you talk to her," he said. "I can even let her come back for a few days, but I can't make it last any longer than that or things get wonky inside them. I can't let the kid do that to you."

"She's the only good thing I ever had, Johnny."

"Come on, that can't be true," he said, moving his hand across the table towards hers.

"You don't fucking get it!" she screamed, pulling away her hand and slinging the coffee cup on the floor. "I have nothing. NOTHING. She was the only one I ever loved."

Johnny leaned back, his hand withdrawn, his heart aching for her. He understood.

Trixie spent the night.

Johnny wasn't surprised. She always did when she came looking for him. She never wanted to be alone after he told her he wouldn't bring her daughter back.

It had shocked him the first time. He'd looked on her body with reverence, a worshipper before his god. Now, he still loved her, enjoyed the nights he spent with her, but it was more a holiday than a holy day.

Johnny watched her as she dressed. She was always

shy the morning after. But of course she was. For her, this was the first time it had happened. She didn't have the memory to ease her nerves.

"I guess I should go," she said. "Unless—"

"Unless I changed my mind?"

She nodded, shrugged. She walked towards him, steeling herself to say the words she always said. "You could do this thing for me, and I could do some things for you. A body for a body."

He'd considered it the first time. But now there was no hesitation when he shook his head.

"I can't, Trixie."

She nodded. She was on the verge of tears, unable to speak. Johnny knew she would start crying if he didn't interrupt it now, so he did.

"There was another, Trix. One more person I didn't tell you about."

Her eyes found his, wide and excited, her hope igniting in her chest. "Did they, I mean, was it the same?"

Johnny shook his head. "Worse."

"Oh, Johnny, how could it be worse?"

He sighed. "When I heard you died, it broke me, Trix. I mean, I always loved you. Even when we were kids. Even when you didn't bother looking my way. So when I read your obituary, I had to do something. I wrote to the *American Institute of Necromantic Arts,* got them to agree to let me do a course by mail. It was hard, but I was motivated. Got my certification real quick, Trix, real quick for you.

"We talked first, your spirit and me. But it wasn't enough, when I knew I could do more. So I brought you back. You were my first. I didn't know what I was doing, so I didn't bind you well enough. I didn't know how to keep your need in check. You went back to your little girl and..." he trailed off.

Tears were rolling down her face. "This isn't funny, Johnny P. Nash. You stop it right now."

"I covered it up for you. Car accident. I put you down to rest, until I thought I was ready to try again. So I raised you from the dead a second time. It was better. You were under control. You started making a life for yourself. Then your memories started to surface about your girl, and you ended up coming to me. It was part of the controls I'd put in when I brought you back the second time. You come to me before you hurt somebody."

"This is cruel, Johnny. I never thought you'd be this cruel."

He stood and crossed the room. He picked up a

plain box sitting on his mantle. Dipping his index finger in the box, he began to trace shimmery black circles across his bare chest.

"I've tried so many times, Trix. Everything I know to do, I've done. But I keep trying. Monday night like clockwork, I raise you up. By Friday—Thursday this time, so maybe things are changing—the memories are back, well, at least partially; you know she's dead, but you don't remember doin' it. So I put you back in the grave and raise you again the following week, hopin' to get it right the next time."

Trixie was inching towards the door. Johnny flicked his wrist and she stopped, unable to move. He turned his hand, and as he did, Trixie's body rotated towards him.

"I can't bring her back, Trixie. Necromancy has rules. If one of the dead destroys a person, they can't live again."

Trixie's whole body was trembling. "You're sayin' my Josie is gone for good? And it's all because you couldn't let go of a schoolboy crush?"

Johnny pressed his lips together. He crossed the room and smeared a shimmering black thumb across her cheek.

"I love you, Trixie. I always have. I'm gonna help

you sleep now, and you're gonna forget all about this. We'll try again to get rid of those pesky memories."

"Don't you dare," she spat. "If you take away the last I have of my little girl, I'll never forgive you."

Johnny sighed and said, "I'll see you soon, babe."

"You'd better hope you never see me again, Johnny. Because I swear to you, I will find a way to kill you."

Johnny smiled. She always said that, every time. People are always people.

Johnny P. Nash was waist deep in grave dirt for the third time that week. He laid out his tools and began his work. He didn't need to check the name on the headstone this time; it was there inside him, written on his heart.

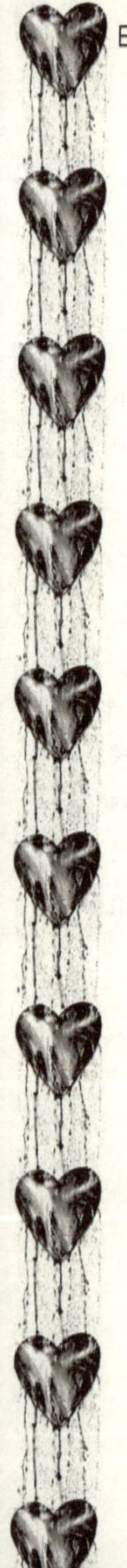

City of the Hungry Coyote

by Vonnie Winslow Crist

She chopped off the heads of her family. *Snip! Snip! Snip!* Then, Bellarosa Carrillo cut through her fiancée's neck. Humming a guitar tune she remembered Diego playing when they were children, Bella arranged the heads among a bouquet of sharp-beaked bird of paradise blooms.

She was precise in her placement, because she wanted a blossom cluster to frame each familiar face. Once she was satisfied with the arrangement of heads and flowers, a few quick strokes of a brush loaded with decoupage glue later, the collage was complete. Next, Bella rinsed out her brush, set her loved ones aside, and picked up another old greeting card.

In *Ciudad Nezahual-Coyotl*, the City of the Hungry Coyote, greeting cards were usually purchased from off-world peddlers, and quite expensive. Bella received more cards than anyone else in the city because Diego Sanchez thought of her on every holiday. She recycled them by gluing the card's front onto heavy paper and re-gifting, or by using the card in her collages.

Occasionally, neighbours would give her their old cards. It was her policy to utilise every scrap, so the odd bits which weren't right for collages were placed in warm water and whirred in her solar blender. Then, the resulting mixture was poured through paper-making screens.

With pressure, time, and patience, Bella had managed to supply The Hungry Coyote Emporium with handmade paper. But the Emporium, along with every other business in *Ciudad Nezahual-Coyotl*, had closed months ago. Bellarosa was the only remaining resident.

"You *must* leave," Diego had said last week when he'd visited. "Bella, I have waited nearly twenty-five years for you to become my wife. Now, is the time to marry me and come live in the Outlands."

"You're right," she'd responded. "I'll marry you in ten days' time."

In love with her since childhood, Diego had cried with joy. "Shall I come to pick you and your things up?" he'd asked.

"No, I'll say my goodbyes, then drive myself."

"It's no trouble. I—"

"I said, no," she'd replied, perhaps a little too forcefully. But Diego knew to never cross her.

He'd nodded, muttered, "Whatever you want, Bella, as long as you marry me."

She rolled her eyes. Diego Sanchez was a fool. A modestly well-to-do fool, but a fool nonetheless to pine for a woman who didn't love him as much as he loved her.

As she picked up another card, Bella sighed. She thought Domatilla's hazel eyes would look lovely peeking out from the purple cockscomb blooms that crawled across this card, but with time ticking away, so she decided to wait and clip off her half-sister's head next week. She pushed her chair away from the desk, stood, brushed the paper trimmings and who knew how many microbes off her lap and into a waiting bag. Next, she packed her collage materials into a suitcase and rolled it to the top of the cellar steps.

As she walked across the hand-braided rugs, Bella mentally checked off the tasks which had to be completed today. The list was long, but she had already packed most of the things she treasured, wheeled the items to her van, and neatly packed the vehicle.

She grunted as she stepped up into the kitchen and then crossed to the gas stove. Bella flicked on the back burner, went from stove to refrigerator, opened the squeaky door, and tugged out a casserole dish of cold baked beans and rice. Next, she took a gleaming butcher's knife from the one-handled drawer.

A thick slab of beans and rice on bread is just what I need, she thought. But before she could make a sandwich, the teapot began to sob. She reached over and twisted the knob on the stove counterclockwise. The blue flames popped and disappeared. After dumping some instant coffee and canned sweetened condensed milk into a stoneware mug, Bella added hot water from the kettle.

She dipped her forefinger into the mug to test the temperature, pulled it out quickly, and popped the slightly burned finger into her mouth. She'd always thought boiling water would kill all microorganisms, but she, like most Martians, had been wrong.

Bellarosa made quick work of slathering two slices of bread with spicy mustard, slicing the cold bean-rice mixture, and making her sandwich. She got a chipped plate down from the cupboard and placed the sandwich on it, along with a handful of popped popcorn and two pickle slices. As she ate lunch, Bella rocked back and forth and thought about the town.

Ciudad Nezahual-Coyotl had been founded by miners and their families over eight hundred years ago when Mars had first opened for settlement. People looking for a new beginning, and companies eager for big profits had arrived—full of hope and enthusiasm— on the partially terra-formed surface of the red planet. But indigenous viruses and bacteria, sloppy mining and agricultural practices which mutated fungi and protozoa, and plain old greed ended up making huge swaths of land uninhabitable. The City of the Hungry Coyote was smack dab in the middle of one such swath of poisoned ground. Even before the evictions, the town's population had dwindled. Mental disorders and diseases caused by pathogens apparently were the culprits.

Bella sneezed before stuffing the last of the sandwich in her mouth. Meal eaten, she finished her coffee and set the mug down with a loud clatter. She coughed, spitting some blood-tinged mucus into a tissue.

The tainted water I have been cooking with all my

life will probably kill me if an airborne organism doesn't, she concluded.

"No matter."

Shocked by the sound of her own voice, Bellarosa pushed up from the kitchen chair and strolled to the sunporch. Idly, she rotated the spinning wheel a few times before reaching for the one remaining record. She rubbed her hand across the dusty surface of the record player, then impaled the record, cranked up the player, and settled back in the sunporch's faded velvet chair to listen to the lament of a jilted lover.

As the vocalist sang about a woman whom he loved though she thought of him as nothing but a friend, she thought about Diego again. He swore he loved Bella enough to convince her to love him in return. But she had her doubts. If that technique hadn't worked to date, how was marrying him going to alter her feelings?

"Oh, Diego," she said and shook her head.

It is almost time, but before I go, I need more coffee, Bella thought. "And I will have a frycake with this mug," she mentioned to a stuffed raven perched on the sunporch's Formstone mantle. Her beloved pet until he had succumbed to a microscopic fungus, Sam still watched over her.

Grabbing the carrion bird and record, she carried

them to the craft suitcase and placed them in a basket next to it. She made one more trip to the sunporch for the record player, then returned to the kitchen and sat down.

As she chewed the last doughnut, she thought, *The store-bought kind can't begin to equal frycakes hot from the grease. But they're edible.*

After licking the confectionery sugar from her fingers, she glanced down and noticed the sweet powder now speckled her clothes. Bella brushed away the offending particles and countless dust mites which nibbled endlessly on her shed skin, stood, and moved into the hallway.

I have got some old frames for those photo collages in my bedroom, Bella remembered. She climbed the twisting stairs, shoved open the door at the top, took a deep breath, sneezed twice, then walked to her bedroom. In her room, the tang of drying herbs smothered the stink of leaking gas, the mustiness of the sunporch, and the stale air of the remaining upstairs rooms.

Metal rings squealed as she slid the closet curtains aside. Shelf by shelf, Bellarosa searched for the frames.

"Not here."

She pivoted and started to exit the closet but paused for just a moment to pick a speck of lint off of Emilio's best suit. He had looked so handsome when he'd sauntered onto the deep-dig shuttle dressed in his uniform. It had taken weeks to retrieve the miners' bodies from the deep-dig tunnels after the poison gas leak. And Emilio's casket had been locked closed. Not that that had stopped Bellarosa.

With a sigh, she scuffed to her bed and flopped down. Bella studied the quilt that covered her blankets and kept her warm on the coldest of nights. She ran her fingertip around the carefully sewn edges of a mauve triangle that had been cut from Mama's favourite dress. Next, she caressed a forest green square of fabric that had come from Alvaro's Sunday shirt after he and Emilio had outgrown it. Finally, she rubbed a swatch of yellow gingham which had come from a set of curtains that used to hang in her half-sister's bedroom.

"Enough." She jerked upright. With no additional woolgathering, no more delaying the inevitable, Bella snatched the quilt from her bed, sending an invisible cloud of single-celled and multicellular organisms into the air, and stuffed it into a waiting bag. She hurried from her room, dragging the canvas sack, and clomped down the winding stairs.

"Those frames must be in a trunk in the cellar," she informed no one.

Bella slid several buckets of stones aside. She yanked on the door handle. The basement door opened with a scrape-creak. Bella fumbled for the light string, located it, and pulled the cellar into day. Ghost town or not, at least the *Ciudad Nezahual-Coyotl* solar array still functioned. She dragged the canvas bag and the craft suitcase down the cellar stairs. Upon reaching the bottom, she stepped onto the packed dirt floor.

As she studied her mother's canning efforts, Bella rubbed her temples to alleviate the throbbing. She couldn't bring herself to empty out Mama's hard work, so she had saved those glass-preserved summer hours of gardening, preparing, and preserving. The tomato slices reminded her of happy lips. The cucumber pickles were reminiscent of mouldy fingers pointing every-which-way. And the pickled onions looked like floating eyeballs. No newfangled jars on Mama's shelves, only glass-lidded containers with their seals faded to brown.

Bella witnessed her distorted face reflected in the jars again and again. She nibbled on a cuticle, knowingly ingesting thousands of simple animals. Once moistened by her saliva and warmed by her mouth, the long-dormant creatures would reanimate and join their kin already living in Bella. With no more than a flutter of her eyelashes to acknowledge her newest passengers, she tried to recall which trunk held the old frames.

"Ah, yes," she said to the tomato slices. With a cluck of her tongue, she moved a stack of shingles, and found the frames in the first chest she checked. "I've got a memory like an elephant," she bragged to the pickles as she selected three frames, then closed the trunk's lid.

Though I wonder what those extinct creatures had to remember? she mused, as she sat down on top of the trunk to enjoy the cellar.

She tilted her head back. Cobwebs netted the sagging wooden beams. Watching the ravenous spiders rope off their territories was always a pleasure. She glanced down at the small black beetles scurrying from shadowy place to shadowy place. Bella had no idea how many of the quick little insects lived there, but they seemed harmless enough—unlike the fungi and protozoa that lived in every part of this planet's biosphere. She suspected they crept into the cellar via the secret tunnel which led to the old barn.

Bella pressed her palms against her bosom. Here, in the basement, Bella was with family. She chuckled. No one had ever suspected anything unusual when they lowered the caskets into the ground. Who could tell what weighed down a coffin? Rocks or corpses? And no one still living knew about the tunnel, except Bellarosa and Diego.

They were all here: Mama, Poppi, her brothers Emilio and Alvaro, poor Domatilla. She and Diego had even managed to sneak Cousin Juan out of Grimmelo & Sons Funeral Parlor & Crematorium.

For a moment, she considered Diego's role in the theft of the corpses—it amazed her how much the man was willing to do for her.

"You were right," she told Mama, "love is a powerful thing."

No one—not Mama, Poppi, Emilio, Alvaro, Domatilla, or Juan responded.

"Look at how it's kept us together," Bella said as she glanced around the room.

Each of the posed cadavers had smelled horrid for a time, but over the years, the stench had diminished. She knew, whatever the cause of death listed on their death certificates, her family members had died from the microbes which had hitchhiked to Mars on the settlers' ships. Or, scarier yet, the organisms had been waiting for humans in the air, the deep water tables, even the crusts of the moon and Mars.

Still, Bella liked the way her family always smiled now. It made her feel glad.

She stood, walked upstairs to gather the last load

leaving Hungry Coyote with her. Once everything was piled into the waiting wheelbarrow, she studied her family. It was time for farewells, but Bella wasn't sure she could go through with her plan. Maybe, it would be better to stretch out on the horsehair sofa and wait for the bulldozers.

Diego will never allow such a thing, she mused. If she didn't reach his cabin by tomorrow afternoon, he'd be on his way to find her, save her from herself.

Nevertheless, she closed her eyes and imagined the dirt and debris closing around her in a dusty embrace. Thus entombed, her bones would rest with her family's remains deep in the belly of Mars as long as the cursed orb circled the sun.

A spider creeping across her cheek brought Bella back to the present. She brushed the arachnid to the floor. It paused, raised its two front legs, and seemed to beckon to her before it scurried down the tunnel.

"You're right!" she exclaimed. "We must push forward and find a new home on this bloody planet."

Once again, the spiders and beetles had come through for her. She knew she could always count on them for the best advice.

"Bye, Poppi," she murmured as she kissed her father's bony head. "It is time to leave *Ciudad*

Nezahual-Coyotl."

Her father's smile seemed halfhearted, as did the grins of the rest of the family. Dutifully, Bellarosa kissed her relatives on their cheeks.

The skeletons, each holding a *calaveras de dulce* in their finger bones, were surrounded by marigolds. On a table in the centre of the family gathering, a clay bowl was filled to the brim with *mole pasole* garnished with crisp tortilla strips. Chayote, jicama, tomatillo, and ancho chilies surrounded the stew. On the right side of the table, a small tin of *pepitas* and chocolates was positioned in front of a pitcher of *horchata.* On the left side of the table, a vase, overflowing with baby's breath and lit candles, finished the tablescape.

"I know you can still hear me," said Bellarosa Carrillo. "I remember and honour you, but the butterflies return no more to *Ciudad Nezahual-Coyotl.* I leave for the Outlands, a place that still welcomes *mariposa.* Still bakes *pan de muerto.* Still sends fireworks into the sky over the heads of a mariachi band on *Dia de los Muertos.*"

Without another word, she picked up a canning jar from the floor beside Mama's feet. Last week with Diego's help, she'd plucked one tooth from the jaw of each family member and placed them in the jar. That way, when she abandoned their homestead on the edge of the City of the Hungry Coyote to finally marry her longtime admirer, she would have something to remember them by, and there would be something for their spirits to track.

She believed her family's spirits would track the teeth. There was some dried blood and tissue attached to the roots of each tooth so, as the angry winds swept across Mars, their ghosts could hitch a ride and meet her in the Outlands.

Bellarosa wiped away tears with the back of her hand. She was the city's last resident. Her family and most of her friends were either dead or had departed Mars in great hospital ships to float in the blackness of space until their passing. The City of the Hungry Coyote was empty.

The Mars Public Safety Officers had delivered multiple eviction notices to her. Four months ago, Bellarosa was certain she was between a rock and a hard place when the mandatory stipend for homestead seizure had been deposited in her credit account. For the past week, she'd heard the bulldozers working to level the town before sealing it beneath countless tons of concrete. By daybreak, Bellarosa expected the bulldozers to begin demolishing the homes of her former neighbours. The day after tomorrow, her home would be rubble, too.

But all was well. The final wheelbarrow load waited by the tunnel entrance. She had never trusted bankers, so most of her credits—including the recently withdrawn homestead stipend—had been stored in a tin box by the jars of canned vegetables. The credit box and other items leaving with Bella were already in her van. The fully-charged vehicle was parked in the barn just steps away from where the tunnel ended.

She'd be joining Diego Sanchez in the Outland District and bringing a little femininity to his mountain cabin. A miner, he was a basically decent man, though in her opinion he drank and gambled too much. But Bella felt certain she could get him to toe the line.

Though, if he insisted on continuing his foolish ways, she would have to put an end to him. Then, the cabin would be hers. From Diego's letters she knew the cabin's pantry was well-stocked, its well provided drinkable water, its walls were thick enough to hold off night chills and keep out daytime heat, and it had a regular basement plus a root cellar. What more did she need?

Bella picked up the container of kerosene and rags she always kept in the corner of the basement, just in case. She smiled. The government didn't control her fate—she did. The last Carrillo, she intended to make the best of an unfortunate situation.

She placed a kerosene-soaked rag in each of her family member's laps, poured the remaining liquid over the various storage boxes and chests stacked nearby, and set down the metal can. Second, with utmost gentleness, Bellarosa Carrillo placed the jar full of teeth in the wheelbarrow. Next, she paused for a few minutes while a swarm of spiders and black beetles ran into the tunnel. Finally, she struck a match and tossed it onto the nearest fuel-soaked rag.

Singing an up-tempo rendition of her favourite fiesta song—the one she and Diego had danced to dozens, perhaps hundreds of times—Bellarosa Carrillo ignored the flames behind her and pushed the wheelbarrow through the tunnel. If her calculations were correct and she drove through the night, by this time tomorrow, she'd be on Diego Sanchez's doorstep in the unregulated Outland District of Mars.

Her wedding dress was riding shotgun in the van's front seat. She'd freshen up, slip on the dress, and she and Diego would be married tomorrow evening.

Pathogenic organisms be damned. She would not surrender to a quiet death in space. And maybe, just maybe, there was a happy ending awaiting Bellarosa Carrillo after all. The spiders and beetles who chose to ride along in her van would find new homes in the less toxic Outland environs. Her family would follow their teeth and piggyback the next wind that swept towards the west.

Perhaps she'd manage to love Diego as much as he loved her. If not, there were Bella's collages, paper-making, stuffed crow, and insect pets to keep her company. There were fiestas and *Dia de los Muertos* preparations. And there was her axe and a cabin cellar in the Outlands ready to be filled with the dead.

Imagining millions of microbes smashing against her windshield as she drove down the road, Bella thought of her wedding day, kissing Diego in his fine cabin, and a new life with him constantly by her side. She shivered.

Then, Bella imagined how nice she'd look in widow's clothes and the sympathy offered to her by her new neighbours. She glanced at her wedding dress. Next, she studied the axe handle visible beneath the gown's sheer lace sleeves.

She sighed. Unfortunately for Diego, Bellarosa Carillo suspected romance wasn't her thing.

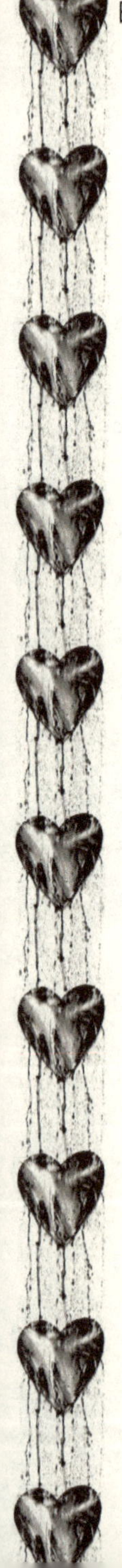

Cold Love

by Stephen Herczeg

Of all things, it was my stupid phone that destroyed our lives.

I really did love Kaitlyn. We'd been together for a couple of years and almost every minute of our lives was spent in each other's company.

I think it might have all started when Kaitlyn brought up the idea of a wedding. The whole having a girlfriend and lover thing had been great. Before I met Kaitlyn, I was a borderline drunk. Every Friday and Saturday night was spent down the pub, drinking until I dropped and trying to crack onto anything in a skirt. My hit rate was as phenomenal as could be expected.

Then one night I met her at the bar when I was buying another round of beers. We got talking while we were waiting to be served and wandered off into a dark corner and carried on for hours. I don't think my mates ever got their drinks.

Six months later, we moved in together, and our lives have revolved around each other ever since.

I don't think I ever thought any further than just being boyfriend and girlfriend. I've virtually given up drinking. I don't need to get wasted every week anymore. I've got something to look forward to during my time off from work.

But of late, Kaitlyn has been getting really serious. She leaves bridal magazines lying around. She watches those stupid reality shows about people getting married at first sight. She watches travel programs and keeps hinting about romantic honeymoon locations.

I don't want to lose her, but there's been something nagging in the back of my head. It's like an itch I can't scratch. The words form in my mind *Total Commitment*. My brain screams out the words as if they are some sort of death knell.

I think Kaitlyn feels it too. As the hints have grown, the sex has died off. It used to be every night. We were as randy as rabbits. Now, I'm lucky if it's once a week, and that's only if we've had a couple of wines and watch the naughty channel on a Saturday night.

For the last couple of years, I hadn't even had eyes

for any other woman. That's probably why I locked onto Chanelle when I first saw her.

The boys had decided to go into the clubrooms after training one Friday night. I normally didn't join them, but this week I thought a couple of beers would go down nice. It was hot, the season was almost finished.

Then I saw her.

Blessed with a gorgeous face, framed in dark hair that hung down to her tight bum, and perky breasts defying gravity under a tight t-shirt. And better yet, she looked at me with interest.

In a complete replay of the night I met Kaitlyn, the boys never got their round, but I got more than I bargained for. Luckily, what happens on the field or in the bar afterwards, stays there. *The boys' code*. None of them mentioned anything to Kaitlyn.

Chanelle and I carried on for months. She didn't want anything more, which suited me fine. I managed to load a couple of apps onto my phone that were hidden from Kaitlyn but kept me in contact with Chanelle.

Then it all fell apart.

After all the talk of weddings and honeymoons, I managed to move the conversation to a smaller hint at amalgamating our lives.

A joint phone plan.

Simple, not really a major commitment, but it made Kaitlyn happy. We switched our Sim cards out for a couple of new ones. I culled my address book and made sure there was nothing awkward in there. The messaging app that I used to contact Chanelle was hidden beneath a series of menus and passwords. I thought I was safe.

How wrong I was.

A month after the phone plan merger, I'd left training and was about to make my way to Chanelle's for a quick tryst. I sent her a message and headed over.

How was I to know that the stupid app would perform an auto-update when I used it?

A message popped up on Kaitlyn's phone, asking her to install and update the app. She had no idea what it was, and intrigued, she pressed *accept*.

The app installed itself, opened up without using my password and displayed the latest message trail between Chanelle and me.

Kaitlyn flipped.

She somehow managed to trawl backwards through weeks of messages and found Chanelle's name and address. She already knew I was heading over there and made a beeline to catch us in the act.

And did she what.

Now, Kaitlyn is no shrinking violet. When she has

a bug up her butt there's nothing stopping her.

She somehow managed to bust the door open and stormed into Chanelle's bedroom where we were performing the dance of the two-backed beast.

What followed was lots of screaming and shouting. Kaitlyn found a cricket bat—did I mention that Chanelle is quite a good cricketer—and brought it down on the back of her competition's head. I think Kaitlyn was dead before she hit the ground, but the second blow certainly finished her off.

I jumped off the bed, took one look at Chanelle, then saw the bat heading towards my head. Many years of playing football gave me reflexes quick enough to avoid a swinging arm. I grabbed the bat in mid swing and pulled Kaitlyn off balance. She tripped over Chanelle's body and flew across the room. Her head slammed into the brick fireplace against the far wall and she fell to the floor and lay still.

I was gutted. I stood gobsmacked. I couldn't scream. I couldn't cry.

I checked and confirmed. The two women that I loved were both dead.

I didn't know what to do. All I could think was to bundle them into my car and bring them back here. I've had the air conditioner cranked up for days, even grabbed some bags of ice and plonked them around their bodies.

They're sitting on the couch, just staring at me. Their eyes have gone a strange colour. Their skin seems to have gone a bit green. I've tried makeup, but I'm no good at it.

They've become a little squishy of late, especially when we do it, and we do it a lot. I figure I've got to keep them both happy.

And there's the smell. I really could live without the smell, even the perfume won't cover it.

I don't want to leave them here on their own. Somebody might find them, but it's Friday again, and I've got to go to training.

I wonder if the boys want to come around.

Eternity

by Eddie D. Moore

Alan rested peacefully in his bed. His breathing slowed and became shallow before stopping altogether. He found himself standing over his own body. A tunnel of light appeared, and a sense of warmth filled him as he walked into it.

A man standing in front of an ascending staircase greeted him. "Welcome to eternity." Another stairwell appeared that descended about fifty steps into near darkness. "The time has come for judgment."

Alan glanced up the stairway and saw someone move in the distance. "Who was that?"

"Your ex-wife. Wait—" Alan ran down the descending stairway two steps at a time.

 BLACK HARE PRESS

Belladonna

By Raven Corinn Carluk

Chris read the latest text, taking an angry pull from his cigarette. Dave arched one brow as he exhaled his own smoke, and waited patiently for whatever his co-worker was going to say.

"Fucking Jodi," Chris finally swore, tossing his phone onto the bench beside him.

"Another Valentine's request?" Dave drew in another lungful of smoke and held it.

"Yes!" Chris dropped his butt, ground it out with more vehemence than necessary, but didn't leave the patio yet. "Already demanded roses and chocolates, and now she wants reservations at that steak house downtown."

"Thought she didn't like red meat?" Smoke roughened Dave's voice, curled up around his face.

Chris began his post-smoke ritual. His girlfriend hated that he smoked, wanted him to quit. Apparently refused to kiss him if she even caught a whiff of cigarette. Dave laughed to himself as the young man used sanitiser on his hands and face, then popped a of couple mints.

"She heard her sister was going to some nice seafood restaurant," Chris said, standing and slipping his phone into his pocket. "So, she *has* to go somewhere even more expensive. Eighty dollars a fucking plate."

Dave shook his head, dropping his butt into the bucket of other stubs. "So, what are you going to do?" They started back inside toward the rest of their shift.

Chris shook his head. "I don't know. Try to get reservations, I guess." He held the door to the backroom open.

"See, this is exactly why I don't date bitches at Valentine's. Or any holiday."

Chris's gaze bored into the back of Dave's head. He turned to look at his co-worker. The younger man stared in confusion, caught off-guard by Dave's statement. "What do you mean?"

Dave chuckled, shrugged, and put his smokes back in his locker. "Every *one* of these bitches is comparing their Valentine's against all their friends. Who went where, whose man gave them what, and how much money was spent on them. They post to their Facebook, and they brag on their Instagrams, and they look at everyone else's posts." He turned to nod wisely at Chris. "And woe to the man who doesn't outdo those other men."

Chris couldn't respond at first, just frowned as he put his own stuff back in his locker. When he looked back up, his brows were drawn together tightly. "You really think women are that shallow?"

Dave snorted, ready to make his way back onto the sales floor. "Look at what your girl is asking for, then tell me you don't agree."

"What about *your* girl though? Haven't you two been together a few months?"

He smiled and nodded. "Since just after Christmas. Texted her that it was over this morning, though. After all this hearts and chocolate bullshit is over, I'll give her a chance to get back together."

"Cold blooded, dude."

"Or really clever?" Dave winked and finished his shift with a smile on his face. His heart remained light the entire drive home, without a care in the world except kicking off his shoes.

Bella was a great girl, had been almost two months

of fun, but he wasn't going to get caught up in the hype of the day. She'd replied to his text with a sad face emoji, nothing else. Not that anything really needed to be said.

He'd hit her up next week, and they'd either be back in bed or they wouldn't. Girls as hot as her weren't that common, but it wasn't that big a loss to him if she wasn't around anymore. Having a girlfriend and getting some on the regular was great, but he did look forward to the alone time. No one to nag him if he just lounged on the couch to watch the Blazers game while drinking beer and eating pizza rolls.

Dave opened the door to find lit candles and sweet incense filling his apartment. He stood in the doorway while trying to understand what was going on.

Bella stepped out of the kitchen wearing skimpy black lingerie and holding a plate of brownies. Bright red lipstick gleamed as she smiled, her black hair laying in waves down her back. "You're home just in time."

"What are you doing here?" He closed the door, still frowning. She was probably trying to win him back, but he'd just eat her brownies, rock her world again, then kick her to the curb for the weekend.

She bit her lip, lowered her eyes, and extended the treats. "Well, I thought maybe some edibles and a little nookie would, you know..." Bella giggled, met his gaze. "Maybe we could just have our Valentine's early. Who needs to go out with all the others when we could have more fun staying home?"

Dave nodded his head, dropped his keys on the coffee table, and made his way toward Bella. Lust warmed his blood, and he started to think of all the things she'd do in bed if she thought he could be won back. He took a big bite of one of her pot brownies, smiling at her.

Bella wrinkled her nose, giggled, and set the plate down. She took his free hand to lead him into the bedroom. Dave chewed, savouring the musky flavour, appreciating how strong she'd made them. He watched her taut ass beneath the lacy panties, the first flush of intoxication racing across his skin.

She'd clearly spent most of the day getting things ready. Had he even given her a key? Dave couldn't remember, but the smell of her perfume kept him from caring. More candles, more incense. Red satin sheets and rose petals on the bed, black lace curtains over the window. Even a mirror hanging on the ceiling.

"Damn, baby," he muttered, words slurring. "What's all this?"

Bella turned, began tugging at his clothes. "Only a

little something. But you just need to lie back and let me do all the work." Her eyes glittered in the candlelight, lips the colour of blood.

Dave tipped his head. Why would he think that? Then she was kissing him, and he didn't think of much else.

She kissed and sucked at his lower lip, her tongue dancing in ways he'd never felt before. By the time she had him undressed and in bed, Dave's head was spinning.

Bella followed him into bed, still kissing him. Crawled on top with her mouth locked on his. Dave sighed, shivered, and couldn't resist as she slipped his hands into silk ropes. Didn't want to. If she really wanted to do all the work *and* get freaky, he wasn't one to complain.

She straddled him and leaned back, arching her spine. Only a thin piece of cloth separated their flesh, kept her heat from enveloping him. Dave tugged against the restraints, another wave of intoxication swimming up his spine.

"You like that?" she asked, pushing her breasts together, lips coming together in a sexy pout.

His heart pounded and his breath hitched when Bella ground her hips down onto him. Dave moaned, eyes rolled back into his head. "Yeah. Just like that. Damn, girl, that's good."

"You haven't seen anything yet." She moaned and he echoed her. Bella still had her clothes on, but she was doing things she'd never done to him before. He pulled against the restraints, wishing he could put his hands on her constantly rocking hips.

A cold edge pressed against his throat, stinging him.

Dave's eyes flew open. Bella bit her lower lip, eyes mostly closed, and continued to rock on top of him. Something trickled down his neck, too hot to be sweat. "What the hell?" His voice held little vehemence, his head fuzzy from her brownie.

Bella smiled slowly, a wicked curling of lips. She lifted a black knife from his throat, a small stain of blood on the glinting edge. "You never had a chance to see my athame. I was going to show you my altar and my herb garden, and even let you meet my familiar."

He tugged harder, trying to get angry, to push away the fog of intoxication and lust. "Bitch, what's wrong with you?"

She stopped moving, pouting as she sat on his manhood. Dave squirmed, her weight uncomfortable, pinching but not hurting. "See, Dave, I was really hoping we could work this out."

"Get off me, you stupid bitch." Dave managed to yell, to buck her up briefly, but it caused his head to spin. He groaned, collapsed back in his bonds with tingling limbs. "What the fuck did you give me?"

"Nightshade. Belladonna, just like me. Delightful, isn't it?" She laughed, traced his breastbone with the tip of her knife. "Small doses aren't lethal, only mildly hallucinogenic. I find it really opens a person's energy channels right up. Opens them up for the bonding."

Dave tried to speak, but his tongue seemed glued to the roof of his mouth. He groaned and tossed his head, tears of frustration blurring his vision. The sweet incense smoke grew thicker, cloying, with a hint of rot underlying it.

"Yes," she whispered, nearly purring. "Struggle. It makes it all the more painful when Beleroth begins taking over." Bella sliced his chest, and the stinging pain crawled over every inch of his body.

Something else crawled across Dave's body. Unseen, but thick and sticky, like a toad's belly. His stomach threatened to flip, and the last vestiges of desire faded away, seeking refuge inside him. Tendrils of clammy cold followed, filling each of the man's openings.

Bella moaned, writhing once more, and made another slice in the hollow of his throat. "You really are cute." She leaned forward, breasts against his chest, and licked at the blood running from the latest tiny wound.

"Fuck you, you fucking bitch." Dave's vision began to fade as his mind slipped away beneath a cloud of rotten stench.

"But we really need to do something about that personality of yours." Bella laughed, and the sound followed him into blackness.

The Best Part

By G. Allen Wilbanks

The best part of a relationship, William thought, was the very beginning. There was nothing better than meeting someone new, feeling that flutter of butterflies low in the stomach, and wondering if this person was going to be "the one." He loved those fragile, fleeting moments. It was a time of firsts: the first date, first kiss, and yes, the first time tumbling into bed together. It was all so fresh and exciting.

William stood in the garage and surveyed the awful mess. *The worst part*, he thought, *was cleaning up all the damn blood when the relationship was over.*

BLACK HARE PRESS

Mr Right

by D.M. Burdett

The moonlight glimmers across the lake and I feel the wind lift my hair as I watch him pull his shirt over his head, my eyes following the line of his pectoral muscle across his tanned, waxed chest and the arched back of the lizard tattoo that sweeps up over his shoulder.

He's always looked after himself—eating healthily, going to the gym, twice daily jogs—it's one of the things that attracted me to him in the first place. That and those beautiful, clear sea-blue eyes.

I wait for him on the grass—crisp, golden autumn leaves under my bare back, and my white-blonde hair a halo around my head—as he unbuckles his jeans and pushes them down his legs, his eyes sliding up and down my body.

As he bends down to me, he whispers, "Happy Valentine's Day, darling." He pushes my knees apart, looks at me with lust-filled oceans, and I remember back to the exact moment we met.

It was in the Hilton Hotel, Park Lane, London, January 17th, 2016. The time was precisely one minute past six—I know because the clock behind the reception desk was where I focused my attention while I waited for my heart to steady after that first encounter.

We were both checking in, patiently waiting in the queue. As I fumbled about in my handbag for my purse, I dropped my car keys on the floor. We both bent down to pick them up at the same time. His hand got there first, but mine accidentally closed over his. When he looked up at me with those dreamily delicious aqua oceans beneath envious dark lashes, a blush spread from my cheeks to my groin, and my knees literally went to jelly.

Pathetic, isn't it? *Just one look, that's all it took*, as the song goes. My fate was ultimately sealed in that nanosecond.

We met again in the restaurant the following morning, bumping shoulders over the breakfast buffet. One shared joked at the waitress's expense led to an evening in the bar, a hot first kiss, and a night of rampant passion in his hotel room.

We were inseparable from then on.

Those early days were so romantic; all I'd ever dreamed of in a relationship. He bought me flowers, turned up at my work with lunchtime picnics of champagne and cheese, swept me off to Paris at a moment's notice for our first St. Valentine's Day. It was all so charmingly breath-taking.

I'd found my Mr Right.

He was so successful and charismatic; a high flyer in a big PR company in the city. Everyone who was everyone knew him and loved him. Doors opened for him wherever he went, and we dined in the finest restaurants, at the best tables, got invited to movie premiers, stayed in the swankiest hotels. I floated on clouds when I was with him.

Just six weeks after that first kiss, we moved in together. I know! Mad, huh? It was the proverbial whirlwind romance.

Of course, that's when everything started to go wrong.

I hadn't realised at first just how obsessive he was, how controlling. It started with him telling me—not just suggesting, but *insisting*—what I should wear to work.

No more sexy pencil skirts and high heels, just dowdy trouser suits with flats.

"You should wear those little grey shoes," he'd said, lounging sexily in bed and watching me dress.

"What's wrong with these?" I'd asked, slipping my feet into my usual four-inch heeled work pumps.

"People will take you more seriously if you don't wear the hooker shoes."

"Hooker shoes…" I had looked down at the Louboutin's I'd coveted for months and eaten dust to save up for.

"And why don't you wear trousers more often? You don't want to look like you're giving it away, you'll never get that promotion you want. Or, if you do, people will think you only got it 'cause you're blowing the boss."

Tone down the lipstick, wear my hair up, show less cleavage; his demands became countless. To be honest, I was a bit annoyed, but I thought he was being cutely jealous…and I loved him…so I did what he asked.

He had his secretary buy me all new clothes; I came home one day to a dozen beautifully wrapped packages of new, dull workwear, and plastic bin bags of my old clothes. At that point, I still thought of them as gifts rather than facets of his controlling behaviour.

Then he started dropping me off at work in the morning and picking me up in the evening. He always brought flowers, or a gift, or we'd go somewhere special. So it took me a while to realise how stranded I was during the day. No more meeting friends for lunch, getting a manicure or facial. I was stuck at work, out in the sticks, until he picked me up.

And, more and more, I seemed to be failing him. I ruined everything; special days out, date nights, meals, conversations. I would laugh in the wrong places, or to the wrong person, forget some small detail he'd told me about weeks before, wear the wrong dress, the wrong underwear, the wrong necklace, the wrong perfume.

I'd have an innocent conversation with one his friends—politics, the weather, ask after their kids—and he'd insist something I said had embarrassed him. He'd be furious for days, berating me for being stupid, or insensitive, or cruel. He'd tell me he could do much better, that he did so much for me, that I was ungrateful.

But still I loved him. I adored him. I wanted to do better, be the person he wanted me to be. I stopped seeing friends; I pushed back my family; I went nowhere unless he was by my side.

Then just before St. Valentine's Day last year, the day before we were due to leave for a romantic weekend in New York, he dropped a clanger. He insisted I give up my career and stay at home. My dream job, the one I studied for four years to get into, that I'd worked up from a junior to senior over the years for.

I raged and ranted for days. To myself, in the bathroom mirror; I didn't dare do it in front of him. *I won't do it! It's everything I've worked for!* I hated the very idea of it. My career was my passion, not just a job.

But then he proposed on the observatory deck at the top of the Empire State Building, just like in my all-time favourite film, *Sleepless in Seattle*. Of course, my heart melted. I imagined it dripping over the side and blowing away in the wind.

I said, "Yes," and resigned from my job on our return.

But I was so lonely. I'd spent all my life surrounded by people, colleagues and friends, and I was thrust into hours spent alone, interspersed by the time I spent with my fiancé when he got home from work. Even then, he was often too busy to give me any attention, secreting himself behind his office door while I watched sad rom-coms and got drunk on expensive wine.

I went stir crazy. Literally.

I spent hours on the internet just scrolling through inane rubbish. I made invisible friends on Facebook that

I'd never meet but that I could talk to about anything. I purchased things I didn't need from websites, and ordered groceries to be delivered, just so I could see another face at the door.

I even invited the Jehovah's Witnesses in for coffee rather than politely turning them away like a normal person would. Oh, yes I did! That was the depth of my loneliness.

I became depressed. I cried a lot, stopped showering every day. My wardrobe comprised of pyjamas and housecoats.

And just when I'd stopped getting up in the mornings—preferring to mope in bed all day, only dragging myself up in time to make dinner, and then floating in a sea of Chablis in front of late night TV on my own—I met Jack.

Wonderful, handsome, young and intelligent Jack. Jack who was also a very good listener.

I missed the postman while I slept off the usual hangover, and he'd left my parcel—another delivery of things I'd never use—at the neighbour's house. Their son, Jack, came over to drop it off. Grasping at that moment of social interaction, I kept him at the door; asked him how his parents were; how university was; how his sister was getting on in her new job at the local lawyers…anything to keep him there longer. He was all politeness and smiles and chatted away merrily.

Just as I'd run out of rubbish to ask him about and we were about to say our goodbyes, the bulb in the light above my head suddenly exploded and showered us both in glass.

I was at such a low, that insignificant incident reduced me to tears and I started bawling like a baby, much to Jack's startled surprise. But, what a darling! He ushered me into the kitchen and left me to change my clothes in the laundry while he went and cleaned up the mess, sweeping and vacuuming everything away. He even replaced the bulb.

And then he poured us both a glass of wine, and I poured out my soul to him while he listened sympathetically.

And that's how our friendship started. After that, he came over most lunchtimes he wasn't at university and we'd sit and chat the day away. Sometimes just over coffee, sometimes the odd glass of wine. He gave me something to look forward to, something to get up, showered, and dressed for. It was all purely platonic though. I know that seems strange—the thirty-year-old and the twenty-one-year-old—but it really was. Despite everything, I still loved my fiancé, I wanted to do my best for him, for him to love me too. We had a wedding to organise, a life to live.

And besides that, Jack was gay.

Of course, my fiancé didn't know that. So when he dropped by in the middle of the day to collect something from his office and found us giggling in the kitchen over a picture in a magazine and a bottle of wine, he literally hit the roof.

He'd been angry at me before, but I'd never seen him as angry as that. He snatched the magazine from the kitchen counter and threw it on the floor as he yelled and screamed at us, spittle flying, his face purple. Jack looked scared—he was right to—and cowered in his seat. Wine glasses and bottles went across the room, along with the bowl of fruit, bananas and apples everywhere. All the time I was trying to calm him down.

"It's not what it seems?"

"You're fucking him!"

"No, no. This is Jack from next door."

"I gave you everything! This is how you repay me?"

"He's just a boy, don't be ridiculous."

"You're a whore."

"I love you, I wouldn't do that."

And on and on it went. But he wouldn't listen.

Eventually, he stormed from the room, went back to his study, returned with his gun.

"Holy shit," Jack had breathed—his last words—as he backed up against the wall. The bullet passed through him, lodged itself in my beautiful Italian tiles, and he dropped to the floor, blood and gore pouring from the exit wound in the back of his head.

Then the gun was turned on me, but my world had already gone black even before the trigger was pulled.

And now here we are, in this cold forest at midnight, spending our third St. Valentine's Day together.

We're not alone for this one; the depression in the earth where Jack's body lies is just feet away—I can feel his spirit some nights, hear his ghostly cries for his mother.

The filtered light from the moon steals between the branches high above my head, glistening on the sweat on my handsome fiancé's cheek as he thrusts and groans his way to climax.

Despite everything that's happened, I'd still reach up and touch his face if I could, rake my nails down his back. Pull his buttocks into me. My craving for his attention is still intense. But I just watch from behind cloudy eyes as he finishes and collapses against me, his hot breath on my bone-white cheek.

At last he breathes, "You'll always be my girl," as he caresses my face and presses a wet kiss to my cold, bloated lips.

And then he pushes my body back into the shallow grave, tenderly re-covering my swollen, black flesh, and I know I'll yearn for his touch until next Valentine's Day.

Heartbreaker

by Michele Freeman

May I hold your hand?

It's been so long since I've touched someone who offers kindness instead of pain. Your hand is warm. Soft. Please forgive me if I squeeze too hard. It's nice, even for a little while, to connect with a human being who gives a damn.

I know you have questions. But it's probably better if you just let me tell you everything I can. It's weird. Talking, I mean. I haven't had a real conversation in…well, I don't know how long I've been in this basement.

Peter. Yes. That's the name he told me. We dated for about six months. I was wildly in love with him. He seemed so…perfect. Like a handsome hero who'd stepped off the pages of a romance novel. I guess that's how naïve I was. So starved for affection and intimacy, I fell for his pretty words and slick veneer.

You know what I mean?

Peter told me he had something special planned for Valentine's Day. I thought he was going to ask me to marry him. I'd even bought some bridal magazines, thinking we would soon be planning our wedding together.

We went dancing. Made love under the stars. Then we went to his place. Music. Laughter. Wine. I felt strange after one glass of merlot. Absolutely giddy after the second. The world spun and burst into bright colours.

It never occurred to me that he'd drugged the wine.

Peter said it was time for the surprise. My heart leapt. I thought he'd show me a ring. Pop the question. Instead, he brought me down here, stripped me naked, and chained my ankles to the wall. By the time he made me his prisoner, I was too out of it to put up a fight. It felt like a nightmare.

And it was.

An endless waking nightmare.

It's Valentine's Day again? So, it's been a year?

It feels like a hundred years. I wish it had been possible to escape. In the early days, I screamed until I lost my voice. Broke my fingernails trying to pry off the manacles. Begged for my freedom while he taunted me.

What? Yeah, it really does smell awful down here. I'd say you get used to that spoiled garbage stench, but I never did. Not really. The floors are filthy. Bugs are everywhere. They crawl on me and get in my hair. I've fended off the occasional rat, too.

It's always dark. I used to be able to tell the difference between night and day. See this wall? Near the top is a small rectangular window. The sun would shine through it and chase away some of the shadows. But now it's covered with a black garbage bag and duct tape. Once Peter realised I had a tiny bit of warmth and light to enjoy, he took it away.

I stopped praying a long time ago.

If men like Peter exist, then trust me, God does not.

I don't have clothes. Not anymore. I'm lucky I got a blanket. He used to take it away. To punish me. Because he hated when I fought him. *Don't disrespect me, you whore.* He used his words like knives—slicing away at my soul until I felt like a raw, pulsing lump of nerves. Hurting my body wasn't enough. He fucked with my mind, too. I hate to admit it, but I was surprised how much humiliation I was willing to endure to have the smallest comfort. I started keeping my mouth shut because I'd rather have the blanket, you know?

He feeds me once a day. Usually a bologna sandwich and a glass of milk. Sometimes, the meal's drugged. GHB, I think. Yeah. The date rape drug. I almost never remember what happens, but afterwards…I wish for my own death. Especially when my body aches from the burns and cuts and bruises. I'm not a person anymore. Just a plaything.

He loves to break his toys.

You'll see.

I'm sorry. So sorry.

But you'll see.

Stay

by Stacey Jaine McIntosh

It's an overcast Saturday in June when he walks through the door at just after 2pm. I greet him as I always do, but something is off, and his anger rises to the surfaces quicker than normal. I retreat to the bedroom, only for him to follow. And as I sit on the bed, he begins to yell and scream, putting me down again and again until I'm sobbing and scared. So scared. I want to leave, but I can't. The kids are playing with the neighbour's kids out in the street. I can't leave them. I won't.

I'd take them with me before I'd ever consider leaving them alone with him, but the point is moot, because there's nowhere else for me to go. I have no choice but to stay.

The fight escalates to a dangerous degree, and

before I know it or understand it, his hands are wrapped around my neck and I'm fighting. Fighting to breathe and fighting to stay alive.

As I struggle, my arms and legs flailing, I see my eldest son pass by the window. But he doesn't enter. He doesn't turn the knob and step inside.

If only…

I don't remember the world going dark, but it does, and I lose consciousness.

When I come to, my husband is standing with his back to me in the living room. I can see him through the open bedroom door.

I was unconscious. The thought bubbles up as my brain wakes up as if from sleep. But I hadn't been sleeping. He did that. He was capable of that! I don't process it, I can't. My brain was starved of oxygen. I should call an ambulance and go to the hospital, but I don't.

I stay. And like a moth to a flame, I'm drawn to him. I feel sick and fatigued but one question plagues me.

"Why?"

He doesn't answer. Perhaps he can't, because he doesn't have the words. He looks defeated, but beyond that, he looks angry.

His grief over the loss of his mother days ago is so raw that I know he must be feeling vulnerable and alone, but even as I think that another thought occurs to me.

I could have died. Before my husband has even laid his mother to rest, I could have died.

That's the thought that keeps me up at night.

I could have died.

I don't probe too deeply within the depths of my mind over that thought. It hurts too much. Death scares me. I don't revel in it.

I don't talk about it.

Instead, I bury it. I shove it so far down deep inside that if there was a lock, I wouldn't have the key to open it, because it's just too hard.

I almost died and it scares me.

He scares me.

Leaving scares me.

There're too many variables.

I can't stay. I shouldn't stay, but I want to.

I love him. I shouldn't, I know that, but I do.

I could kick him out, but I won't.

I'll stay because I love him.

As twisted as it is. I do.

BLACK HARE PRESS

Romance on Wheels

by A.L. Paradiso

No matter how many times I insisted, "That's not what I said!" she couldn't hear it.

Six months earlier

Though I wanted a classic 1957 Chevy Bel Air for my first car, my dad ruled it out when he learned about the *slight* engine mods. Instead of the stock 235 CID, 140 horses or even the top upgraded small block 283 V-8 with 245 horses, the one I found had a big block 427 with dual quad carburettors and 500+ horsepower. It was a tyre-smoking monster. I might as well have replaced the Chevy Bel Air moniker with *Chevy Trouble*. If only we knew then that the car would be worth $65,000 today!

What dad found acceptable was a much smaller four-cylinder car with only 100 horses for $250. When I checked her out, I found her acceptable also, but I knew I couldn't tell him why. My research showed the car had a low top speed of just 105 mph, but she out handled almost everything.

We took her home that day, my 1960 Triumph TR-3. Despite the small *chink* in first gear, she was glorious. If not for the flawed first gear, she could smoke her tyres in first, break them loose in second and chirp them in third—with sticky, Dunlop tyres—exactly the power profile I wanted. All that with beauty and class.

It took some practice to find a comfortable way to climb inside her tight space and not bruise or jam a leg in the wrong place. Once I learned it, it became a graceful dance—open the low, sculptured door, lift right leg to point it into the long gap under the small dash, pivot on left foot, glide butt onto the bucket seat, pull left leg into her embrace, close the door. 1-2-3, 1-2-3-4 cha-cha-cha! A smooth, simple, two-second dance. Once inside, she was comfortably and surprisingly spacious. You don't climb into her; you slip her on like a snug glove and merge with her.

Rushing along—top down, wind in face, scalp massaged by whipping hair—inspired my exhilaration and well-founded confidence in her. Besides the adrenalin upsurge from tight turns on rails, despite her never complaining or resisting, another sensual transition happened at 3000 RPM. The classic lady changed her gentle purr into the sonic surge of a relaxing, euphoric symphony—a powerful, sexy, confidence-inspiring, muscles-rippling growl that always made me sigh in tranquillity. Entering any overpass at 55 and accelerating through 70 in fourth gear manipulated that purr-to-growl change for me, with overtones, and we both enjoyed it.

She made it easy to stay focused on her and her unique soundscape. Her Spartan interior had leather bucket seats which were simple yet comfortable and effective; simple, white on black gauges; a large diameter steering wheel to compensate for lack of power anything. Simple controls, tight shift pattern, and no radio helped keep the focus where it needed to be. Even the gauges were simple health monitors I always tracked. I never ordered her to handle curves, I just saw the line I wanted, and she shrugged and followed it regardless of the speed. The strong disc brakes were always a blessing.

Windows, rag top and frame were all in the trunk until needed. Though the snap-in windows allowed the doors to scoop low to the ground, they also created delays in sealing me against the rains until I found an overpass for shelter. That caused a few *hilarious* moments neither of us appreciated.

Like any *haute classe* being she excelled on nurturing, though never demanded it even when injured. The simple, primitive engine needed frequent attention to keep her at her peak. I drove her many miles; so, once a month, I checked, tuned and encouraged her good health. She inspired a friend to get a newer model (because it had roll-up windows) and we spoiled our cars together.

Love isn't always easy, and some serious problems came to my TR-3. Despite them all, I never lost faith in her…even at the end.

Many months after bonding with my sports car, I met Merci, a girlfriend who became more and more jealous of my TR-3. She hated my doting and the comforting time I spent with my car. One day she asked which end I kissed when I went to bed. *None of your business,* I considered saying, but thought better of it since she was not in a humorous mood.

Isn't that love? Confidence in her loyalty and support, respect, care, concern for the other being, putting her needs first... My girlfriend didn't agree.

Though she knew I loved her, she got ever more demanding and wanted proof I loved her more than the Triumph. *The Triumph is not confrontational, always cooperates and is always there for me, unlike you!* Again, that thought never left my mouth. Knots in my gut told me this was a troubled relationship, a bad romance.

She accused me of loving my car more than I loved her. It's possible that was true. Perhaps the Triumph was a more comforting step ahead, but I couldn't clarify for her that it was different. All she heard was, "I love the Triumph first, you second, and that's how it will always be." No matter how many times I insisted, "That's not what I said!" she couldn't hear it.

Came Valentine's Day, and she wanted just one gift. She insisted I sell the car...or else! My next girlfriend was much more understanding!

My good romance with my Triumph came to a screeching halt on September 2, 1968. When someone tried to steal the left rear wire wheel and left it loose, it slid off the hub at the only critical, nearly lethal spot on the Belt Parkway. There are still gaps in my memory of that grotesque incident and I still have injuries from it.

The briefest highlights are these. My new girlfriend was with me. Since I was taking the Triumph for a thorough painting after a summer of nurturing, everything was loose: seats, trunk and hood; carpets were also out. Seconds before the incident, I pointed out we were cruising gently at exactly 60 and the sonic symphony began to surround us as we passed over small bridges in the left lane. Her perfect, confident purrrrr was perfection. Just three feet from the dividing wall, I expected the symphony to echo beautifully as I gently accelerated past the next wall. After a small rise and drop approaching that final bridge, my memory vanished.

I woke in a hospital asking over and over, "What happened." Bits came back over the next week, many more took years to return. Dad had been following me and his description is the best I have. He said the wheel slid off right after that rise just as I reached the steel wall with I-beam dividers which separated traffic. The car spun on its bare rear drum, at 60, and immediately hit the wall, slid along briefly, hit an I-beam and bounced back violently.

My girlfriend flew over the side and tumbled on the Parkway; the pedals seemed to trap my right foot thus ripping my Achilles, but kept me from meeting the opposing traffic head first; my face bounced off the corner of the windshield and split open; the loose hoods and exposed rust seemed to explode in a huge cloud as if in a movie.

Skipping all the hospital details, when I got out, I wanted to visit my TR-3 and figure how to fix her. There was no fixing. The crash bent the solid frame at the driver's seat; the engine and transmission were wrecked. I cried. Eventually, I visited the wall we hit and saw the rusty scrape that killed my metal mate. I cursed it and the thief who caused all this grief. Had that wheel come off thirty feet farther, beyond the wall, we would have controlled the spin with no damage.

I married that girl, and we had a son. Yet, I still rue Valentine's Day and Labor Day. Was my metal mate another bad romance? It became that for me, and I still grieve the loss to this day.

The Anniversary Dinner

by Angela Zimmerman

From somewhere deep within his slumber, Greg was able to smell food.

Not just any food, but roasted chicken, carrots, and *maybe, yes that was it*, sweet potatoes. The scent of his favourite dinner guided Greg out of sleep and towards the crest of wakefulness.

It was when he tried to lift his arms to rub his eyes, he realised that his arms were tied to the chair he was in. Suddenly, the trip to wakefulness hit him like a brick wall. He was fully awake and fully aware that something was drastically wrong.

Before him was a table full of a beautifully

prepared dinner. A perfectly roasted chicken sat on a silver platter with a side of buttered, multi-coloured carrots. A bowl of steaming sweet potatoes joined two glasses and a bottle of wine on the table that was lit by candles burning in a crystal candelabra. Greg was seated at the head of the heavy oak table, tied to a wooden chair with thick nylon rope.

As he frantically struggled against the ropes, feeling them bite into his skin, he tried to make sense of his surroundings. Other than the beauty of the table, the room was dark and damp. There was no light anywhere else but from the table. From what he could see, the room was a small cellar, but the combination of his fear and darkness made it seem like a vault.

He rocked the chair back and forth, trying to find some leverage in the tightness of his binds. There was none. Frantically, he struggled until he realised that nothing was working. Then he slowly gave up fighting and started yelling.

"HEY!! HEEEY! Somebody! Somebody help me!" he yelled into the dark. He continued to yell until his words dissolved into whimpers.

From somewhere in the room's darkness, a door opened. With squinted eyes, Greg watched as a figure walked out of the light and through the darkness of the room to the end of the table.

She stopped at the edge of the table, opposite to him, and folded her arms. Her brown hair hung loose down her back and the light from the candles made her face soft and delicate. Her sundress was entirely out of place in the dark coldness of the room. *Everything about her is out of place*, Greg thought. She tilted her head and smiled lovely at him.

"You're awake! You were out for a long time. I was worried that maybe I gave you a little too much sleepy-sleepy."

Greg was struck by how childish her voice sounded. She must have been a woman of 20, maybe 25, but her voice and her sing-song speech pattern made her sound so much younger. He stared at her with eyes wide.

"You did this?" He had to work to push the words out of his dry mouth. He was exhausted, not just from struggling, but from being racked with fear and confusion. None of it made sense to him and none of it felt safe.

"Of course I did, you big silly head! How else would we celebrate our anniversary? Especially," she giggled as she started to round the table and walk towards Greg, "when you won't answer your cell phone." She made a pout face at him. "I've been calling you all week. You never even answer."

She stopped walking when she got to the side of Greg's chair. She paused for a moment, then began stroking his hair.

"It's ok though. I know how busy you are. I've been following you and oh, boy! Do you have a jam-packed day! You are so dedicated to your job, and your art! Oh, and your kitty cat! Felix, right? He's so cute!" She almost purred the last words.

She stepped back to the side of the table and held her hands under her chin, "So I thought, since it was our anniversary, I would make you your favourite dinner so you didn't have to worry about doing anything special. I wanted to show you how much I care and how much I value you. So, I saw this dinner in a picture at your house, the one with your family all around the table? And I thought I'd make it for you." Her smile, huge and saccharine, made Greg want to vomit.

"You followed me? You know about my cat? YOU WERE IN MY HOUSE? Who the hell are you? Why are you doing this?" The questions tumbled out of Greg's mouth as he began to struggle again.

Her smile instantly turned into a look of disgust. "Don't talk like that. You know me, Greg. We've been together for a year. You gave me your pen at the post office when I was trying to mail a letter to my mama back home. Remember?"

"I have no idea what the hell you are talking about," Greg said through gritted teeth. "I don't have a girlfriend. I'm not even into girls, you freak!"

She stormed around from her side of the table and slapped Greg hard enough to make his lip bleed.

"But you said you liked my sweater! And you let me use your blue pen! AND I KEPT IT!" She struck him again as her voice grew louder. "I could see it in your eyes! You were in love with me from that moment!"

Her blows came fast and hard until her palm was pink and Greg had blood dribbling out of the corner of his swollen lips. She walked backward around the corner of the table, eyes never leaving Greg's now red and spotted face.

"Why are you men always like this? I do everything for you, I carry the weight of the entire relationship, and for what? For NOTHING!" Her voice seemed too loud to come out of such a small body. "It's always like this! I give my heart, I give EVERYTHING! And what do I get? I get someone who doesn't even know who I am!"

The tears that streamed down her now red face left behind black pathways of mascara.

Greg spat blood onto the floor. "That's because I

don't fucking know you! Maybe we ran into each other once before. And maybe I liked your sweater. I try to be a nice guy, so I like to compliment people. But look, lady, trust me, we have never and will never be a couple! I don't know why you have this idea in your head, but it's not true. Now, GET ME OUT OF HERE!"

"I'm sorry, Greg, I really, really am." She snuffed her nose and wiped the tears and mascara from her face. "But if this is how you're going to treat me, how you are going to treat our love, then this is goodbye. We'll just have to break up."

From the table, near the now cooled and forgotten chicken, she pulled a knife from the platter.

"I won't let any man break my heart. You can join the others that have tried."

She started walking closer to his chair with the knife extended in her shaking hands. Greg felt bile rising in his throat as fear replaced the anger that had been colouring his vision.

He tried to rock the chair, twist his arms, move his body; anything to get away from the glistening knife and the eerily calm woman making their way towards him. Bloody spittle flew from his mouth as he worked against his restraint. She closed the last few feet between them and then climb up and straddled his lap. His breath came in short gasps as she sat on him with the knife between their chests.

Her light blue eyes looked deeply into his as she used the tip of the knife to trace the line of his jaw.

"We were so happy together, Greg. I had so many plans for us. We were going to be together forever. But you ruined it. And now…now it's all over."

The knife caught on his chin, opening the skin just enough for a small drop of blood to emerge. Greg saw something shift in her eyes. Her anger and betrayal had been replaced by something more primal, more urgent. Instead of heartbroken, Greg fearfully realised, she now looked hungry.

She leaned her head forward enough, so her mouth was almost touching Greg's.

"I have to do this. But I'll tell you a secret." Slowly she licked his chin, cleaning the small cut with her tongue. Greg closed his eyes in disgust.

"When it has to happen, I kind of love this part."

Then fireworks went off in Greg's chest. A rush of hot pain began to radiate from under his sternum to his ribs. He opened his eyes and looked down.

The knife from the table was no longer in her hands. She had buried it, handle deep, in his chest.

Blood poured from the wound as she slowly

climbed off his lap, leaving her dress and legs stained with a dark rich crimson. Greg tried to scream but could only force out a gargle as she put her fingers in the current of blood coming from the knife. When she slowly brought them to her mouth, he felt his consciousness slip away.

With a swift tug of the handle, she pulled the blade free of Greg's chest. Blood began spilling out at an alarming rate as she turned her back on the twitching and gasping Greg. She made her way to the head of the table, straightened her dress, and sat down. She used the knife, blood and all, to cut into the chicken. She plated the meat, served herself a few of the carrots, and got a huge spoonful of sweet potatoes.

Then she ate dinner while she watched Greg, and their relationship, die.

Up in the Tree House

by Archit Joshi

God, she looks beautiful!

He leaned against her wardrobe, admiring once more the fine conjugation of pure beauty and silent moonlight. Half her face was in darkness, the other half illuminated by a solitary beam of moonlight. He marvelled over the many obstacles the beam would've had to fight to make its way through her curtains. Perhaps the celestials loved her as much as he did.

She always slept peacefully. Somehow, she had learned to disrobe her troubles off her shoulders, with her clothing, before getting into bed. Not a care in the world. Her dark curls would fall to her shoulders and then disappear under her blanket, like a coursing waterfall fading along its tumultuous descent.

He shifted his weight, waiting. Any moment now, out of some weird habit, she would curl up into a ball, bundling up her blanket between her legs. Seasons didn't matter to her, and she always slept with a blanket tossed over her body. Every night, he would gently gather the blanket by its corners and douse her with its warmth.

If only she knew.

As if on cue, she snuggled up in a ball. Rearranging her blanket, he was tempted to graze a swift finger over the small of her back. *No!* With unearthly self-restraint, he pulled himself away. Blowing a kiss in her direction, he sauntered to her bedroom window. With the sure footing of someone who'd done it a hundred times, he climbed down a pipe that ran down the wall and plopped down with a soft thud onto the gravel below. Vaulting over the wrought-iron doors of her building, he walked home, a merry tune playing in his head.

It wasn't that they didn't try. They tried everything they could to make him feel loved, feel safe. And he would've felt like he belonged too, if he hadn't found out

the truth so...unceremoniously. The mistake had been his. He shouldn't have been snooping around in his parents' closets in the first place.

Hrishabh was bored out of his wits that lazy Sunday. He'd already broken the fire truck they had bought him after he'd begged for it. His mother was out in the backyard, hanging the laundry on the clothesline. His father was out with his friends, enjoying his day of bliss. Looking for things to do, he'd found the door to his parents' room open. Curious, he'd gone inside. He'd practically grown up in this room, but something about the secrecy and the sneaking sent a tingle down his back. He went to his parents' cupboard and started rummaging through everything he could find. Nothing was out of sorts until he found a strip of pills, only two of which were remaining. The details had been scratched off the wrapper and he had no way of knowing what they were for. He considered popping one in just for fun but decided against it. They'd notice. Putting the pills back as they were, he wondered what else he might find. Drawers were hurled open, clothes were thrown amok.

His groping hand found something, a sheaf of papers, hidden deep under layers and layers of folded clothes. He pulled it out, smacked the dust off it.

As he read the first couple of lines, he found out his entire life had been a lie.

As soon as Inspector Vyom Rane entered Room 406 of the ladies hostel, the rancid smell hit him like a punch in the gut. Gloving his hands, he approached the body.

"The maid discovered the body, sir," Constable Omkar Shirke reported.

"Id?"

Shirke produced the woman's driving licence.

Padmaja Pawar, 26.

"Twenty-fucking-six." Turning towards the waiting constable, Vyom barked, "Notify the closest relatives, I'll be at the station shortly to interview them. Have the maid wait there too; I need to talk to her."

Shirke gave Vyom a half-assed salute before walking out of the hostel bedroom.

Sub-Inspector Sanat Bawade appeared in the bedroom.

"No signs of struggle, sir," he reported. "Doors weren't forced open, but I did find a tree that runs down the building. Very close to the window. Padmaja must've left it open to let some air in. Summer's a sucker this year."

Vyom grunted an acknowledgment, thinking about the numerous windows the killer must have passed on his way to the fourth floor. What must the other girls be going through?

"Anyone aside from the maid see anything?"

"No sir. The hostel doesn't appoint a watchman."

"They will, now."

Vyom turned towards Padmaja. *What secrets do you have for me?* He brought out the photograph from the first murder and compared it with the current crime scene.

This woman, too, had been left lying on her stomach, face stuffed into the pillow. Bruises on the naked body indicated signs of rape. But the killer hadn't wanted to face her during the act. *Low confidence, guilt. This guy wants to stop killing but doesn't know how.* The killer would probably call out to the police after his next murder, leave signs asking for help. What Vyom couldn't explain was the missing hair from the victim's head. The bald spots were more noticeable this time. It was as if the killer had pulled out entire tufts.

He gently turned over the victim's body to inspect the cut at her throat. Alternating between the photograph and the victim, he noted the obvious surety with which the killer had used the knife on this woman. The first victim had bled to a slow death; the cuts to her throat had been sloppy and unsure.

"Seems like he's evolving," Vyom announced to no-one in particular.

"Evolving, sir?" Sanat asked.

"Bawade, the two murders are connected."

Sanat didn't respond, but the disrespect hung in the air.

"Out with it!"

"Well," Sanat hesitated. "The two victims look nothing alike. The first one was dark, chubby. Padmaja is fair, slender."

"Something else connects them, something symbolic only to the suspect." Vyom pinched the bridge of his nose and massaged it. "But the MO screams of the same person."

Sanat fell back into silence. He wondered whether Inspector Vyom's excitement was clouding his judgement. His superior had been reading a lot of Roy Hazelwood these days. But they couldn't declare a serial until they ran background checks on the new victim, found some connection between her and Sakshi Potdar, the first victim.

"I'm all for your modern techniques, boss. But I'm

afraid we'd need more concrete evidence to dismiss any possibilities yet. Unless, of course, your psychological hoo-hah can tell us who did this..."

"I can't tell you who did this yet," Vyom snapped. "But I *can* tell you this; he's someone who keeps a menial job, where he feels disrespected. He does...this," Vyom gestured towards the victim, "to enjoy being in control. The first murder was incidental, probably to keep the woman from identifying him, but he found murder brought him more satisfaction than rape. He feels guilty about killing, but at the same time, he needs to compulsively chase after that gratification. This is just the beginning, and it's going to get messy."

Sanat admired the boss's conviction, but the only way Vyom could be certain of his theory was for another innocent woman to lose her life.

"For the sake of young women out there, let's hope you're wrong," he said solemnly.

"Let's hope I am," Vyom agreed. *But patterns don't lie.*

Debanshi awoke to find a parrot chirping at the window. Stretching herself out of slumber, she hunted around for her clothes. Throwing on a nightgown, she trundled to her kitchen, groped her way to some biscuits and picked one out for the birdie. Making little crumbs of it, she laid them out gently at the windowsill, frightening the bird away. A while later, the bird timidly trotted back, and began pecking at the food.

Debanshi smiled. Today was such a lovely day! The sun was out, the air was clear, not a single cloud up in the sky. All good signs. Debanshi believed in them a lot. She had to. What else is there? Isn't it scary, knowing so many things are out of your control? Much more relieving to believe that God doesn't play dice. Her life had been uprooted once when she'd been twelve. Her father's job transfer had torn her away from everything she knew. Since then, a series of incidents had brought her here, during which she had found herself, found her true calling. It was too overwhelming to even think that anything other than fate was at play.

Today, she needed the signs to be in her favour. The interview was going to change everything. Finally, she could leave her stupid job at the call centre and have a more sophisticated lifestyle, bring in more money for her side-hustle. After all, she had her father to prove wrong.

Preparing a cup of coffee absently, she thought of the vicious fight eight months ago. Her father's undermining voice still rang in her ears. *You'll never make it in the business world. Just get a job, make some steady money.* One part milk, two parts water. *Marry into a good home, don't dream of too much.* Two tablespoons of powdered coffee. *I don't need your help, Daddy. I'll make it on my own.* Set it to boil.

Well, she was far from 'making it', but getting a side job for the steady cash-flow was almost a page out of the Entrepreneur's Guidebook.

After the very last dregs of coffee were tossed down, she hurried to her bathroom to draw a bath. *Shit!* Her ankle twisted at an ugly angle as she slipped across the bathroom floor. Moaning, she clawed at the walls for support.

"It's alright, sweetie," she said to herself. "The universe is just testing your will." She winced with the effort of standing up. Sidestepping the wet blotch on the bathroom floor, she bent down to inspect it.

Just a few drops of shampoo.

After a cleansing bath, she dried herself, fluffed her dark curls, slipped into carefully ironed clothes and blew a quick kiss at her reflection in the mirror. Grabbing her bag, she locked the door to her apartment and limped down to catch a taxi.

She felt confident about the interview. Her ankle

hurt, but her wits were still about here. She inhaled deeply and allowed the positive energy to fill her mind and body. Yes, she could feel the goodwill in the air. It was almost as if someone was lovingly watching over her.

Climb, climb, climb!

Panting, Hrishabh finally plopped down on the thick rug they'd spread out over the tree house. He loved it here. His father had taken two whole days off work to build this for him, with him. His father might have many flaws, but not trying was definitely not one of them. They'd had loads of fun building this tree house. Mother had plied them with lemonade. Hrishabh had felt like a grownup then, hammering nails and lifting logs.

The tree house had two gaping holes, acting as windows. One faced his house down below and the street. He would spend many an evening here, amazed at how tiny everything looked from up here. With his chin resting on the 'window' sill, he would gaze at the people below, imagine stories of random passers-by.

The other window overlooked the neighbouring building. The height of the tree house matched with the bedroom window of that Sinha girl. He quite liked her.

They'd hardly ever talked—he hardly ever talked much with anybody—but she would smile at him whenever she saw him, and her eyes were always kind.

This window was where he sat right now, hoping he would catch Debanshi in her room. He needed to speak with someone. Ever since he'd found out he'd been given up at birth, he had shut himself off. His parents—adoptive parents—were worried sick. But they were the last people he wanted to vent in front of. He was bitter, confused. Angry at everybody and nobody. It was all too much. How dare they keep such a big secret from him?

He stared out the window, wishing Debanshi to come into her room. As if by magic, she waltzed into her room, playing with her ponytails.

"Deb...Debanshi," Hrishabh croaked, his voice barely audible. Before he could raise it and call out again, he noticed that she was in a hurry.

In so much of a hurry, in fact, that she forgot to draw the blinds before changing her clothes.

A part of Hrishabh wanted to peel his eyes away, but another mischievous part of him wanted to watch on. One by one she took off her clothes, until nothing remained but bare skin. She let her curly hair loose against her bony back. She kicked the clothes away and took different ones from her wardrobe. Putting them on, she scurried out of her room. Moments later, he heard the familiar roar of Mr. Sinha's rusty old motorcycle. He rushed to the other window just in time to catch her speeding away with her father.

That night, Hrishabh had a hard time hiding an awkward lump under his blanket.

It had been a busy day at 'Arora dernier cri Clothing'. He sat alone in a corner, winding down after a harrowing few hours. Soon, they'd all leave without as much as a courtesy glance at him. It was all fair, he supposed. He didn't do so well at his job.

"Distracted by God knows what..." Mr. Arora had shouted in an hour-long rant. He'd listened, his blood boiling inside, but hadn't uttered a word in defence. Later on, he'd returned to the shop floor to a room full of sniggers and nasty looks. The men, he didn't care about all that much. It was the women whose contempt ate away at him. He wanted to please them so bad, he didn't quite know how to behave around them.

It wasn't any different today, except that the boss was in a particularly foul mood. After the shop closed to customers, and most of the other employees had left, he stomped down to the shop floor and cornered Arpita, the unfortunate customer service assistant who'd been tasked with following up with the police.

"Any luck?"

"No, sir." Arpita had her gaze glued to the floor. "They...they shooed me away."

"Shooed you away?" Arora spat. "What are you, a bloody pigeon?"

To anyone not in the close vicinity of an angry Prakash Arora, the colouring of his skin would seem quite comical. Like a cartoon character, his face would go from red to purple. But to those poor souls who were caught in the man's crosshairs, the anger meant a lot of personal insults and flying spittle.

"They said they're understaffed...murder," Arpita mumbled, hardly audible to her own ears.

"Speak up, dimwit!" Arora thundered. "You can't even address MY grievances, how're you going to fare with angry customers? We have wigs and mannequins stolen, and you care about the daft police staffing? It's my pockets the money goes out of..." And so it went on for another seven minutes. The remaining few employees hurriedly stole away. Somehow Arora managed to bring Arpita's mother-in-law into the argument and left her flustered out of her wits. In his anger, before storming out, Arora pulled out the plugs from all the sockets. The ignored employee in the corner grew very happy at this. After the thefts became more frequent, they'd installed security cameras as a precaution. Generally, they left these on, but in his rage, the boss had shut down every system connected to the power supply.

After Mr. Arora left, Arpita turned towards her fellow worker and decided to pass on some of the rage down the ladder. But Hrishabh didn't care. He'd listen to her crap for as long as she wanted to vent. Then she'd leave him in charge of pulling down the shutters.

No one around, in a room full of mannequins and curly-haired wigs. Hrishabh was so delighted, he decided to cancel his nightly visit to Debanshi and stay here in the shop instead. It would be good practice for tomorrow night.

His glare could've burnt a hole in the letter he clutched in his hand. It was Debanshi's appointment letter. *Welcome to CS Pophale and Associates. We are eager to have you on board.* Yes, he was happy she'd nailed the job, but the office policy had required her to cut her hair short. Idiots!

He sat alone in her room, wearing nothing but underwear. She'd gone off to stay at a colleague's house; for some business proposal for her baking. The letter crumpled at the ends where his finger bore into them. His rage was starting to get the better of him. It'd made him do curious things recently, pleasurable things, but left him feeling disgusted at himself afterwards. He needed help with his urges, and so he'd left the police a little note today, in some stranger's bedroom. He hadn't planned on it becoming so messy. But the sight of his beloved with her curls chopped off had caused him to over-react.

The thought of that event made the blood that was making his veins pop flow someplace else. He decided he needed to vent. Who knows what he might do otherwise? Twice in one day? Hmm... But where would he find a girl at this hour? Every girl took meticulous planning. Impulsiveness would probably ruin the experience.

He finally went into the bathroom. He was in there a good ten minutes, and then came out drying his hands on the underwear. He took it off, folded it neatly and placed it back in her wardrobe. Then, he put on his own, followed by the rest of his clothes, and then climbed out the window and shimmied down the drainpipe.

Inspector Vyom sat in his office, feet propped up on his desk. It was past dinnertime, and he would've loved nothing more than to wrap things up and go home to spend some time with Shruti, who was probably waiting on him for dinner. But his laptop screen glared at his face. He was reading the Board of Director's reply to his request for formal training in profiling. Needless to say, they'd turned it down. Again.

We are the police. We catch criminals through good old legwork and clues...

As he was getting to the end of the letter, his phone buzzed. Sanat.

"Sir, there's been another one."

We do not use psychobabble to draw predictions out of thin air.

Sanat sounded perplexed.

"It's exactly how you predicted, sir. And it's messy. Get here, ASAP." The line went dead. A text from Sanat followed, bearing the address of the crime scene.

What's next, a crystal orb?

Vyom flipped shut his laptop in one angry motion and grabbed his helmet. He quickly fired a short text to his wife and hurried out the station. Hopping onto his Royal Enfield Bullet, he sped off towards the scene, allowing the nippy wind to take his mind off of the BD's obstinacy.

The first thing Vyom noticed as he got to the crime scene was the neighbourhood. Although the bungalow was last in a row of houses, it was still a residential area, unlike the previous two girls' hostels located in remote areas. *He's getting restless.* This time, the perp had hit a modest bungalow. As he parked his motorcycle in the bungalow's driveway, he noticed a huge crack in one of its French windows. That would've made some noise.

He went inside to find a sobbing woman being consoled by Sanat.

He found Constable Shirke nearby and took him aside.

"Who's the lady?"

"She's the neighbour. She was at a party and came home a while back. She had plans with our victim for drinks tonight. Came here to find the window cracked. Reported the body soon after that."

Vyom sent Shirke to join Sanat in calming the neighbour down. He put on his gloves and found his way to an inner bedroom. As soon as he went in, his gaze was caught by something on the wall.

Help Me Stop

The p's were dripping downwards, the blood becoming a dry coagulation as it raced down the wall. This time too, the victim was turned face down, but he hadn't placed her dutifully this time. The legs were sprawled apart, the sheets all cluttered under the woman's body. All signs of frenzy. Sanat soon walked into the room, followed closely by Constable Shirke.

"We've sent the neighbour back to her home and given her strict instructions to be available for further investigations," Shirke announced.

"The victim's name is Shivanjali Desai, 27. Unmarried. Lived here alone," Sanat reported. "Notice the hair," he continued "This time, he shaved the woman bald."

Vyom followed Sanat's gaze and found straight, reddish dark hair stacked in a neat pile by Shivanjali's head.

"So, our killer hates hair, then?" Shirke said.

"No, Shirke, think," Sanat replied. The slight gleam in his eyes told Vyom some leg pulling was to be expected. "If he hated it, would he have arranged it so neatly?"

"No sir, it would've been scattered around the room."

"Exactly, my friend. Think like the killer, get all up in his head. That little detail is going to crack this case wide open."

"Stop it already!" Vyom growled, but some gears had started to turn in his head. Something scintillating was glimmering in his mind, some little detail that wanted to be remembered. After a moment of biting his lip, Vyom called it quits. *It'll strike when it strikes.*

Leaving his subordinates with orders to cordon off the area and notify the next of kin, Vyom decided to head home. He'd interview the neighbours first thing in the morning. People aren't always cooperative when the police come knocking at doors late at night.

On the ride back home, it struck.

Could it be?

"What're we doing here?" Shirke whispered. "Shouldn't we be interviewing the victim's neighbours?"

Sanat didn't reply. *Inspector Vyom and his hunches. Why was he following up a petty theft complaint when they had a murder at hand?*

Vyom seemed riled up.

"That little detail, Bawade?" he'd said on the phone. "It just might crack this case wide open." He'd hung up with orders to report at Arora dernier cri Clothing.

When they arrived, Vyom was already present and was barking off a list of characteristics to employees at the shop.

"This man is in his late twenties and shows poor performance at his job. He has difficulty communicating and shies away from interpersonal—"

"This is a customer-facing job," the owner, Arora, jutted in, rather rudely. "Why would he hang around if he hates talking to people?"

Vyom gestured at the mannequins placed around the shop and continued, "He often shows up late for work, is distracted most of the time. The women in your store might have complained about his indecent workplace behaviour..."

Vyom's voice trailed off on noticing a few timid female employees gazing at the floor.

"Something I should know, Arora?"

"Well, sir, I don't want to cause anyone any trouble..."

Rubbish, Vyom thought. All Arora wanted to

protect was his shop's reputation.

"This man might have killed three women and might possibly be out looking for a fourth. He's in enough trouble already."

Arora agreed to talk. There *was* someone matching Vyom's description at the shop, but he hadn't reported for duty today.

"Doubtless, he'll report late, as if his father owns this shop," Arora continued, backed by the female employees to recall instances of lewd workplace behaviour, making passes at the ladies and touching up the female customers who went to him for fitting and measurements.

"Address?"

Arora gave it to him. Before Vyom and his team could storm off, Arora clutched at his elbow.

"Sir, what about my stolen wigs and mannequins?"

Vyom glared until Arora released his grip.

Hrishabh watched flecks of golden and blue dance in the flame of his lighter. At his feet was a bag of leaves he'd raked up in the early morning. His back hurt from having to remain uncomfortably on his haunches. It didn't matter. The tree house looked exactly as the one his father had built with him, complete with the two makeshift windows. At length, he opened the bag wide and selected a few fresh leaves.

Dried leaves, they catch fire easily. It's almost as if they're awaiting a kiss of the flame, to burn and wither as they fall to the ground. Greener leaves take a tad more time to be consumed. When you pluck a healthy leaf from a tree and set it aflame, you're essentially claiming a piece of the universe's creation for yourself; it was those leaves he enjoyed burning the most. The leaf might have created life and energy for its tree. It might have flirted with dew drops of the dawn. And yet, it was his hand that would seal its fate.

He sat at one of the windows and watched as plummeting fire turned a lustrous green to the pale grey of ash. With every little fire he set, his heart burned with equal anguish. *Debanshi.* Every cell in his body was longing for her, and yet he had to stay away. He feared what he might do to her once she was in his embrace. He feared that his gentle fingers stroking her cheek would find their way around her throat. When he'd accidentally heard from some of her relatives in Calcutta that she'd settled in Pune, he'd left home in search of her. He'd wanted to confront her, confess his love. But now he had no such forceful intentions, only fear. *What will I do to her?*

His mind, wandering over the memory of Debanshi's slender body, was jerked away from the daydream by the sound of sirens in the distance.

Ah…help at last.

The crumbling house was nothing more than a few rooms and a small terrace. Fallen into the right hands, it could've been turned into a quaint little bungalow, but now it was in total disrepair.

Sanat was the first in through the door, gun raised. Before the others could storm in after him, he took an involuntary step backwards.

"What in God's heaven is this?"

The room was a stinking mess. Strewn across the floor were dolls of all sizes, in different levels of undress. They were marked with 'x' at questionable places and were glistening with a repulsive wetness. In a dusty corner, Arora's precious mannequins lay violated, the plastic cracked in a grotesque circular shape, the wigs from the shop stuck to their heads. Above the bed, three strands of hair hung separately from nails hammered in the wall. Even more terrifying were the rows of other nails lining the walls all around the room, waiting for more hair to join them.

"A man with a mission to complete," Vyom muttered. He poised his gun and stepped around the dolls to check the bathroom. No sign of Hrishabh. A waft of wind carried smoke through an open window. For a split second, Vyom closed his eyes, pained to think of where the smoke might be coming from. Reluctantly, he walked to the window, squinted his eyes. He could see a dark outline of someone sitting in a tree house in the backyard.

He motioned with his gun. "Let's go."

Feet thundered back around the house to the backyard. A face peered from a hole in the tree house, eyes expressionless. Shirke and a few other uniforms took position below the tree house and trained their guns on the man above.

"Hrishabh Sengupta!" Sanat raised his voice. "You are under arrest for the murder of Sakshi Potdar, Padmaja—"

"Don't bother with the names." Vyom cut him short. "I don't think he saw those women as people."

Her heart could've fluttered right up to the sky. She'd made her first sale! Debanshi's dream of her very own patisserie had inched one step closer to becoming tangible. Granted, the order had been for a simple children's party, and the pay cheque—divided between her partners—could buy a luxury no greater than the next month's Wi-Fi bill, but she had made something with her own hands and sold it. After the party, she'd hurried off to an unfocused second shift at work. From there, she had raced home, took a long, blissful shower and hopped right into bed.

The adrenaline made it difficult for her to sleep peacefully. She even woke up in the middle of the night to rearrange her blanket.

The next day, the sun shone extra bright to cheer for her little victory. Readying herself for another day of slogging, she found she had a few minutes to spare. She fell back on her bed, and opened her Instagram. Her celebratory post had gotten over 300 likes. Her scrolling was disturbed by a notification from her Daily News app.

Women of Pune, you can breathe safe again...

She clicked on 'Read more.'

Disturbed killer Hrishabh Sengupta arrested for the rape and murder of Sakshi Potdar, Padmaja Pawar and Shivanjali Desai...

Debanshi heaved a little sigh of relief. All the

negativity of the murders had taken a toll on her aura. But well, all was good with the world again. She decided it was time to leave for work and slipped her phone into her purse. All along the cab ride, she felt something nag at the back of her mind. Something was amiss, and it always bothered her when placeless emotions like this picked at her pure energy.

At the office, all anyone could ever talk about was Hrishabh Sengupta. One of her co-workers had spread out a newspaper article over his desk. Debanshi was hurrying by to her desk when she saw the man's photo alongside the article. And then time flew in reverse.

Suddenly she was back in her old home, looking out the window at her shy neighbour in his tree house. He never talked much, but his eyes were distant, lonely. She would smile at him and he would awkwardly curl up his lips. She'd hoped to get to know him better, but before she had the chance, she'd had to move cities. Before leaving, she'd gone to his door, looking to say goodbye. Mrs. Sengupta had told her he was away, had been for a few hours, and she didn't know where he'd disappeared to. A few months into her new life, she'd completely forgotten about the awkward little kid next door.

Abruptly, she found herself leaving the Calcutta breezes behind and return to Pune's oppressive heat.

The universe had decided to remind her of a long-forgotten friend. Her heart came alive then, and it had only one purpose.

I must see him.

Vyom wiped sweat off his brow as he reported back to the station after lunch. He saw Shirke talking with an athletic woman, who was anxiously playing with her short curls.

"Relation with the accused?"

"I knew him as a child. We were neighbours."

Vyom eyed the Constable. "The artist's muse," he said under his breath.

"I'm sorry?"

"Right this way ma'am."

He wanted to rip his own heart out and caress it, tell it things would be alright, that the end was near. Flies flitted around his mangled hair and the smell of urine didn't make breathing any easier.

Love can be greedy or selfish or hurtful at times, but the only thing it isn't is impure. To love is to allow your inflated self to subside and let another person in.

He'd lost his conquest, but he'd forfeited to keep her safe. Longing can bring out the monsters lurking in us all, and sometimes they take over. But the heart hopes…

He heard footsteps and his heartbeat quickened. He probably should've tried to run. He'd thought the hanging would finally free him of his sorrow, but the waiting and confinement had sowed the seed of doubt.

He looked up at the approaching people and forgot everything that was wrong with his life. Instead of the piss and heat, he could smell her perfume, and instead of the bars of his jail cell, he could see infinity, filled with joys incalculable. Her face was taught with worry, and he wanted nothing more than to reach out and hold it, allay whatever it was that was troubling her.

The Inspector pulled out a key and unlocked the cell. He stepped aside and allowed her to enter.

I am breathing in the same air as her.

She came inside uncertainly, her eyes searching his for answers.

Did you do what they're saying you did? she doubtless wanted to ask.

Yes, he would reply. *For you.*

He stumbled towards her, hands outstretched.

"Distance," the Inspector barked. *Insolent bastard.*

He refrained from taking her into his arms and

bringing his lips to her. His legs gave out under him, and he chose instead to sit down on the mattress in his cell. She towered over him, arms on her hips.

"Do you remember me, Hrishabh?" Her voice was wavering, sweet as notes from a flute.

He smiled. *As if I could ever forget you...* He remembered every inch of her body.

At length, she burst out, "They must have made some mistake!" She turned and glared at the Inspector. "Look how innocent he looks, how subdued! I've known this man as a child. He couldn't have done the horrid things they're writing about in the papers. You have the wrong man in custody!"

"Shush, dear," Hrishabh whispered before the riled Inspector could burst this bubble of bliss. He grunted with effort as he stood up and put a silent finger to her quivering lips.

"Do you believe in love, Debanshi?"

"I will help you! My firm can manage a lawyer—"

He shook his head, his heart now at total peace. This time, he gently grabbed both her shoulders.

"Do you believe in love?"

"I believe in fate, Hrishabh, and it has brought me here, to help you."

"So be it. Trust fate and let all your worry fade

away. All will be well."

"Let me find a good lawyer. I know in my heart you're innocent!"

He shook his head again, with the air of someone wise. *Hearts are funny little creatures. Angelic one moment, filled with demonic rage the next.*

"Stop, stop. All I ask of you is to share a bottle of wine with me."

Before her doubt weakened her resolve, he quickly turned to the Inspector, "Can we arrange that?"

The Inspector hesitated and then shrugged. "Whatever keeps you from murdering more women."

Vyom felt sheepish as he gave the order for a bottle of wine to be bought. This was by far the most bizarre day he'd ever had to face, and as someone who dealt with the bottom feeders of Pune, that was saying something.

The bottle was brought, two of their own teacups fetched.

"Make sure this doesn't reach our kindly superiors," he warned the staff present. He took the wine and the cups to the back of the station where the woman was tapping her heels outside the cell. He made to unlock it again, purposely fumbling with the keys.

"I'm breaching some serious protocols here."

"Inspector, you will have my signed confession if you let me have this."

Vyom smirked. The man's living quarters were proof enough. *Boy, does this man get off on being in control.* But what had Vyom to lose? Perhaps this little incident could allow him to jot down his own little insights into the book he was currently reading.

Hrishabh waited for him to leave. *Fat chance.* Vyom entered with the woman and cuffed one of Hrishabh's hands to the prison bars.

"Is that really necessary?" Debanshi asked.

"Trust me." *What sort of goody-goody world does this woman live in?* "He can enjoy his precious drink with one hand."

He kept the cell door open and stationed himself some distance away, wary.

Not many words were said. They sipped their drink in silence. After a while, Shirke joined Vyom in his vigilance.

"He must really love her."

"Like a ship does a lighthouse," Vyom replied, wondering about the nails on the wall waiting for more victims. "That's not love, that's dependency." *Debanshi*

Sinha was a mere object of fixation, a compulsion. They hadn't released case specifics to the press yet; otherwise Debanshi wouldn't have come here.

Finally, Vyom decided enough was enough. He ordered Debanshi to come out. Before exiting, she paused at the door.

"You sure you don't want me to get help?"

"As sure as I have ever been."

Something about Hrishabh's tone sent a shiver down Vyom's back. Brushing the feeling away, he locked up the cell, forgetting the bottle inside.

"I'll be back for that signed confession shortly."

A self-assured smile.

Vyom asked his constable to escort the lady out. The moment their backs were turned, a shrill noise of glass shattering echoed, followed by Debanshi's guttural scream.

"Open it, open it!" She ran to the cell as more officers scrambled to the back of the station, but the deed had already been done. Debanshi rattled against the cell door.

A bloodied hand snaked through the prison bars. Debanshi took it in hers. With utter incredulity, the policemen stared as she brought it to her face, tears mingling with blood.

She doesn't know, Vyom told himself. *She wouldn't be doing this if she knew.* But he wasn't so sure anymore. He was rethinking everything he thought he knew about people and their behaviour. They must not be teaching this stuff at Quantico.

He watched helplessly as Hrishabh fell limp to the floor, grasping, in his dying moments, the hand of the woman who'd inadvertently caused three innocent women to lose their lives.

A crystal orb would have been very fitting here…this was nothing less than a fairy tale.

The Call

by Chris Bannor

She crawled into his arms and felt his lips against her cheek. She took a deep breath, wanting nothing more than to drown in his scent. They had warned her to stay away from him, but no one understood the pull he had over her. If she believed in love at first sight, she would say her fate had been cast, but she wasn't a believer. There was no such thing as soulmates, no one perfect person in the world. No, this was imperfection and temptation and days of longing buried in overtime and cheap liquor.

"You've returned to me," he whispered into her ear. "I was beginning to worry."

"I tried not to," she admitted. Oh, she craved, but her mind still worked even as lust filled her blood. There was nothing good that would come of this. There was no dinner with the family over holidays, and no happy ending in this embrace. There was passion and lust and dangerous things promised against the tight press of fingers and lips.

"You would deny me this?" He drew away from her and held her back by the arms. He searched her eyes for the truth as if she didn't know what it meant to give in to this.

"No, not for long," she said as she tried to pull him closer. "I needed to think. I can't think when I'm with you."

"Thinking is overrated." His lips curved up into a smile just as they descended to her own. With their bodies entwined, she couldn't think of a reason to stop this. When she had been at home, it had been easier to understand the repercussions. She had still come tonight though. As her thoughts turned to lust and longing, she held on to that. She made the choice to come here tonight. Away from him, away from the allure and magnetism that he invoked simply by being, she made the decision to return.

"Help me forget then," she answered against his lips.

Morning came with the fog. She woke in a strange room, with no memory of getting there or most of the night's events. She remembered him. She remembered the pulsing drive to be with him. She remembered returning to his arms after nights of pushing it down and struggling to tell herself that she didn't want any of this. It never mattered. Her determination never mattered. When the call came, only he mattered.

She pulled on a robe and walked to the bathroom, stopping to look at the mirror on the way. Her face was gaunt and pale, with eyes that stared out of sunken pockets. Her once luxurious hair was thin and dull. Skeletal arms bracketed a too-thin waist and her ribs poked against her skin like a cadaver.

She was ravenous. She could smell food and knew that there was a tray waiting for her once she was out of the shower. She would eat her fill (it was never enough; food wasn't what she craved), then return back to her life as if she hadn't spent the evening with a myth. She would lie to herself that she was strong enough to resist his call. That when next he beckoned her into his arms, she would resist. That it really was her choice to return.

The door opened slowly behind her and she saw him enter, pushing the hotel cart of food before him as he positioned it near the bed. "You look hungry, my love," he said with a warmth that was sincere and welcoming. "Come eat with me."

"I was going to shower," she reminded him. Their routine never faltered. She came to his call. In the morning, she showered, and when she came out, he was gone. She ate alone, then she went back home.

"This morning, come eat with me," he said. "I'm feeling just as hungry as you are."

She should say no, she knew that, but his call was already too strong. He had taken her strength of will in a long, slow courtship before she'd ever realised what he was. He had taken the strength of her body with each press of lips. She went to him anyway, dropping her robe as she joined him on the bed, his kiss as hungry as ever.

As their lips met and his hands gripped her carefully, she realised this was the end. There would be no more. She would not survive his last kiss.

The coven was right. Not even a witch's love could tame an incubus.

Red Fallen Snow

by Cindar Harrell

"Most women love Valentine's Day, but I'm not most women. I hate it with my very soul. It brings me nothing but rage now. Rage and darkness. And all because of *him*.

"I used to envy people who had someone. I would see their pictures, taken as they played in the snow on Valentine's, their eyes filled with love, no other thoughts for anyone but each other. While they were making precious memories, I stared out into the beautiful world of white alone, longing to run out into the snow, but having no one to join me.

"I was always alone. But then *he* came."

"How did you meet?"

"We were in a library. I dropped my books and he stopped to pick them up for me. Our eyes met, and I knew then that our love would be eternal."

"Go on."

"Our first date was kind of awkward. One of his exes dropped by and kept hogging all of his attention. She was jealous of us.

"He gave me roses the day before Valentine's. My heart stopped as he handed them to me over the counter. The snow had just begun to fall outside, covering the world like a fluffy blanket. He said that he would carpet the ground with rose petals for me. Just for me. Finally, I would be the one making beautiful memories on a snowy Valentine's Day. It was going to be perfect."

"What happened, Maggie?"

"Well…"

"Your body language just changed. You became tense and your eyes narrowed. Did he do something to anger you?"

"I went to the park outside the library where we met. It was our favourite spot, like it was made just for the two of us. Since it was snowing, no one else was around, we would get to be alone, just like I wanted. The ground glistened, beautiful and white, just like my dress.

But then *she* showed up."

"Who?"

"His ex, who do you think? She just couldn't take it! She couldn't stand the thought that he had chosen me!"

"What did you do? Did you ask her to leave?"

"Of course I did!"

"And did she?"

"She didn't want to, but in the end, I finally convinced her."

"And how did you do that?"

"I have my ways."

"All right, and did he show up?"

"Yes, on time and perfect as always. He had arranged for the ground to be covered in red rose petals, the red fallen snow looked so beautiful in the moonlight."

"The snow was red?"

"Yes."

"Not the petals?"

"No, the petals were."

"What about the snow?"

"The snow was white."

"He spread the roses while you stood there?"

"No, he had done it before."

"But I thought you were the first one to arrive? You said the snow was white and bare then."

"No, I didn't! You're just trying to confuse me!"

"I'm sorry, please continue."

"He was shocked by how beautiful I was, nearly speechless in fact. I wore my red dress and had my raven hair down in loose curls. I picked up some of the rose petals and put them in my hair. He really liked that, I could tell because he shrieked with joy. We embraced, and it was better than anything I've ever felt before. It was like we were a couple in a fairy tale. He absolutely fell to pieces when I gave him his present."

"What did you give him?"

"A silver pocketknife. He loved it! He held it so tight, like he'd never let it go."

"So, everything went well?"

"Yes! It was magical! I wish I could relive that night again and again!"

"But you said that you hated Valentine's Day, that he was the cause. What changed, Maggie?"

"He did! I went to all that trouble getting him his present and he hasn't come to see me! I've called him so many times since that night, but he never answers and never calls me back! I just want to hear his voice again, to go out into the snow! I remember how warm and slick it made everything. Covering everything, but he won't call!"

"Do you think maybe something is stopping him from seeing you?"

"Like what? That bitch! Yes, she must be stopping him! You're right!"

"You're referring to his ex?"

"Yes!"

"Maggie, I want you to think carefully back to that night, again."

"All right, I can do that."

"Now, you've mentioned several times that the snow was red, and your dress was red. It seems to be a prominent colour in your memory of that night."

"Of course, everyone knows that Valentine's Day is all about red roses and hearts!"

"Yes, but you describe the snow as red, not white."

"That's because of the heart petals, I already told you."

"Heart petals? What's that? Blood?"

"What? No! Why would you say something so horrible! It was red because he spilled rose petals all over the ground!"

"But you said heart."

"I meant rose!"

"'Spilled' is an interesting word choice. It usually implies a liquid, not something like petals."

"Well, then whatever you would call it, I don't know."

"Where did the roses come from?"

"From them."

"Both of them?"

"Yes."

"Why would his ex give you roses?"

"No, not her! You're confusing me again!"

"Calm down, Maggie. I want you to think of something else now. The knife you gave him as a present, you said it was wet?"

"Yes. Everything was because of the snow."

"What colour was it?"

"Red."

"The knife or the snow?"

"Both, the snow made the knife red."

"Red?"

"No, wet! They were wet and white!"

"Calm down. Close your eyes and really focus. You've given him the knife. What does he do?"

"He gives me a present."

"Are your hands wet?"

"Yes."

"What colour are they?"

"Red."

"Where is he now?"

"On the snow."

"Where?"

"To my left. No, right."

"Which one?"

"Both!"

"Where did his ex go?"

"I got rid of her, so she would never bother us again."

"What colour is your dress?"

"Red."

"What colour is the snow?"

"Red."

"What colour is the knife?"

"Red!"

"Open your eyes. One last question, Maggie. What present did he give you for Valentine's Day?"

"His heart."

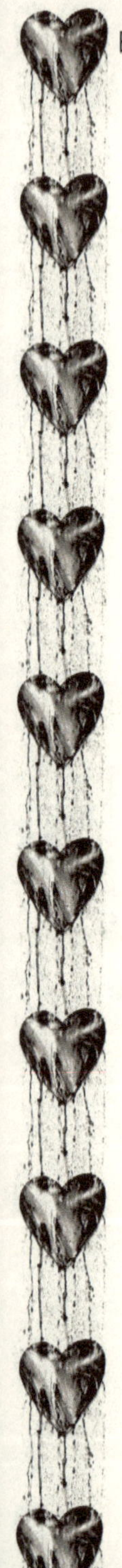

Second Date

by David Bowmore

Paris, 1985

For their first date, Julian had chosen an expensive restaurant. It was exquisite.

For their second date, she suggested the Jules Verne on the second level of the Eiffel Tower. Men threw longing glances in her direction and women envious ones. She was used to people looking at her and knew how to draw their attention; fortunately, she also knew how to blend into the scenery. However, right now she wanted to be seen. Being six feet tall in four-inch heels helped. Striking looks and cold blue eyes ensured people didn't forget her in a hurry. She wore a faux fur but preferred the real thing.

Julian was a gentleman. He stood when she excused herself. He ordered the right wine for each dish, and he treated the staff with respect. He kept the conversation neutral, staying away from topics of business and politics. They had a lot in common—a love of travel and old TV programmes—and he made her laugh. It was such a shame he would be dead before the night was over.

Given a choice, she would have picked a more secluded spot. It's easy to kill a man in the privacy of his own home, but Romanov was paying good money, very good money, and besides, it was unwise to refuse him his little indulgences. Romanov wanted Julian to die on the Eiffel Tower. Still, he must have been losing his marbles to think it would be possible to kill in such a public place and get away with it.

Her plan was simple. Lure Julian to the top under the pretence that she had never been there. In return, she promised—with heavy sexual innuendo—to satisfy his every need and succumb to his every desire. She would offer him a line of top quality coke to cement their forthcoming union.

The cocaine, of course, was cut with a not-so-healthy dose of cyanide and would ensure a quick but painful death. Then, as he lay dying, she would head to the rest room at a sedate but brisk pace, turn the reversible coat inside out, take the wig off, shake her hair out, remove the coloured contact lenses, unscrew the special heels and hopefully be on the Jardins du Trocadéro before anyone noticed the dead lawyer at the top of the most famous tower in the world. Tricky, but it was what Romanov wanted.

It was close to midnight when they got to the top. Fortunately, not many sightseers came up at night, especially at this time of year. The wind buffeting the tower took one's breath away. Finding a spot where they could shelter from the wind, she took a moment to marvel at the beauty of the great city by night.

"Come over here, Julian. I want to kiss you."

He clung to the iron frame by the elevator. She was sure he was about to bottle it and said, "Keep your eyes on me. Just look at me. That's it, Big Boy. Keep coming."

She put her arms around him, drawing him into a tight embrace and then looked down into his face. His forehead glistened with a fine sheen of perspiration. She kissed him long and sensually. After all, if a man is about to die, he might as well die happy.

"There. Wasn't that worth it?"

He smiled, his lips now shining with some of her red lipstick, and nodded.

"Fancy a line?" she said, opening her clutch and

waving a little paper sachet under his nose. He smiled again as she formed the fine powder into a thin line on the mirror of her compact.

She offered him a rolled up two-hundred franc note.

"Ladies first," he said.

"I couldn't possibly."

"I thought so." He took a step back from her. "How much is Romanov paying you to kill me?"

Her mouth opened a fraction as she tried to take in the full meaning of the words. How had he known? She didn't even have a back-up weapon with her. The alternative—beating him to death with her bare hands— was not only messy, but her only option if she was not to become one of Romanov's targets herself.

"I'll double it," he continued, unaware of her fist clenched in readiness to strike, "if you turn your unique skills on Romanov. Kill him and you'll be doing me and my associates a tremendous favour. How about it?"

She smiled and let the wind take the poison.

"This might be the beginning of a beautiful relationship," she said and kissed him again.

Roasted

by Dawn DeBraal

He married her on a whim. Met her on a dating site and she checked all his boxes. Independent, sexy, smart, beautiful. She had a great job and didn't want children. Paul was pushing forty and didn't want to raise children. Melanie had never married, so there were no kids for her to worry about either. A match made in heaven, or so he thought.

The first indication Paul had that something was amiss, came a few months after they were married. He happened to take the afternoon off from work and was lying on the couch watching some nameless talk show. The phone startled him. He picked it up with trepidation.

There was a moment of silence, and then, "Mr. Sandler?" *Robocall, dammit.*

"This is him."

"This is the Foster Collection Agency, on collecting a bill for Dr. Soloman. Can we make arrangements for a payment plan at this time, or are you disputing the bill?" She caught his attention.

"Soloman? I don't know a Dr. Soloman. You must have the wrong Paul Sandler. It happens all the time." He was about to hang up when he caught, "Melanie."

"Yes, Melanie is my wife." He was intrigued.

"This bill is in Melanie's name. She put you down as a payee."

"Well, how much is the bill?" Paul was now interested.

"Six thousand and thirty-three dollars, seventy cents."

"What is that for!" Paul raised his voice. "Did you charge the insurance company? She has a policy for us both."

"I'm sorry, sir, I don't have records here. I have been hired to collect the debt. If your wife signed a waiver, you might call the doctor's office directly for information. Would you like to set up a payment plan? If not, we will be putting up a red flag on your credit." Now, he was pissed.

"Look, I don't know what this is about, but if you want to set up a payment plan, I will look at that. How much a month?" Melanie had some explaining to do when she got home.

"With this amount, we are looking at five hundred and three dollars a month."

"Five hundred!" Paul shouted back at her.

"And three dollars. There is also an initial payment to divide this bill into a yearly payment plan. We can roll that into the payments, or we can put that on your credit card today."

"I am not giving you my credit card number over the phone, roll it into payments. Are we done here?" Paul was on his last nerve of civility, the relaxation he experienced on the couch was long gone, replaced with ire and angst.

Paul went out and started the lawnmower. So much for his half a day off. He needed to destroy something, and the lawn needed mowing. He thought of strategies to bring this up with his new wife in at least seven different ways, but all of them ended with, *why didn't you warn me?* The lawn done, he got out the hedge clippers and trimmed the whole front of the property. At least the yard was in order.

Melanie came home at five-thirty. Paul had a roast in the oven. He decided he would approach this civilly; they were still newlyweds, and he wanted to keep it that way.

"Honey, that smells wonderful. Pot roast? My favourite?" she said, opening the oven. He hated when she did that, it let all the heat out and had to start the build-up again. She hummed when she smelled the aroma, and then kissed him on the cheek.

He tried to start a conversation, but she said, "Hold that thought. I'm taking a shower; it was so hot at the office today, the air conditioner broke down, and you don't want to be around me." Melanie skipped out of the kitchen, and he heard the shower turn on in the bedroom. Sighing, Paul decided it could wait a little longer.

Dinner was lovely, they opened a bottle of wine, and she told him all about her day.

Then it was his turn.

"I got a strange call today."

"Oh, from whom?" Melanie looked interested.

"Dr. Soloman's collection agency."

"Hmmm, Dr. Soloman. Yes, I do remember seeing her a few months back."

"They want six thousand dollars." Paul looked to see if she flinched. She didn't. Melanie shook her head.

"There must be some mistake. I will call the doctor tomorrow. The insurance should be billed."

"It's in collection. It's too late for that. Have you

been getting bills?" Paul was losing patience.

"Yes, I put it in the file as you told me to."

"What file?" He didn't know what she was talking about.

"Our *pay the bills* file. You know, the expanding folder."

"Where is that?"

Melanie opened his desk drawer. There next to the whiskey bottle in the lower left-hand side was an expanding file. He flipped the cover. Six months of bills had piled up. She never opened a letter. Luckily, he had auto pay on the utilities and the house payment, otherwise they'd be standing in the dark. He pulled at his hair. *How could she be so stupid. She was an intelligent woman!* Paul sat back at his desk and used his letter opener to open all the bills. There was quite a stack.

"Honey, who is Dr. Soloman anyway? Are you alright?"

Melanie laughed. "I'm pregnant!" When she realised that was the worst thing she could say, she took it back quickly. "I'm sorry that was supposed to be funny. It was for botulin toxin injections. I had a mini facelift. We had wedding photos, and I wanted to look my best."

"Bot— A facelift? Six thousand dollars for wedding photos, are you kidding?" Melanie shrunk back as if he'd hit her and started to cry.

"Oh, honey, don't cry. It's ok. We'll pay it off. Insurance will not cover botulin toxin injections."

He spent the rest of the evening going through the bills. They were behind with everything; this wedding cost them a fortune. He went online and established accounts for all the new creditors. It took a big chunk from their savings to pay down the debt. Paul was doing a slow burn. As they went to bed, he mentioned to her to not put any bills in the bill file, just to lay them on his desk and he would take care of them and then put them in the expanding file.

"I'm so sorry, honey. I thought you knew the system."

Paul rolled his eyes in the dark. She snuggled up to him, but he was in no mood to snuggle back. He yawned deeply and turned on his side.

"Goodnight, honey." He could sense her frustration. He didn't care about that right now.

The unpaid doctor's bill was just the tip of the iceberg. Paul was watching his decent savings dwindle.

In studying their finances, he realised that Melanie's income was not coming into their joint account, and he decided to ask her about it.

"Mel, when do you get paid?" he called out to her.

"I got paid last week, why do you ask?" she called back from the bathroom.

"Well, I don't see it in the account."

"Which account?"

Paul rolled his eyes again. "The joint account."

"I don't have a joint account. I have my old bank account."

"Melanie, you were supposed to get that changed. Your job should be depositing your check into the joint account." He tried to sound non-judgmental, but he might not have passed that test. Melanie came out of the bathroom, blowing on her fingernails.

"After I talked to bookkeeping, she told me that I'd pay more in taxes if I paid them married filing jointly, so I told her to forget it."

"You can't do that!" shouted Paul. Melanie turned on the waterworks again. "Mel, you either pay a little out of each check, or a lot at the end of the year, it's less painful." He tried to take it down a notch.

"Alright! I'll change it tomorrow." She walked off in a huff.

He went to put the paid bill in the expanding file. There sat another bill she hadn't left on the desk! Paul almost blew a gasket.

"Mel." He stopped himself. He was going to say something in anger that he would regret later.

"Yes?" she sounded on edge.

"I love you." That was a hard eat.

"Love you, too!" She chirped back. He secretly flipped her off, Paul was that mad.

Valentine's Day was coming up in a few weeks. They had nearly survived a year of marriage. Paul realised he not only had to take care of his business, he had to take care of Melanie's, as well. He paid Dr. Soloman off—finally—so that freed up a good sum of money each month. At least he could get back to the art of saving.

The phone rang.

"Is Mel there?" A man's voice. Why was a man calling his wife?

"No, she's not home. Can I take a message? This is her husband, Paul."

"Husband!" The man sounded genuinely surprised.

"Yes, husband. Can I take a message?" The phone

clicked, no one was there. Paul checked the phone. 'Not Provided' was the number given. Paul had those kinds of calls screened and blocked, unless Melanie had that particular number unblocked.

The seed was planted.

Paul watched his wife like a hawk from then on. He drove by her office, no car. *Where the hell was, she? A noon quickie?* It became an obsession. He couldn't stop himself.

"I went to your office today." Paul tried not to sound accusatory.

"Oh? What for?" She sounded scared.

"To take you to lunch…a surprise," Paul lied. Melanie started into a lie about a meeting across town. Paul stopped her.

"Let's not make us both fools. You weren't at work, and you haven't switched to a joint account, I asked you months ago to do it." Melanie started the waterworks. "Stop it! Now. For once tell me the truth!" Paul stood up and faced her.

Melanie answered very quietly, "I lost my job."

"What? When? How? Why?" He sounded like a newspaper reporter.

"A long time ago, I just was too ashamed to tell you."

"We don't have insurance! How could you be so ignorant? What if we had gotten into an accident, or had an illness? I can't believe you, Melanie! What do you do all day?" Melanie shook her head and ran for their bedroom. The cheap lock on the door opened with a poke of the nail in the hole of the doorknob. Paul had put nails on top of the door trim for every door in the house. Melanie looked up at him and put her head back down crying as he came in.

"The lying stops now." Paul wasn't even surprised. This scenario was the way their whole marriage had been going. He wondered, *if she lied about this stuff, what other things was she lying about?* Perhaps he would find out when the private eye he hired last week met up with him. He couldn't trust her anymore.

Paul sat at the desk across from Tom Spitz, Private Detective. Eight by ten glossy photos, one after the other, were laid before him. Each one filling him with disgust. Melanie was a stripper during the daytime. She was selling her body to drunken cowboys at the Hitching Post. Yes, the parenthesis was in the bar's name. They lived in Nevada for heaven's sake. Prostitution was legal. He wondered if she used protection, or had Paul had sex with all her johns? He wanted to vomit. He felt like he'd been roasted. *Take the fork out, I'm overdone.*

Ironically, it was Valentine's Day—their anniversary— and he'd just found out yet another lie. No wonder their sex life had waned; Melanie was so tired at the end of the day from having sex with other men, she didn't want to put in the overtime.

Paul stopped for wine on the way home. When he pulled up to the florist shop for a dozen roses, he was formulating a plan in his mind.

Finally, he pulled into the driveway with steaks to put on the grill, roasted mushrooms, a salad, wine and roses—nothing but the finest for his high-priced whore! *Wife,* he corrected himself.

She was all dolled up—they had talked about going out for dinner—but what he had in mind would not be proper to display in public.

"Hi, honey. Every place I went by is packed. I forgot to make reservations, so I bought a couple of steaks and your favourite wine…and these." He handed her roses. "We'll go out tomorrow, I promise." Melanie's face fell, but she put on a brave one. Smart girl, she might survive the evening.

Paul started the grill, and opening the wine, they toasted to one year. He thought about adding "of Hell," after one year, but didn't want to blow the surprise just yet. "How about I clean off the grill and you bring those steaks out?" he said sweetly.

Melanie took the steaks off the store trays and seasoned them. She put them on a lovely platter and carried them out with the meat fork. Paul opened the grill, took the meat fork from her, and pointed for her to put the platter down on the side wing of the grill. Melanie did. Her hand was leaving the plate when Paul came down with the fork, piercing her hand through.

She screamed.

"Oh, honey, I'm so sorry." Paul pulled her in close and held her head inches above the grill. She screeched, scratching at his hands with the one good hand not shish kabobbed by the large meat fork.

Paul felt nothing as he watched the blood that flowed from the scratches sizzle as it hit the grill rack. All he felt was the shame and anger of the pictures, one after the other, like a silent horror film playing out before him. Pictures of his wife messing around with other men. Melanie stopped screaming a minute or so after the cover went down on her head.

"Happy Anniversary, honey!" Paul shouted, followed by maniacal laughter. "Oh yeah, Happy Valentine's Day too, bitch."

Paul wondered briefly if Melanie had paid the life insurance up.

The Tuesday Night Special

by Hari Navarro

My name is John De Lellis and I sit on the soft edge of my never-made bed and I gently stroke my exposed thigh with the back of my fingernails. It makes the hairs bristle. But it soothes me. It calms me.

"Not yet, John. Cool your jets. Not just yet," I say or, maybe, I just think these words as anticipation manifests as a gel-like sheen in the deep pores that pock at the ruined smash of my nose. I swallow. I taste the red wine in the flesh that I pull. The strips that I chew and swallow from the snarling curl of my lips.

Not long now. Not long now.

My apartment is small. Big city small. Actually, it's

not an apartment at all but rather a converted storeroom in which, for many years, scented meats were hung. Sausages. I think it was a curing room for sausages. It is perfectly square and as tall as it is wide. A cube with a toilet and a bed and a window. Oh, but listen as I afford it such disservice. It is not just a window. It is *the* window.

My sweet escape.

Such a wonderful thing, this hole in the bricks. This balm for the cracks in my thoughts. And this room from which I am allowed to gaze, it is perfect too. This meaty hole in which I hide. This is the reason I came here, you know? To hide. To shun those who would reach out and try to gather me in.

Like family. Fucking family with their sanctimonious fucking grooves into which I must slot. Collectors of pretty husbands and handsome wives. Makers of dirty babies and spotless money. Whisperers that hone the edges of their knives with the grit of their contempt before then plunging them into my back.

Like friends. I never had real friends or, at least, not those bone-ribbed flesh holsters of blood and piss and shit that pass themselves off as real. Don't worry, I never wanted those type of friends anyway. You don't have to worry about me. Not ever.

I don't like people I can smell. This is why it is a well known truth that, on-line, I'm a social fucking god. I'm a dirty digital deity to the fleeting fools that I scoop up and I tally and I wear at the top of my feed. It's numbing how fucking deluded they are, really, don't get me started. Following me. Clicking on my junk. Friending me as if the sum total of their mass is some sort of validation of my worth. It's a joke, and not a very fucking funny one.

A god, I say. A god.

I had thousands of them, you know? Fucking thousands. But not any more. The internet connection here is shit. It's actually all but non-existent. I get flashes sometimes, images and sounds. Puffy sweaty memories of chat-rooms past. My digital tales of woe and my cringe-worthy login names, but then they did serve their purpose. Bait, and in did swarm my flock.

I get a few dribbles of porn too from time to time. Actually, I never really liked porn. But I did still stalk through the filth and step over the writhing bodies of the dirty slut trash to find the special few. The naturally beautiful, you know? The ones who take your breath away and leave you to wonder just what it is that lays smashed and broken beneath the pit of their perfectly bronzed pores.

Why aren't they married to some guy who owns fifty-three cars and a monkey that dresses like a Barron in a top hat? Why aren't they models? Or weather readers, or any number of other jobs where the perfect mould of their skin becomes a key that opens all doors.

Anyway, fuck them all, but fuck her the most. She who told me she knew who I was. Which is, on reflection, a pretty obvious thing to say. So she fucking well should know me. I opened up and told her everything. I told her things I'd never told anyone. Things that I hated to hear. Truths. Festered, dripping, horrendous truths. Things I know now are not true.

What am I saying, of course, they fucking are.

She was that fraction of the thousands that I actually thought thought like me. To her I gave my all. All access to my deepest thoughts. My perversions. This twisting sickness. My hated skin. I did try to change with her, for her, but I cannot deny this thing that I am.

That is why I am here. Here.

This is why I live now in this far away city that stinks of the shit that seeps from stacked bags and the stale fungal taint of wet bricks. I came here to protect myself, not from what I feared I'd become, but from what I have always been.

Fuck her. I didn't need or want her anyway. I have

this now. I have someone else. Now that I have my window.

I sit on my bed and I gently draw the backs of my fingernails across my thigh and I look out of my window and across the steaming alley and down the ruddy steel grate steps of the fire-escape ladder that jags down from the roof and passes through the landing that sits just beneath the dancing gossamer stir of her curtains.

"Not yet. Wait. Breathe. Wait."

I look at the sweating face of the clock on my wall. It's so hot in here. Moisture has breached its curved glass and stained and peeled at the paper backing that tells me that the time it is near.

Not long now. Not long.

Actually—and you are going to think I'm fucking deranged; OK, I'm no fool, I know how I look to you already, but you will seriously think me in need of help—because, you see, to me, my new friend, she who lives out through the hole in the bricks and down there in her little lonely room, to me, she is already home.

She is safe and she is in here, with me. Here.

She covers every inch of my walls. I purchased a new camera, and it takes the most fantastically clear shots from a distance. I don't get out much but when I do I follow her. I even sat in her place of business once and had her bring me a big cup of black coffee and the special—a great gooey slice of pecan pie. Best damn slice I ever had.

You should see her in her uniform. It's so complementing to her form. Beautiful, in fact. She is quite simply the most beautiful woman in this world. In this little world of mine, at least. Soon you will see. You will see her, and she will be wearing her uniform. You must tell me what you think.

Not long now. Not long.

I took a little bit of artistic license with her images. It's crude, I know, but I plastered her face to the perfect bodies I gleaned from magazines. They're not all porn. Some are just famous actresses and models in swimsuits and lingerie, but yes, some are just skin. I do love swimsuits. I don't do that any more though, that's old school. I've gone to digital video.

I've gone to deep-fake. It's fucking seamless. The manipulated frames; they look just like her, exactly like her. And besides, my walls are all full, and the production of paper takes a terrible toll on the environment. Did you know that, for every one thousand high-end glossy magazines, fifteen trees are consumed? Fifteen. I know I'll come off sounding glib, but I truly believe I'm doing my bit for this ungrateful fucking planet. And if we all do a little then we can change a lot, am I right?

"And there she is. Perfect, punctual and home."

You know, I worry about her. Living in this shitty city. Having to navigate this filthy rotten alley just to get to her front door. Did you hear that? Say what you want of this place but the acoustics in this man-made ravine are fricking fantastic. That there is the click of the key in her lock.

So now she will take a few minutes to check her mail. Her box is the third from the top on the left. It's got her name on it, but I've never read it. I just look at the number.

One eighty-nine C.

The light in the landing at the base of her stairs has just turned off, so she'll be climbing. She's trudging her tired soles up the shared staircase to her third floor room.

I was just thinking that you're very lucky to be here. Tonight is a special night. It's Tuesday. Swimming practice, you'll see. You'll see.

She will soon enter her room, and her shoulders will drop and she will swear at the nothing at her feet. She will walk to her fridge, and she will take out a blue labelled bottle of sparkling mineral water, and she will sip it down and wipe her lips with the back of her hand.

Then, she'll take a tray of ice-cubes from the over-frosted cave of her freezer and she'll crack them into a bowl.

She will unzip her uniform and peel it away. She will take off her underwear, and she will fall back on the bed she pulls down from the wall and she will masturbate. She will lose herself, and she will find herself, beneath the cubes she melts down and into her flesh.

This is what I'm waiting for. The special instance where I reach down and into this most personal intimate moment. Where I reach down and I help myself to a slice.

She does not know that I watch. But I know that she loves when I do. She has no reason to think that anybody even lives in my building. It's mostly abandoned and I have tinted the glass so not even it's perpetual blue glow can escape. I do make a lot of videos, you see. You can watch some of them later if you'd like. Remind me.

"The Tuesday Special. Not long now, John. Not long."

After she has finished, she'll stand in the window and she'll rub a wedge of lemon all over her body. And then she'll go to the battered suitcase that sits atop her tiny fridge and she'll take out her swimsuit. She will peel it on like a reclaimed shed skin, and then she'll hide it away beneath her thick bulky clothes. She will hide her perfect body, and she will hide her blood-red suit. She is shy, you see? Too shy to change in front of the other girls. It's kind of sweet really. Those bitches have no idea what they're missing.

Any moment now. You'll hear it. How the hinges at the threshold of 189C catch ever so slightly, and how she has to give it a helping nudge with her shoulder. Any moment now. This is our thing, but you are welcome to stay. Just keep everything you see to yourself. You understand, right?

The more, the murkier.

OK, quiet now, she's at the door. Hear how it sticks? I've been meaning to, maybe, nip over there and oil it. But, then, I kind of like it. It's a part of the play. It's a part of this thing that we have. It's a character in and of itself. And there she is. There she is.

Lovely, isn't she?

She had her hair cut last week. It used to be long, and I wasn't quite sure at first, but it's really grown on me. A cute little French bob. Don't mind me while I ready myself here. It's not easy, you know. I have to time this just so.

Wait, what is she doing?

No ice?

No sparkling water?

No fridge?

She's toying with her hair. Listen, that's her phone. I have the exact same ring-tone, not that it ever bloody rings. Who is she fucking talking to?

OK, calm,

calm,

easy.

Well, this is a bit different, but at least now she's taking off her uniform. Her beautiful breasts. Cupped in my favourite bra. It's what I think is called a balcony bra in that it holds the breasts in low-cut cups like little lacy-fringed balconies. I love it so much, I once thought about stealing it. Though I'm not sure what I'd have done with it if I had.

I've spent quite some time down there in her apartment. Actually in it, not imagined, actually there. I like to touch her stuff. To smell her perfume, not her skin but her perfume, and even the waft of the blue chemicals in her bowl excite me as I flush. Well, not excite, but they do fill me with a kind of happiness.

It's a joy to be there. To be that much closer. To be breathing the air that she does, you know? You know what I mean?

What in the actuality of the fuck! She's dressing. What is this? A new red sweater from the brown paper bag on her bed. She's struggling. Peeling it over her head and then wrenching it down over the jut of her breasts. It's so tight. This is not her style. She does not dress like this. Not ever. And now a skirt?

Thin black tube.

No.

No.

This is not right. Who the fuck is that on the phone? I know her smile. I've seen it before, but never on her with its flushing shades of freshly breached shyness. Somebody or something is making her happy. Fuck that. No fucking way am I to be allowing that.

I am going to end her. Another fucking corpse. Damn, I thought this one was different. I did. I really fucking did. How dare she? What we have here is special. She is broken, and I am broken, and together we make a beautiful and ancient cracked pot.

How dare she do this to me?

I will go down to the street and I will hoist myself up to the rungs of the rusty ladder. She will hear it screech but think nothing of it as she talks to the thing on the phone. I know how to move. I know how to shift my weight just so. I won't be silent but I will be very, very quiet. I've been there so many times. So many times.

And I will stand on her landing, and I will listen as she laughs through the mesh of her curtains, and they will filter out her betrayal and, for a moment, I will turn and I will start to leave. But then I won't, and I will climb through her window and will tear myself into her flesh.

The door behind me opens and in walks a man in a suit. I hear him but I remain transfixed on the window. On her new red sweater and her little black dress.

"Hello Frances," says the man in the suit, milking his greying beard to a point. He makes a sucking sound with his lips as they part, and he cups his hand beneath my chin and gently he turns my face. Away from the window. Away from the sweater and away from the little black dress.

"Why must you torment me? And please don't try this tiresome trick of conjuring names. I have a name. My name is John," I say.

"Frances, we have worked on this. Try to focus. Try to remember. John James De Lellis stalked and raped and very nearly killed you. Touch the scars on your face. Run your finger along the bridge of your nose. You know this. Inside your head, crumpled inside you, lays the ruin of this information. Maybe we cannot fix what he did, though I most certainly hope that we can, but I know what I can do. I know what we can do. You and I can help you face it. It's horrific. But turn toward it you must. It is the only way in which to return to some modicum of reality. To peace."

"Real as real can be. Frances is her name, you say?" I say, turning my head and, once again, drinking in through my window, the tight cling of her sweater and the grip of her little black dress.

"Yes, yes remember, we've been this close before, Frances. Find a hint of yourself and reach for it. Cling to it."

"Frances... Frances, so that's little red riding whore's name."

"Please, Frances, you must find a crack in this delusion. Sift through the details. If it were true, and you are John De Lellis, then surely you'd know the name of your obsession. And who am I? Why do I have access to your room? Look at it. Look at this room, really look at it. Open the window and feel the breeze on your face. There is no window. Feel the walls. They are padded for your protection. There is no window, Frances. There is no window."

A deep sigh and a muffled half snorted laugh secretes into the room and the doctor bites at his lip. He, too, sighs and his back straightens and he braces.

"I don't know her name because I couldn't care less. Do your research, people like me we don't want them to have faces or homes or families or fucking pets. All that I want is her flesh. And her love, that too would be nice. So just stop. I know this is your game. I know this is our naughty little game. But just stop. Please, just stop it, Father. Stop."

The man in the suit's eyes look sad, and he puts his hands together and up to his lips and he inhales deeply through their clasp. He knows what is now to come.

"You know full well why you come here. You know why you come into my room at night. It's why you are here right now. You're the doctor and I'm the nurse, right? Is that what we are tonight, Daddy? Don't worry though, I know just how to shift my body so that we make but a whisper. Just stop tormenting me, and we can play and not Mother nor anyone else will ever, ever, ever have to know."

One Perfect Love

by J.W. Garrett

Ben sat at the bar, nursing his third beer, waiting for his girlfriend—correction, soon-to-be ex-girlfriend—to show. It would be better this way, in public. Hopefully she'd not freak out again. After last night's episode, he was done. Here, what could she do really? They would be surrounded by people.

Rubbing his forehead to ward off his impending headache, he glanced at his watch again. Damn, he wanted this over and done with, so he could move on. Clearly, he'd let this woman hang on to him for way too long. Still, it had been easy and relatively comfortable. He'd gotten what he needed from her with little trouble.

But the strange mutterings…? And the odd things that happened occasionally…? Something was off with this woman, and hell, he didn't want to catch it. Last straw—last night, when she'd used the word *love*, and then stared at him, like she expected to hear it back. That's always when he knew it was time to call it quits.

The noise level in the bar had kicked up by the time he'd ordered his fourth beer. The music, yelling, dancing, large-screen TVs blaring—all of it blurred into a loud steady monotone. "Shit, if she's not gonna show, maybe I'll just find me another, and the night won't be a total loss."

"Ben! So sorry I'm late. You wouldn't believe the day I've had. My car broke down." Julie rolled her eyes, catching her breath. "I was planning to charge my phone in the car, so my phone died also." She laughed. "Almost funny, right? I convinced the tow truck guy to drop me here."

Ben cocked his head. "Yeah. Almost."

Leaning over, Julie planted a kiss on his cheek. "Anyway, I'm really ready for that drink now."

"Sure. What'll it be?"

"Uh, gin and tonic." Ben motioned for the bartender and ordered. "So, looks like you got a head start."

"Well, yeah. You were late."

"Forget that. Want to get a table, or better yet, head back to my place? Just give me a minute to finish my drink. We'll continue at home."

"No, I don't think so."

"Okay. Here's good too."

"No, Julie," he said, twisting to face her. "This is it. I'm done."

"Done? What do you mean? Why? Because I was late?"

"No. Six months is a long time. I'm ready to move on. Last night just drove it home for me."

Ben watched as Julie shifted in her seat and avoided his gaze. "I explained. We talked about it," she whispered.

"Yeah, and it's freaking nuts. You're nuts. I don't want any part of it."

"So, you're breaking up with me?"

"Yeah, now you're catching on… That's the gist of it." He ran his hand through his hair. "Look. Do what you need to do. Mumble those…spells—or whatever they are—while you get someone else off. I need someone more…suited to me."

She twisted her hands in her lap. "In what way exactly?"

Ben was impressed. Even though she looked like she might cry, maybe she wouldn't lose her shit right here in the middle of the bar. At least there was that.

"Why are you doing this to yourself?" He threw cash on the bar to cover the drinks. "Have a little pride." He bent low, close to her ear. "But since you asked… I need someone smart, not crazy… Someone sexy, not eccentric… Someone strong, not pathetic. Someone beautiful too," he added. Ben swivelled on his heels to leave, then turned back. "Come to think of it, I can't even remember why we got together. The sex isn't that great."

"My smile."

"What?"

"You said you loved my smile."

"*Huh…*" He shrugged. "I need to remember to use that line more often. I'd forgotten it'd worked on you. Listen. We both deserve a clean slate. I need someone, different. You need…" He shook his head and chuckled as he stood. "Well, who knows what the hell you need, but I'm not hanging around for it. Maybe you're better off alone."

Beating a trail to the door, he heaved a breath. "Free. Finally." But as Ben cleared the door and set off at a brisk pace through the misty rain that had started to fall, he couldn't shake the growing sense of unease creeping up his spine.

By the time Julie reached her apartment, she was soaked to her skin. A puddle surrounded her feet, growing underneath her as she stood in her tiny entryway. Catching a glimpse of herself in the mirror, she paused, taking stock. Mascara ran down her cheeks; her long black hair clung to her face, and her eyes were red around the edges from crying. Her lower lip trembled. Ben's words to her last night after they'd made love seared her heart. *Together we can be anything*, he'd whispered. A sob rose in her throat. Was she destined to be alone? Did nobody want her?

Peeling out of her wet clothes, she let her thoughts roam. He was so cruel. She'd let him in, just a little, to share a small glimpse of who she was, and he'd thrown her out like what they'd had meant nothing. He'd spoken of a future together. They'd made plans… Well, only *she'd* made plans. Clearly.

The warm glow of her bedroom called her. She shivered and swiped again at the wetness on her cheeks. Once inside, she pulled on a robe and lit the candles that circled the bed. Ben could have been a part of this with her. She steeled her heart for the task ahead of her. Now, well…now he'd get everything he ever dreamed of. A gift. For a short time.

Letting her fingers trail down the spine of the grimoire before placing it in her lap, her thoughts drifted, guiding the magical book, the pages flying by, fluttering, standing at attention, as if uncertain which one would receive the weight of her wrath.

Whispering softly, her eyelids drooped shut. The pages settled. The lights flickered out, and the flame of the candles danced in the unnatural wind. Outside, thunder rumbled and lightning struck, while she muttered under her breath. She drew the darkness from the night to her, fortifying the ancient spell spilling from her mouth. Then yanking a knife from her nightstand, she slid it across her palm and counted the drops hitting the pages, sealing her words in the deep crimson of blood magic. Exhausted, her conjuring spell cast, she cradled the tome against her chest, and with Ben's name still on her lips, she curled into a tight ball and slept. *We could have been the best…*

In a tiny graveyard, secluded behind a weathered wrought-iron fence, a mist escaped the damp earth, unleashing a putrid stench, along with the demonic spirit. Long dead—but not at rest—the demon answered the calls of those powerful enough to draw its essence from below.

The mysterious fog elongated, pulling and gyrating as it took shape. A sinister atmosphere clung to the space, bracing for the creation to come. The steady rain didn't deter the mass as it birthed arms, legs, chest, and head, writhing under its spell to cast itself in an image which would garner its specific prey.

Yet only for those deeds to bring the damned soul nearer to closure in this world. Only for twenty-four hours to snare its target and to gain another life force to feed its own, allowing the demon's journey to an eternal rest to continue. And the living soul must willingly give itself to the demon. Otherwise the conditions of the spell wouldn't be met, and the human would maintain its ties to the living.

The spirit escaped the confines of the cemetery; its long lean legs filled out, leading to perfectly proportioned breasts and black hair that curved over athletic arms and shoulders. With each successive step, the vision perfected itself, coming closer to the facade which would solidify the illusion.

The cheery bell danced a hello as Ben pushed

through the door of the diner, cursing the noise under his breath. One hell of a hangover and an empty bed had him in a piss-ass mood. He scooted into a booth and didn't raise his head when the server appeared by his table.

"Coffee?"

"Yeah. And eggs over easy, toast, and sausage."

"Coming right up."

Ben gave his attention to the dreary morning outside the window. *Maybe I was too hasty…* He shook his head in answer to his own question. *Hell no, she was messed up… Had long since served her purpose.*

"Your order's up. Here you go. Like for me to warm up your coffee?"

"Sure." Taking one more sip before setting down his cup and lifting his gaze toward the woman's voice, he choked down his mouthful of coffee, sputtering drops on the table.

"Are you gonna be okay?" The woman patted him solidly on the back.

"Yeah. Never seen you here before…uh, Mandy," he said, reading from her name tag.

"It's my first day. Don't mind telling you that I'm a little nervous. If you'd put in a good word for me on your way out, I'd appreciate it. I'm hired only on a trial basis. Every little bit helps. Ya know what I mean?" The woman placed her hand on her hip, straightening her stature and thrusting out her breasts in the process. Her long black hair bounced animatedly as she shifted her weight from side to side, narrowing her eyes at the man behind the register.

"I'd be happy to, if you let me buy you a drink after you get off to, uh, celebrate your first day. What do you say?" In the silence that followed, Ben waited for the rejection that surely was headed his way. The woman was knock-dead gorgeous. All the men staring at her in this café obviously agreed. No harm in trying though.

"How sweet. Just getting over a breakup though. So, if you're okay with a casual drink, I'd love to. Plus, I study in the evenings. I'm working my way through law school."

Damn, a knockout and smart. "Fine. Sure."

"Great. I'm off at six. Meet you here?"

"I'll be here."

The day wore on, dragging hour by hour. Ben changed, then decided to wear something different and changed again. He needed to impress her. Tonight had to go perfectly, so Mandy would agree to a real date. The words he'd spewed last night kept churning in his mind. Maybe this was meant to be. His reward for turning Julie lose, so he could find the woman of his dreams—smart, beautiful, and sexy. Three outta four…not too shabby. And, with the toned muscles she sported on her arms and her to-die-for legs, she looked pretty damn strong too, so consider it a solid four outta four.

Now, let's go get her. Fate was finally on his side? Hell, it was about time.

As the evening progressed, Ben prayed silently that this goddess beside him would agree to dinner with him. If he played his cards right, one thing would lead to another, making dinner an easy transition to his bed. The pair of Jack and Cokes that the waitress had brought them earlier sat abandoned, only half empty, condensation pooling underneath their glasses.

Numbing his senses with alcohol wasn't necessary with her. Her words fed him, and he hung on each one as Mandy opened up before him. "Look. I know you said just drinks," Ben began, averting his gaze to their watered-down drinks, "but you gotta eat. How about we grab a table and have a bite together?"

"I'd love to. Studying can wait. I hardly ever have any fun." She let out a little giggle, freaking music to his ears. "Tonight with you has been a nice break."

A couple of steaks later, completely lost in the

discovery of each other, the conversation still hummed along. And as the minutes rushed by, he let himself hope that maybe she felt the same way, and he could push further with an invitation to come home with him.

"Ben," she said, reaching for his hand, letting her fingers linger over his, "I've had a wonderful time. Thank you. But I should be getting home."

"Sure." He motioned for their check. "Mandy… I'm just gonna toss this out there, 'cause I'd hate myself if I didn't. I feel this connection with you. It's hard to explain. It started in the diner, when we met, and hasn't let up since. And, if you feel this…energy between us too, well, I thought maybe we could go to my place, or yours, and continue what we've started." Avoiding direct eye contact, he waited, while the seconds eked by, each one seemingly longer than the last.

"Actually, I'd love to. I thought you'd never ask. Let's go."

He slipped his hand around hers as they left. "How did I get so lucky?"

Once inside his apartment, Ben threw his keys on a side table then turned and pinned her to the wall. He pressed his lips to hers, softly at first, but when she yanked on his shirt, pulling him closer, he deepened the kiss. Stepping back, he sucked in a breath. "I'll be right back, kitten," he gritted out, tugging at his tie. "Get comfortable."

"Oh, I can help with that." She launched herself at him, pulling his tie free and ripping his shirt open, buttons pinging to the floor along the way. When she circled her legs around his waist, he was a goner. "Here. Now," she demanded.

"You don't have to tell me twice," he murmured. "Perfect. You're perfect. And now you're all mine." Against the wall, as he pumped into her, they had their first tryst. Eventually, they made it to the bedroom for round two, where her nails drew first blood, exquisitely raking a path down his spine. "Woman, you are intense." He nipped at her lip before she scooted to the edge of the bed.

"Be right back…" She scraped her nails down his arm. "Don't go anywhere."

Fifteen minutes later, still waiting for her return, he called out. "Kitten?" Ben got up and knocked on the bathroom door. "Mandy? You okay in there?" He turned the knob and walked in.

She stood in front of the mirror. Lifting her gaze to his, she flashed a wicked grin. "Just couldn't wait, huh?"

Mandy's image winked out and, in its place, was Julie's face, suspended there only an instant before dissipating into a formless mass.

I'm coming for you…

"What did you say?" Ben blinked, leaned forward and refocused on the mirror again. His woman reappeared, but then his eyes widened as her skin slipped slowly down her cheeks, her eyes yawning wide in the remnant of her face.

Mandy swivelled and raised her arm high. In the second before the knife sliced into Ben's neck, the once-beautiful face deteriorated into bones and loose flesh, oozing blood from the cavities where her ears and mouth had been.

His heart hammered in his chest, and his knees went weak as he struggled to stand. "What's happening!"

The knife ripped through him with a wet sickening *smack*. Blood poured from his gaping wound and slid over his fingers as he tried unsuccessfully to staunch the flow. A gurgling noise escaped his throat. For a second he was weightless, suspended almost. Then the floor rose to meet him.

"Perfect."

He heard the whisper from the form who had been Mandy.

"*Perfect*," she chanted, repeating his own word back to him.

The spectre stood before the grave, her skeleton body dissolving, soon becoming mist again, slithering and seeping through the dirt with an audible hiss. With the ghost came its new companion, the two dragged beneath the earth in tandem, destined now to roam, searching for other lost souls to feed their own lifeless existences.

"Well, let's hear it. What do you think about what I've done with the place?"

"Julie? Where the hell am I? How are you here? I was just with—"

"Mandy. I know. Her time's up."

"What?" He clawed at his destroyed neck, manically jerking his gaze about, desperately taking in his surroundings. "How do you know? What have you done with her? And why can't I breathe? What a crazy-ass dream."

"This is no dream." Her lips twisted into a demented smile.

"What have you done?"

"Given you what you wished for—Mandy. But

dreams come at a price."

Ben fell to his knees, gasping, then lunged for Julie.

"Oh, I'm not actually here with you. Think of me like an apparition. But your beautiful Mandy? That was all me. Here she is."

A conglomeration of bones, skin, and blood coalesced before him, mingling at his feet.

"You don't recognise her?" With a whip of Julie's hand, the vision of Mandy formed again, only for a few seconds.

He retched.

"You're with your love now for always, your souls bound together as are your destinies. You died in her arms. Remember? You've finally found your *perfect* love…a dead restless soul to match your own cold heart. I just wanted to give you a moment to fully comprehend your fate… Your choice…"

"Wait… I can do better." He convulsed. "Please! Give me another chance. We can try again. Just the two of us."

Dirt and rotting flesh filled his mouth, stealing away his last Earthly seconds.

She gave him an empty smile. "Don't worry. Might take a while, but time will give you a chance to redeem yourself, over and over again, until you're perfect. Just *perfect.*"

His body went translucent, a silent scream frozen on his mouth, until he faded into nothingness.

Then summoning her power within, she bowed her head and gave in to the mist.

If I Can't Be Loved...

by Jasmine Jarvis

I was at my wits end. I needed to figure out a way to resolve things so I could get my life back to normal. The situation I found myself in was unique, and after months of ongoing fighting, tears, threats and the trashing of my personal property, enough was enough. If I had known I was moving into a flat occupied by a miserable married couple from the afterlife, I would have opted to live on the street instead. My life was absolute misery as I worked my existence around the poltergeist pair that were bound for eternity in a wicked love-hate relationship.

It started out with random banging and slamming of doors just after I moved in. I would get up to investigate, terrified that I was about to come face to face with a home intruder, but find nothing. As the slamming intensified, I had the landlord send out a builder to check the flat from top to bottom for possible points where a draft could get in, but he found nothing that could explain the noises. I made sure all the doors were closed at night, and to my horror, the doors were still being opened and then slammed shut!

Then came footsteps and thumping along the walls. It sounded like a scuffle between two people. Up and down the hall, I could hear soft thumps of fists landing, bodies being pushed against the walls, and what sounded like a body being dragged down the hall towards my bedroom.

The night that happened, I remember straining my ears to listen to what was going on. My bedroom door was closed, and I was in my bed, surrounded by the thick darkness of the night. When I heard them approach my bedroom door, I climbed out of my bed and took up a baseball bat I kept by my nightstand. I tiptoed quickly across my room to the door and took up my batter's stance, poised to knock someone's block right out of the park the minute a head poked through the doorway.

With sweaty palms, I flexed my grip on the bat handle, and anchored my bare feet into the carpet, my eyes locked on the closed door. My heart was bouncing around in my chest like a canary trying to escape its cage. All I could hear was the whooshing of blood rushing through me.

I heard the click of the handle as it was twisted, then *BANG* as the door was kicked wide open. It swung with such force, it bounced off the wall, and before I could swing my bat, a freezing cold rush of air hit me and sent me backwards. I dropped my bat and scrambled to pick it back up. When I rolled over, I was frozen in fear; there was no one. Nothing but me in my bedroom. The hallway light cast a soft glow into the room, and there I was, all on my own.

The bedroom was still freezing, and despite being all by myself, I had this feeling I was being watched. Soon I was to learn it was actually *somethings* that were in my room that night. Him standing, her lying on the ground where she'd been thrown into the bedroom. Both of them stopped and were staring at me in shock as I, oblivious to their presence, got up and headed back over to my bed with my baseball bat to try to go back to sleep.

I exhausted my landlord and her builder—no matter what they did, there was no way to explain what was happening in the flat. I was offered the bond back so I could move, but do you know how hard it is to find anything affordable that is close to the city? Yeah, impossible. I wasn't in a position to give up this place which was close to my work and cheaper than all the other flats on the rental market. I had to learn to just live with it.

And live with it, I did.

Soon after, it became the norm to wake to my plates and cups being thrown about. I would turn on the kitchen light to see all the cupboards and drawers opened and all my cutlery and crockery thrown about. I replaced all the broken stuff, and after a few trips to buy new dinnerware, I decided it was probably better to switch to plasticware. I found I was able to sleep much better to sounds of plastic dishes bouncing around my kitchen than the violent smashing of glass and ceramics.

After a few months of living in the flat, I had my first encounter with my neighbour. Her name is Carol, and she is a graphic designer who works from home running her boutique design company. Because it is taboo to ask a woman her age, as she and I chatted away, I estimated her to be mid-forties. She was married, and her husband worked in IT for a bank in the city. No kids, just some cats. She was bright and pleasant, and I don't know why I hadn't made the time earlier to meet my neighbours. She seemed lovely. I told her I had moved from interstate to take up a new job as content writer for a magazine. Carol was thrilled to learn this and informed me she had some great contacts herself within the media industry, and if I was ever thinking of taking on extra work, she would be happy to help me network. I told her I would definitely like to take her up on that offer.

After the niceties, she'd paused and said something that floored me. "I think it is awfully brave of you to move into that place." She nodded in the direction of my flat. "I mean, what happened in there two years ago was terribly tragic. It was a real mess."

My expression must have given away that I was completely clueless as to what Carol was talking about. "Oh! The landlord never told you? I am pretty sure there is a clause that if a death has taken place, the landlord has to inform the new tenant. It was awful. Gavin and I knew Brent and Jane for the time they lived in that flat. Always fighting, so miserable, they were terrible together, but for the life of us we don't know why they refused to separate. It was like they enjoyed making each other mad. We would hear the shouting, the thumping on the walls, things being smashed. I lost count of how many times we called the police, only to watch in disbelief as they left because Brent and Jane insisted it was nothing more than a disagreement and they didn't need to have the police involved. Well, the day they killed each other, the police had to be involved, albeit too late."

I felt my stomach flip as Carol gave me the rundown on Brent and Jane. I asked her if she knew how they had killed each other, but Carol didn't know. At the time of their deaths, she and Gavin were on holiday in Fiji. They came home to find police tape all over the door and the landlord simply informed them that something terrible had happened.

"Anyway, I think you are incredibly brave. I wouldn't be able to do it myself—too much bad juju went down in there." She shuddered and then looked at her watch, politely excusing herself to go back into her home to make a call to a client. After standing on the landing by myself to process the body blow I had just copped, I clumped, heavy-footed, downstairs and out the foyer door to work.

When I returned home later that evening after enjoying a few after-work drinks with my co-workers, I could already hear things being thrown about behind the front door. I hesitated in sliding the key into the lock. Instead, I crossed the foyer to Carol and Gavin's place and knocked on their door. I had this idea to ask them if they could also hear what was going on in my place. I knocked and waited…and waited and knocked…and waited some more. Neither Carol nor Gavin answered the door. Thinking that they must be out to dinner, I returned to my own door and unlocked it.

The noises on the other side stopped as I opened the door and crossed the threshold and into my front hallway. As I approached the living room, I noticed a chill in the air, and the silence was almost deafening. I stopped in shock in the living room—cushions had been torn to shreds, the couch was flipped onto its back, and my coffee table had been turned over. The vase that had originally sat on the coffee table was now in pieces across the room, water marks running down the wall from where it had connected and flowers crushed into the carpet. As I took in the chaos, I didn't notice the plastic cup hurtling towards me until it bounced off my head. It made a *donk* sound as it connected, and I looked down at it on the floor, rubbing the point of impact above my left eye.

"Ow, fuck! What the he—"

A plastic plate came flying out from the kitchen,

like a Frisbee. I bolted from the living room and down the hallway towards my bedroom. I could hear heavy footsteps following me as I burst into the room and slammed the door behind me. My heart felt like it was three times its size in fright, pushing my lungs out between the gaps in my ribs. I felt a *thump* against the door and then whatever had been chasing me was gone.

I slid to the floor. Pulling my knees up to my chest, I tucked myself up and sat there until my heart shrank back to normal size.

"It wasn't always like this," a woman's soft voice snapped me out of my daze.

I looked up and saw a spectre of a woman sitting on the end of my bed, her back was towards me. She had brown hair pulled up in a bun and was wearing a t-shirt and tracksuit pants, her legs crossed and hands resting on her knees as she stared out of the window. She appeared to be flickering; I could see through her.

I didn't respond. I didn't move from my balled-up position by my bedroom door.

"We were in love once. The first few years were the happiest we had ever been…" Her voice floated on the chilly air in the room. "Then we moved into this place and…everything just went wrong. It started with him cheating on me."

I still couldn't speak. It was hard enough work on my brain to process what was happening in front of me. I suspected that my brain may have still been under the influence of a few beers after work that day.

"I'm sorry for the living room. Brent did that Okay, we both did that…but he started it! The arsehole said, if I hadn't been such a nagging bitch, he would not have run off into the arms of her." There was a venomous tone at the mention of *her*, and the woman's presence seemed to appear to solidify in the brief moment of anger and hurt.

This is Jane! Oh crap! I am living with ghosts! My brain hollered at me to stand up quickly and run as fast as I could out the door and down the street. They could keep all my stuff, I just had to get out. *What if they killed me?*

Jane got up off my bed and walked over to where I sat on the floor. She crouched down next to me and I got a look proper look at her. She was petite, and on her right forearm was a tattoo of a heart with Brent's name in the middle of it. Her skin was grey, her lips tinged with blue, and when I looked at her face, her eyes were full of sadness and hurt.

Suddenly my brain allowed my voice box to work again. "Did he… How did he kill you?" I asked.

She looked at me and smiled, baring a flash of white crooked teeth. "Ohhhhhh! You can see me! Wonderful! If I had known, I would have put something else on." She looked down at her t-shirt and tracksuit pants and then back up at me. "No, Brent didn't kill me. Nor did I kill him. Our deaths were accidental—faulty gas connection—we died in our sleep from carbon monoxide poisoning. But I suppose Carol told you that we killed each other, right? Well, I wouldn't take what Carol says as gospel. She is one to stretch the truth. Ask her how she died—every time it is a new story."

My brain decided to shut down. Carol, dead? A ghost too? What the fuck had I gotten myself into? Maybe I should have taken my bond back and lived on the streets.

Jane continued, "Brent and I, well, it's complicated. Yes, he cheated on me, and in retaliation I lied to him, telling him I had cheated on him as a way of getting back at him, but for some reason, no matter how hard we tried to walk away from our marriage, being apart from each other was just as torturous, and like a rubber band we would snap back. We kept snapping back, alright." She winked at me, but I was still stuck back on Carol being a ghost too. "Being together and fighting was less painful for us than living without each other, so we stayed together and fought and loved like crazy until the night we went to sleep after a really big fight, and… never woke up…" Her voice trailed off.

"I am so glad that you can see us. This is a good thing! This means that, finally, we might have a chance to get out of this limbo that we've been stuck in. You can help us." For some stupid reason, my head nodded in agreement.

I needed to stand up and I began to uncurl. Despite being sat with a ghost, I didn't feel in that moment that Jane was going to hurt me, especially as she had just said that I could help her and Brent.

Jane stood up too and she continued talking, "Brent and I are tired of being stuck in this flat. We want to move on to what is beyond this place. Together. We have tried everything we can think of to cross, but just can't work out what we need to do. This place is holding us here, I just know it is!"

I felt the pins and needles hit my legs from the rush of blood as I moved over to my bed. I knew in that moment I was not drunk, definitely sober and definitely in the company of ghosts. "I don't know if I can help you. I don't know what to do. I have never had to do this before—help ghosts cross over." I turned, and she was right next to me.

"Well, we can figure it out together, Roomie!" She went to playfully tap on my right shoulder, her little balled up fist passed right through me, leaving an icy sensation in my bones.

"Let me sleep on it," was all I could say as I climbed into my bed—fully clothed—and reluctantly let sleep take me over as Jane's voice floated away, "Okay. We'll see you in the morning then."

I woke the next morning convinced that what had taken place was nothing more than a dream. I got out of bed and headed down the hall to the living room.

But it wasn't a dream; there was my trashed living room, couch was still on its back, coffee table turned over. The water on the wall had dried, but the shards of the glass vase glittered in the morning light that was popping through the gaps in the curtains. The flowers had been completely mooshed into the carpet and the petals had stained it, their colours leeching out like auras. The plastic cup that had hit my head was there on the floor where it had landed after bouncing off my left eyebrow. The plastic plate was there too.

My stomach flipped and I covered my face with my hands. If my living room was like this from last night that meant that…

"Good morning, Roomie! How did you sleep? Well, I hope; we need you well rested so you can find a way to help us out of this…mess." It was a male voice.

Reluctantly, I pulled my hands away from my face and looked up. There Brent stood, wearing nothing but a pair of boxer shorts. Behind him was Jane, still in the same t-shirt and tracksuit pants from the night before. *Not only were they to endure eternity together, making each other miserable, but they had to endure it in their pyjamas*, I thought to myself.

Brent wasn't as tall as I had imagined him to be, and he was also of slender build, his skin grey, and his thin lips blue-grey like Jane's. His hair was mousey brown and short, and I noticed a tattoo on his chest of a love heart with *Jane* scrawled over it.

"I told you she can see us. I don't know why you have to be such a dick all the time to me," Jane said.

He turned to face her, "Shut it! I never said I didn't believe you. Why do you always want to pick fights with me?"

"Maybe if you hadn't of screwed her…"

"HERE WE GO AGAIN! STOP IT JANE! STOP!"

All I could do was stand there like a spare dick at a wedding, watching them spiral into another fight. When

Brent started looking around for something to throw, I spoke up, "Both of you, cut it out! You are trashing my home! I mean look!" I gestured to my upturned living room. "I am not going to help if you keep destroying my things!"

They cut their argument and looked at me, Brent putting down the TV remote and Jane lowering the coffee table book down by her side.

"I can't promise you anything, but I guess I now have no choice but to help you move on if I am to get my home back."

Jane looked sad; she flickered. Brent moved over to her and put his arms around her. "You have to make this work, Roomie. Otherwise you will end up like us."

My blood ran cold—was this the threat I had been anticipating? *If I don't get them through this, they will kill me? Holy shit, what am I involved with?* A chill ran down my back and froze my feet to the floor. "How long have I got to make this happen?"

"As long as you take, we suppose. Until then, we are stuck here with you, and we can't promise things will be happy and peaceful for you, because, you know, ass hat couldn't keep it in his pan—"

Brent seemed to darken as Jane took the chance to sling the barb.

"Okay! Okay! I will help! Look, it is Saturday so I don't work, so if you give me some space to think, I can start working out what to do." They both nodded and then faded, leaving nothing but a faint outline where they had stood.

I decided to get some breakfast and walked into the kitchen. I slipped on a plastic plate on the floor, landing on my arse. "Jesus Christ, guys! Really! Why?" All around me were cups, plates, bowls, cutlery, fruit. The contents of my fridge covered the walls and floor. All the doors and drawers were open—one drawer had been pulled out and thrown across the kitchen, the broken chunks littering the floor. I got no reply from either of them.

Pissed off, I decided to just go out and get breakfast from the little coffee shop on the corner of the street. I was still dressed from last night, and right now I didn't seem to give a shit that my jeans now had a great big smear of tomato sauce across my backside as I stormed out the door of my flat.

When I came back, it was still in an upturned state. As I set about putting my home back together, Jane and Brent would flicker in and out. When I finally had it all back in a suitable state, I turned my attention to solving my paranormal problem. I sat down on the couch with my laptop and notepad to begin my project.

"Sorry about the mess, Roomie," Brent said as he materialised in the armchair across from me. "Can't help it. We were not like this when we were alive, I promise you. Only since we have been like this…dead…when we fight, the rage makes it so we can actually grab hold of things—it makes us feel like we are alive again."

"Well, couldn't you rage enough clean everything back up afterwards?" I asked, waiting for my laptop to start. I looked at Brent in his… oh my God, he had Scooby-Doo boxer shorts on!

He grinned at me. "Maybe. Yeah, maybe we could, but right now it just feels so good to throw and break things."

I scowled at him and went to slam my laptop shut.

"Sorry! Sorry! Okay, Roomie, just chill! I was only trying to be funny. Fine, fine…" He held up his hands before disappearing again, and the flat was silent as I sat up the rest of the night researching exorcisms, psychics, sage smudge sticks, and anything that could help me in clearing the place out.

I woke on the couch to the sound of yelling and screaming coming from my bedroom. Bleary eyed, I rolled off and headed to the source of the noise.

I opened the door to see Brent and Jane punching at each other, my bedding strewn across the floor and books lying across the floor.

"Oh, for fuck's sake, Jane! I NEVER slept with anyone! I don't know who this woman was, HONEST! Why won't you fucking believe me?"

"Because you always lie! Always! She sent me letters and PHOTOS of the two of you together in bed! You and that…that WHORE!"

A book went flying past my head, hit the wall, and landed on the ground with a thud. A few of the pages had dislodged. My temper was starting to fray.

"I swear I don't know her. I have never seen her! You were the one that went off and slept with another guy. You're the one who has had the affair." Brent, in his Scooby Doo boxer shorts, charged at Jane, but she vanished, sending him crashing through the foot of my bed. He vanished, and I let out a heavy sigh, and then left the room to go and find a way to stop all of this.

Whilst the bickering continued over Sunday, I remained in the living room, determined to find a way to get them out of my life. I decided the first thing to try was a psychic. I trawled the internet for a local psychic with the most positive recommendations; I knew I would need someone strong enough to push my unwanted housemates over towards the light.

I found Madame Blanche, highly recommended by those who had utilised her spiritual skills, and on her web page, she had clips from her appearance on a ghost hunter show. Good enough for me. I decided to email her, because despite rehearsing what I would say over the phone, I felt that I wouldn't be able to even touch on the half of what I had been going through. With an email, I could better articulate my request for help in this situation. I hit the send button and waited. The argument from my bedroom was still going on, and occasionally I would be jolted by doors slamming as they took advantage of being angry enough to feel earthly objects. *I'll clean it up when they are gone.*

An hour later, my laptop made a ping sound as an email hit my inbox from Madame Blanche.

"Extremely interested in your case, and I will be only too happy to help you…for a fee, of course…"

An apple went flying out from the kitchen, across the room, and struck an invisible object. "YOU FUCKING BITCH!" invisible Brent bellowed as a picture frame was pulled from the wall and thrown in the direction of the kitchen door.

I replied to Madame Blanche: "Sure. Name your price. I need them gone ASAP."

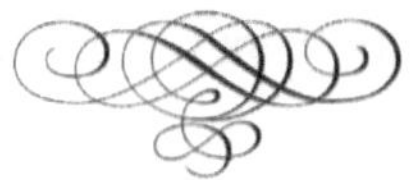

Two days of warfare proceeded, my flat the battleground, my possessions the weapons, and my sanity the collateral damage.

I was woken up from under the overturned couch by a knocking at the front door.

This has to be Madame Blanche. Please let it be Madame Blanche!

I crawled out from under the couch—I'd used it the night before as a fortress from the flying objects thrown about by a couple joined together in misery—and opened my door to find a small, plump woman who held out an old hand, crusted with gemstone rings, her wrists and neck protected with rows of crystal bead bracelets and necklaces. She introduced herself in a voice that seemed too big for her, "Madame Blanche, psychic guide extraordinaire!"

She looked thirty years older than her photo on her website, and she was so short, the shawl she was wearing completely swallowed up her tiny frame. She had short spikey grey hair and huge black-framed glasses.

As she *swooshed* past me and into my flat, I noticed she smelled like the hippie clothing store that I walk past on the way to and from work. I followed her down the hallway and almost bumped into her when she suddenly stopped, caught off guard at the sight of utter devastation that was my home.

In the corner of the lounge, I caught sight of Brent and Jane, huddled together, looking at Madame Blanche. I stood in the doorway and watched along with Brent and Jane as Madame Blanche began her work.

Madame proceeded to make her way gingerly through the mess all over the floor, pausing occasionally to tilt her head and listening, her hands held out in front of her, fingers splayed as if anticipating coming into contact with something ghostly. Suddenly she froze and I could see her trembling. She pulled her shawl round her, beads clinking as she moved. Spinning around to face me, I could see she was visibly upset.

"I am so sorry, but I can't help you with this. This goes beyond what I am capable of dealing with, the spirit involved is stronger than I. I have to get out of this place. I knew when I saw this building from the street that there is a darkness within it."

She pushed past me and headed back down the hall to the front door. I spun on my heel and followed after her. "Wait! Madame Blanche! What do you mean you can't help me? If you can't help me, what can I do?"

She stopped at the front door, a trembling hand clasping the handle, and looked back at me. "You need to get out now. You are the only living soul here, and it is only a matter of time until it takes you too."

"What? What takes me? Is it in my home?"

"Not in your home, but out there." She pointed out to the landing. "It is strong out there, so it must reside close by, but it is not in your home. What it is doing is keeping those two poor souls in your living room trapped here in pain and misery, and if you don't leave now, it will trap you here too."

Before I could beg her to stay and help me, Madame Blanche opened the front door and swiftly made her exit, the door slamming shut behind her.

"Back to the drawing board, Roomie," Brent said, appearing next to me. I looked back down the hall to see the silhouette of Jane standing there, watching us. I could feel her sadness, and it was heavy.

"Please, Roomie, help us. Don't leave us!" The words seemed to float from her closed blue-grey lips and down the hall to where I stood.

There was a yell coming from out on the landing, followed by a loud gasp and growling. I hesitated at first, but then moved to open the front door. Brent vanished, and I was alone as I stepped out onto the landing to the horror on the floor in front of me.

In a crumpled heap, a little body lay draped in a shawl, spikey grey hair poking out from beneath the fabric. Beads rolled along the floor, some bouncing down the flight of stairs. Madame Blanche, the former psychic extraordinaire, was now a ghostly apparition standing beside her broken physical form. She was staring at her body, trying to process what had just happened. She raised her face to look at me, "You need to get out n—" she began, but then suddenly, her ghostly form was pulled through the wall by an unseen force.

I ran back into my flat, slamming the front door shut behind me. I wanted to leave the building then and there, but my brain snapped, and I knew I couldn't bring myself to step over Madame's dead body to get to the stairs.

"Holy shit! Holy shit! Holy shit!" I kept repeating the mantra as I paced down the hall back to the ruins of my living room. I raked my hands through my hair, gripping at the roots, stopping just short of pulling my hair out. *What the fuck did I just see?* A prickling sensation took over me, and the only thing I could think of doing was climbing back under the couch and staying there until I could function again.

From the bedroom, I could hear Brent and Jane winding up for another fight. I didn't care—I was fairly certain by now they were running low on things to break. What more could they do?

The next few days were dark. Jane and Brent had spiralled and seemed to be fighting round the clock. I sought refuge under the couch with my laptop, searching for a glimmer of hope to get out of this situation.

At some stage, I realised I needed to go out to get groceries, and that meant I had to cross Madame's corpse.

Brent and Jane asked me what I was doing as I walked through them in my bedroom to grab some clean clothes—clothes that hadn't been ruined in the fighting. I was left with an old Ramones t-shirt and a pair of cargo shorts I could have sworn I had donated to goodwill at my ex-girlfriend's insistence. "I need to get food to eat. I won't be gone long."

They flickered, and Jane looked panicked. "Promise you will come back to help us?"

"I promise. Look, at some stage I also have to be able to go back to work—I have only so much sick leave

I can take—we need to sort this out soon. Plus, I am paying the rent on this place, so I am not in a position to leave it just yet." I grabbed my keys and wallet and headed down the hall.

"You better come back, Roomie!" Brent called out as I walked out the front door.

The body was quite fruity, flies buzzing everywhere, and a brown liquid had seeped out and was staining the floor. I steeled myself to step over it so I could bolt down the stairs and out the door to freedom. I lifted up my leg, hovering for a moment, but then brought my foot back down and leant on the wall to stop myself from vomiting.

I couldn't do it. I needed to move the body.

The door across the landing creaked open—Carol and Gavin's place. I went over and peered into the hallway. It was silent. I called out to them, but there was no reply. I walked down the hallway to the living room. It was completely empty—there was no sign that Carol or Gavin lived there, or in fact, that they ever had. There was dust on the floor and curtains; a musty mildewy smell hit my nostrils and made me sneeze.

I had an idea.

I went back out to the landing where Madame's corpse lay and grabbed at the shawl, testing it to see it if would hold, and once certain it would, I dragged the corpse over and into the empty flat, leaving it in the middle of the empty living room. I then ran down the hall, out the flat, slamming the door shut behind me and scooting down the stairs.

As I ran to push the double doors open, leading out into the street and to my freedom, I slammed into them, bouncing backward, landing on my backside at the foot of the stairs.

I got back up and pushed against the doors again. They were locked fast; I couldn't get them to open. I searched for security latches to see if there was a bolt I could slide or a lever to flick that would open the doors, but there was nothing.

Behind me I could hear a growling, and I didn't intend to stay to find out what it was making it. I ran back up and into my flat.

Brent was standing in the hallway. "It stopped you too?" he said.

"You knew about this thing?" I asked him.

Brent nodded, "The last day we were alive, it locked us in the building too."

My pulse quickened and I felt dizzy. I turned the coffee table over and sat down on it. My mind was racing; I had to fix this. It was clear I was running out of time.

"If it helps, you can order food online; others can get into and out of the building, but we can't leave it." Jane sat down next to me.

Later that night, I put their advice to the test and ordered myself a pizza while Brent and Jane slammed doors and threw slurs at each other. Thirty minutes after placing my order, there was a knock at the front door. When I answered it, there stood the pizza delivery guy with my dinner. I took it from him, signed the receipt, and then watched as he went down the stairs and walked out the main doors.

I put my pizza and drink down on the landing and went down the stairs to the doors. When I pushed against them, they were locked again. I turned and went back up to my flat to eat my dinner and think of a way out of this mess.

Brent and Jane stopped their fighting long enough to sit with me whilst I ate my dinner. While they no longer needed food, they liked to sit and watch me eat— just as much as they liked to get angry so they could break my stuff.

"Alright. So, you say that you were happy and your marriage was perfect until you moved into this place. When, exactly, did things start going wrong for you both?" I took a swig of my cola and eyed off the apparitions across from me.

Brent looked down as Jane spoke first. "It fell apart when I received the letter from the woman that Brent had been sleeping with. She wrote about how she and Brent had been seeing each other for three months and that he was planning on leaving me so he could be with her."

Brent was shaking his head, "And like I have said every day since you got that first letter, I do not know this woman. I have NEVER had an affair. I wouldn't have an affair, unlike someone else I know…" He vanished, and down the hall I heard a door slam.

Jane pursed her blue-grey lips and closed her eyes. "I saw the photos, Roomie. She sent me photos of them together, in bed. It was Brent in those photos. I retaliated by lying about sleeping with another guy—a one-night stand—to show him how it feels to be betrayed like he betrayed me…but it backfired. We fought more, we tried to separate, but like I said before, there was something that kept pulling us back together. The thought of not being with him, even though he did this to me…" She then vanished. I could hear her crying in my bedroom.

I sat on my coffee table eating my pizza. An idea

was taking shape in my head. I would set about my new plan first thing in the morning.

As it happens, I didn't start my plan first thing in the morning. I was, instead, on the phone to my boss trying to buy more time away from the office. After a discussion (not revealing why I was unable to leave my home), my boss reluctantly agreed for me to work on my assignments from home, provided I meet the editorial deadlines. *Then* I set about my new plan.

In my research on the paranormal, I had read that, in some cases, the haunting was a result of an unresolved issue that tethered the spirit to earth, and that if you can find the resolution, the spirit will gain peace and move on. Brent and Jane had a turbulent marriage in the lead up to their deaths, and they never got to resolve their problems before they died, so…drumroll, please…what if I was to get marriage counselling for them? If I could see Brent and Jane and interact with them, surely they could find the energy to manifest long enough to have counselling? If the counsellor could help them put their issues to bed, Brent and Jane could move on and I could leave this shit place for good and go back to normal.

Nowhere in my thinking did I consider telling

Brent and Jane about my plans, I was so focused on getting out of here.

I found a counsellor who did home visits and booked the appointment for Brent and Jane while they fought like tom cats through the flat.

The following morning there was the knock at my door I had been expecting—the marriage counsellor was here.

I opened the door and greeted him—Mr Gregory Schmidt from Relationships for Life. My saviour!

I ushered him into the flat. I had made an attempt to tidy as best I could, turning the couch back upright, vacuuming up the shards of glass and porcelain, and wiping food off the walls and floors. It still looked like a shit fight, but it was doable to get Brent and Jane over the line. I offered him the armchair that had the least damage to it and told him I would go and get the couple for him. I ran to my bedroom and closed the door behind me. I stood in the middle of my room and called out to Brent and Jane that they needed to come because I had finally figured out how to help them once and for all. They appeared before me, both interested in what my plan was. I quickly explained that a marriage counsellor was in the living room waiting for them, and that by resolving these issues, it would finally open the gates for them to leave this place and be happy. They looked at each other and then at me.

"You really think this will work Roomie?" Brent asked.

I nodded. "Now I need you both to get some clothes on, and, um, I will tell him you are both into the Goth look to explain your grey and blue complexions."

I picked up my jeans and threw them at Brent. The jeans passed right through him and landed on the floor behind him. Jane grinned.

"Oh shit! I forgot; you have to be angry to be able to physically hold things. Crap!"

"So, you want me to get angry then?" Brent asked.

"No. No. Nooooo. Not that. Okay, I will just explain that you have both woken up and are so eager to sort your relationship out, you think that getting dressed is irrelevant to the cause."

"Clutching at straws much, Roomie?" Jane smirked at me.

"I'm not the one in Scooby-Doo boxer shorts for all eternity," I shot back. "Now go, he is waiting, and he is costing me an absolute fortune. Go and fix your marriage."

I entered the living room to see Brent and Jane sitting on the couch and Mr Schmidt in the armchair looking slightly confused.

"Mr Schmidt, please meet Brent and Jane. They really appreciate you being here. Please excuse their attire, they have just woken up…after attending a goth rave party last night." I gestured to where the couple were seated. Mr Schmidt followed my direction and looked at the couch and then back at me.

"Um…there is no one on the couch. You know I totally understand it. Asking for help isn't so easy sometimes, but there is no judgement in getting help. I can help you. I am not just a marriage counsellor; I am also a life counsellor. Do you want to take a seat and we can get started?"

I looked at Mr Schmidt, trying to process what he was implying. The light bulb lit up—he thought I was the one who needed help, and too embarrassed to seek it, I had used the pretence of getting help for my married friends when really it was me that needed the counselling.

"Nice one, Roomie. Here, come sit." Brent slid over and patted the space next to him.

"He can't see us, Roomie," said Jane. She stood up and began to flicker.

"No. If I can see you, he should be able to see you too. There is nothing special about me, Mr Schmidt can see you too.”

"See who? There is no one there. Please, take a seat and let's talk." I looked from the counsellor and then to Brent and Jane. Brent shrugged and Jane shook her head and vanished.

"How can I make him see you then? What can I do? Do you need to get angry?"

Brent shook his head. "I am guessing only you can see us because whatever is holding us here wants you too. The psychic could see us because she is, well was, a psychic. Mr Magoo here is not relevant and therefore can't see us. Unless…" Brent trailed off, his face darkening. "Unless he becomes a ghost too…"

"Are you fucking kidding me? And how do you propose we go about that? No… No, I am not going to do that, Brent. No!"

Brent suddenly flashed in front of me. "You want to help us move on, don't you? If he becomes a ghost, he can then see us, help us, and then you are free to go, because what is holding us here will be no more. Do it, Roomie. For us."

Mr Schmidt was now looking scared. He stood up and began to walk towards the hallway to leave. "I think you need more in-depth help. I can go back to my office and make the calls to have you booked into a lovely…retreat, where you will receive the best care to help you restore your mental health. I will call you with the details once I have them finalised."

Brent looked angry as he watched what could be his chance out of this limbo walk away. All of a sudden, he vanished and then returned to place my baseball bat in my hands. "Do it Roomie," he urged. "We can't move on otherwise."

It all happened so quickly. I ran up behind Mr Schmidt and began to beat him around the head with the baseball bat. "I'm sorry. I am so sorry, but we need to end this now!" I kept saying it over and over until Mr Schmidt stood there looking over his beaten and bloody body. I slumped to the floor next to him, letting out a groan of despair at what had just taken place.

"Why the fuck did you do that? I said I was going to get you the best of care!" Mr Schmidt looked at me with confusion.

"I need you to help Brent and Jane."

"No, I think you need help. You just killed me!"

"You're probably right, yes I do need help, but I will get it when I am outside of this place. Right now though, I need you to go back in there and help Brent and Jane fix their marriage so they can cross over in peace and happiness and all that shit."

"What about me? What happens to me if I do what you ask?"

"I don't know. Cross over with them because you have helped them find peace? Let's put a pin in it for now, and please, please stop them fighting and help them be in love and happy again. I'll wait here…with you." I nudged at his body with the end of my baseball bat.

"Fine. But if I don't cross over, I will haunt your arse, and I promise I will be just as bad, if not worse, than those two."

I sat in the hallway, hunched over with my head in my hands. I hoped like crazy that this would put an end to all of it. Save their marriage and we all go on happy. I could hear the three of them talking. Then shouting. Then my coffee table being flipped over. *Oh, there goes my couch again. Oh good, my kitchenware is now becoming projectiles.* I wonder who is fighting who— Brent and Jane, or Brent and Jane against Mr Schmidt?

Mr Schmidt's suddenly spirit tore past me, headed for the front door. "You are on your own. I can't fix them. There is something else going on, and it can't be worked out. I am not going to stay around to keep trying. I am out!"

I was on my feet and running after him. Behind me

the lovers continued their quarrelling. Mr Schmidt went through the front door, and then I flung it open and pleaded for him to come back. He turned to look at me, but before he could say anything, an invisible force pulled him into the wall and I was standing on the landing on my own, in shock.

I went back into the flat, storming down the hallway and into the living room where I began to verbally tear shreds off Brent and Jane.

"You just can't fucking get it together, can you? Hold on to petty shit, right fighters, you are both doomed to remain here miserable, yet *in love,* as you keep telling me. You are both as sick as each other, and I am done. Mr Schmidt has just been taken by whatever took Madame Blanche, and I want out. LET ME GO!"

"We can't let you go. We don't know why we are here, what is stopping us moving on. We are sorry, Roomie, we really are, but we are just as clueless in figuring out what is going on with us as you are. Please don't give up; we will get there, and you will be able to leave." Jane looked at me pleadingly. Brent tried to look sad, but the Scooby Doo boxers made it hard for me to take him seriously in his remorse.

"Well, after today, I am going to scratch off my next option." I went and flipped the couch over and crawled under it for protection from the next lovers' tiff.

"What option was that?" Brent asked me.

"A divorce lawyer," I replied from my cushioned cave. "Now piss off and let me sleep."

Over the next few days, I moved Mr Schmidt's corpse into Carol's flat, leaving him with Madame Blanche, and then focused on my work—writing the stories and pushing deadlines—while the happily married couple demonstrated domestic bliss, destroying what was left of my home.

Brent's alleged affair was costing more than their happiness now. As I worked away, I stewed on the situation, picking and pulling and trying to tease out clues to a solution. After a high-octane fight—I had noticed the aggression was intensifying more and more as time went on—I had the idea to take my laptop and phone and work across the landing in Carol's flat.

I didn't tell Brent and Jane where I was going, I simply got up and walked out and across to peace and quiet.

When I walked into the living room, I froze. The corpses of Madame and Schmidt were no longer there. There weren't even bones. The room was empty. After everything that I'd gone through, I hardly gave it a thought. Instead, I found a power point and plugged my laptop in. The battery bar lit up—Carol's flat was still connected—so I could get my work done in peaceful serenity.

I thought I might even spend the night there instead of going back into the war zone.

That afternoon, I was able to get my work in for the editor to review; I was enjoying being able to do my job, and it made me feel normal.

I was pulled from my thoughts by the ringing of a phone. Not my mobile—this sounded like an old landline ring tone. I stopped to listen to where it was coming from. It sounded like it was coming from the bedroom down the back. Despite my stomach flipping, I got up from my laptop and headed down the hall to investigate, the air growing colder with every step. The bedroom door was open, and before me, furniture began to materialise. I walked into the bedroom and looked over to where a single bed appeared, next to it a bedside table, and on it a phone.

Carol materialised and walked across the room, picking up the phone receiver to answer the call. I could see her mouth moving, but I could not make out what she was saying. From her expression, I could see she was angry. Crying and shaking, she slammed the receiver down onto its hook and she paced the floor. She appeared not to see me standing there as she went back and forth, wringing her hands and sobbing. Punching at her stomach, she slid to the floor and wept. Then she vanished, and I was alone in the room again.

I didn't move.

Then there was a swirling mist, and from it, Carol appeared again. She was placing a note on her bedside table before taking the phone receiver and dialling a number. Her call was brief, she was crying as she spoke, but I still could not make out what she was saying. She hung up the phone and sat down on her bed. From under her pillow she pulled out a pill bottle and opened it. She tipped the entire contents into her shaking hand and then raised it to her mouth to swallow the pills. She rested her head on her pillow, and then the mist came, and she was gone again.

I forced myself over to the bedside table to pick up the note. I just knew it was a suicide note, and unfolding it, I saw it was addressed to Gavin, blaming him for her unhappiness; wishing he had chosen to stay and make their marriage work instead of running off with another woman; that he will regret hurting her now that she was gone.

"I see you, Roomie," came the voice of Carol behind me. I turned and saw her standing by her desk, her computer was on, and the printer was running copies of photos. "Pretty sad, huh, Gavin leaving me and taking my life? I wasn't good enough for him. Little did I know that, in killing myself, I would be stuck here for eternity, fuelled by the burning of a woman scorned while Gav rode off into the sunset with his new love… Pretty shitty deal, am I right?"

I didn't answer; I was trying to work out what was on the computer screen. An image; one that I was certain I had seen before.

Carol continued, "So I wallow here in this little world of my own misery, waiting and waiting, and then they moved in."

I knew that by *they*, Carol meant Brent and Jane.

"They were so perfect. So happy. So *in love*. I would catch them on the landing as they went in and out of their flat. I saw the way Brent looked at Jane with complete love and adoration, and I wanted that for myself. What can I say, I was jealous of the relationship Jane had with Brent—it was what I had longed for my entire life. I decided that, if I couldn't be happy, then no one else here could be happy either. So, I got…creative." She smiled at me and tipped her head to the computer and printer whirring away.

"Oh Jesus, Carol, you didn't!" I suddenly recognised the image; it was Brent with his supposed mistress.

Carol smiled. "Roomie, I am a…well, before I died…I *was* an award-winning graphic designer. I decided that I had to fix Brent and Jane, and I did so by setting it up to look like Brent was having an affair. I wanted to wreck them; tear their happiness to pieces. I wrote letters, I doctored images, I was the other woman. I took delight in watching them fall apart, listening to their fighting and screaming matches. I kept at it, wheedling myself into their life. They would separate, Brent would leave, and I would be happy, but the fuckers would get back together and try to make it work! Can you believe it? I'd have thought Jane would be the type of woman to kick a man to the kerb and move on— I even suggested she lie to Brent about having a one-night stand to get back at him—but turns out she is just like me. No matter how hard I tried, they would snap back together and work things out. So, I had no choice but to kill them. Gas. They died in their sleep; they didn't feel a thing. Now they remain with me in this building, fighting for all eternity. Look at us, such a miserable lot, aren't we?" Carol comically pouted and then burst out laughing.

"The best part; they found out I was a ghost after they died. They thought I was a legit living human before I killed them. They don't know it was me either." She flickered, moving toward me. "And they will never know it was me, Roomie."

I bolted from the bedroom and down the hall. I wasn't going to stop for my phone and laptop; I already knew now how to fix Brent and Jane.

Carol popped up in front of me as I neared the front door. "I wouldn't do this, Roomie! I have not hurt you, but I will if you do this! Don't fuck up my happiness!"

I ran through her and grabbed the handle. "This stops now, Carol. You can't make others suffer for something Gavin did to you! You had a choice, and you opted to kill yourself. That is on you and you alone."

"Oh, Roomie!" A voice growled from behind me. My left leg was snatched out from underneath me, and I was dragged back down the hall to the living room, where I knew, if I didn't pull some major shit, I wouldn't be living any more. Carol let go of my leg and rolled me onto my back. Straddling me was the rotting corpse of Madame Blanche, a black, swollen tongue sliding out between her dry, cracked lips.

"Give me a kisssssss," Carol growled, leaning in

she changed from Madame Blanche to Mr Schmidt. "I can fix our relationship. We can be happy together, Gavin! Stay with me, please!"

I wriggled frantically, turning my head as Mr Schmidt's lips connected with the side of my face, making his way to my ear where he began to suck on my earlobe.

"Oh, shit, no! Carol stop it! GET OFF ME!" Suddenly I found the strength to fling Carol/Mr Schmidt off me and I made a mad scramble to get back up and to the front door. Carol was fast behind me, ripping at my back, tearing my shirt and pleading with me to stay.

I reached the front door and ripped it open with such force it broke off its hinges. Carol stopped short of the door frame, she looked terrified, wanting to come after me, but there was something holding her back. I looked at her as I opened the door of my flat, and she was furious. She ran out onto the landing, arms outstretched. She screamed at me and then suddenly an invisible force grabbed her and pulled her screaming into the wall.

I ran down the hall and into the living room where Brent and Jane were in another fight.

I yelled at them to stop. It was all Carol's doing. Once I had their attention, I told them everything that

Carol had done. Jane collapsed in tears, Brent crouching down to hold her. Between sobs, Jane apologised to Brent for everything; for the accusations; for lying about the one-night stand to get back at him. Brent held her and told her that it was all forgiven; with the letters and the photos Carol had sent, he couldn't blame Jane for the conclusions she had drawn. He was sorry for lashing out at her too, hurting her with their fighting. They'd had no idea what really lived across the landing from them.

As they held each other, I watched on as a light began to emanate from them. There was a sudden peace in the room as Brent and Jane kissed. The light grew brighter around them and enveloped them so I could no longer see them. Then the light vanished, and Brent and Jane were gone. I sat alone on the floor of the living room, my head rested on the side of the armchair, and relief hit me. I closed my eyes. "Thank you, Roomie," I heard them say, and then I knew they were gone for good.

Once my legs had stopped shaking, I got up and left the flat, walked down the stairs, pushed the double doors wide open and stepped out onto the street.

Boy, was I gonna give the landlord a fucking piece of my mind!

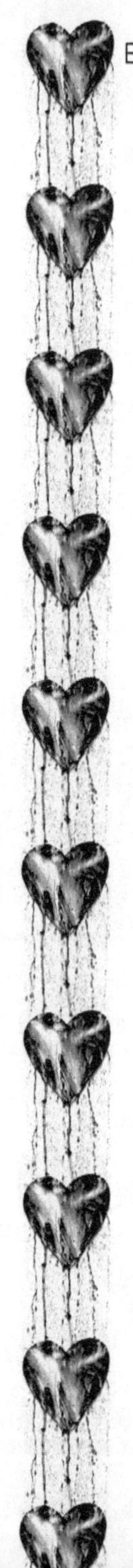

Cecily's Cure

by Jodi Jensen

European Countryside 1665

"The plague—it has returned." Defeated, Aaron dropped his physician's bag on the parlour floor and stared at his betrothed. "The rector has quarantined the village, damning us all."

Cecily rose from the settee, her porcelain face turning an unearthly shade of grey. She snatched her shawl from its resting place near the hearth. "I must return to my village, to my family."

"Did you not hear me?" He took her by the elbow and ushered her back to her seat. "No one is permitted to leave. We've been quarantined."

"Dr. Mauritius!" A muffled shout came from outside, followed by loud banging on the door. "My wife will not wake!"

Aaron frowned at the door, "A moment, please!" then turned back to Cecily. "Wait here until I return. Don't let anyone in and don't go outside. Promise me."

"Just go." Refusing to meet his gaze, she waved a hand at him.

"Cecily, promise me."

Her lips remained stubbornly sealed.

He closed his eyes and issued a heavy sigh. Stubborn, wilful woman that she was, he knew she'd bolt the moment he left. She didn't understand the dangers to her out there. He had to stop her from exposing herself to the sickness.

"Doctor!" A fist pounded the door again.

His eyes flew open. "Just a moment!" he roared.

Cecily startled and sprang to her feet.

Unsure what else to do, and desperate to protect his beloved, Aaron grabbed her arm as she tried to stalk past him. He dragged her to the kitchen and kicked the rug out of the way, uncovering the trapdoor to the root cellar.

"What're you doing?" Cecily struggled against his grip. "Let go of me!"

As he lifted the trapdoor, she tripped over his shoe, lost her footing and tumbled down the stairs.

"Mauritius, open up!"

The rector.

Much as he wanted to tend to Cecily, the rector couldn't be put off. Aaron went down the first two steps. "I'll be back as soon as I can. This is for your own good, dearest. I will not let this plague touch you."

The soft sounds of crying echoed in his ears and his heart panged at her distress as he climbed the two steps and closed the trapdoor, leaving her in the darkness.

Filled with regret, he hurried to the front door, where the banging had grown in urgency. He took a deep breath and flung open the door. "William, wait here while I get my bag."

The rector stepped a foot over the threshold.

"Please." Aaron moved in front of the man. "We are quarantined, under your authority. If I'm to continue treating the sick, I would keep my own household *cordon sanitaire*, same as the village."

"Very well." William frowned, but retreated to the porch. "Make haste, I shall await your arrival at the Howe residence."

Aaron hurried to the parlour and snatched his bag from the floor. His only comfort was that Cecily was safe—for now.

For a woman as near death as Elizabeth Howe, she was surprisingly strong. "Hold her arms!" Aaron grasped his scalpel and sliced into the swollen lymph node in her armpit.

Elizabeth screamed and kicked her legs, flailing on the bed like a landed fish as blood and pus saturated the blanket beneath her.

Aaron's gaze darted to the rector. "Her feet—hold her feet!"

The rector's eyes were wide, his jaw clenched, but he grabbed her ankles and Aaron turned back to his patient. He set the scalpel aside and pinched under the egg-sized lymph node, squeezing until the diseased lump popped out of the incision and landed with a wet *plop* on the bed. "Vinegar," he demanded, without looking up.

One of the seven Howe children huddled in the bedroom doorway, left and returned a moment later with a half-filled glass jar.

"That's it?" Aaron frowned at the offering. "That's all you have?"

Benjamin Howe cleared his throat. "Lizzie was making pickles last week, used up our stores of vinegar."

"I see." Aaron glanced at the jar, thankful his own

stores were far greater. "Remove the lid."

The young boy with the jar did as he was told, then passed it to Aaron, who splashed Elizabeth's armpit with the remainder of the jar and waited for her screams to subside.

"Keep your windows and doors shut and burn rosemary," Aaron said as he stood and gathered his bag. "She should be bathed in vinegar, but since you don't have any—"

"The pickle juice!" Benjamin declared, nodding at his son. "We'll douse her with that. Go on now, take your sisters and bring all the jars in here."

Aaron bit his tongue. The woman likely wouldn't make it to sundown, but he didn't have it in him to dash their hopes. Still, with the quarantine in effect, no one should be wasting food like that. "You and your children, eat the pickles. The vinegar in them may help ward off the sickness." He looked at the rector. "May I speak with you?"

"Of course. I shall return shortly, Benjamin."

Once outside, Aaron turned to William. "She won't live to see morning. If you can, remain here, pray with them."

The rector nodded, though his forehead was creased in worry. "There are many others in need of…something…whatever we can offer…"

Aaron nodded. "I'll do everything I can."

"I'll join you after…after poor Elizabeth is gone."

"Remember, burn rosemary and make them all eat the pickles." Aaron turned and walked away, only one thought on his mind.

Cecily.

Her tidy bun had come undone and her dress was smudged with dirt, but Aaron found Cecily otherwise fine, though in a foul temper.

"You left me…in the *cellar*!" She marched up the steps the instant he opened the trapdoor and pushed past him. "That is unforgiveable."

Aaron ran a haggard hand through his hair as he followed her to the parlour. "No, dearest, unforgiveable would be allowing you to be exposed to this vile plague." He paced the room, his patience wearing thin as the horrors of the sickness he'd witnessed in the village filled his mind. "Now, let us see if there is a rational discussion to be had."

Cecily wasn't interested. "The only thing we have to discuss is how to get me back to my family." She held up a hand to stop his protest. "Take me in your carriage.

We won't stop or even look at anyone."

"I cannot—"

"You can—"

"Doctor?" A small voice called from outside, followed by a timid knock at the front door.

Aaron recognised the eldest Howe child's voice immediately. He went to the door but didn't open it. "Yes?"

"My mum has died." The boy sniffled, then continued, quieter than before. "I'm to find out if we must burn the—the—her body…"

"Christ," Aaron muttered under his breath. He glanced over his shoulder at Cecily. One hand covered her mouth and her eyes were huge and round. He cleared his throat. "Tell the rector he may conduct a proper burial, but her clothing and bedding must be burned."

"Yessir."

Aaron waited a moment to be sure the boy was gone, then leaned heavily against the door.

"A child," Cecily croaked in disbelief. "They sent a child…?"

Much as he wanted to shield her from this too, it might just be a good thing for her to have overheard. "There are six more children in that family, their mother won't be the only one to die."

"How can you say such things?" She paced the parlour, her gaze darting everywhere but on him.

"It is simply the truth. I've seen it. This plague, it's everywhere, in practically every house," he said. He pushed away from the door and went to her. "I know your family protected you from knowing such ugly things, my love, but now do you understand why I can't let you leave?"

Cecily nodded, then backed away from him. "But—but you were in that house. You've been exposed." She took another step back, bumped into the settee, and sat down abruptly. "It isn't safe out there, and it isn't safe in here."

Aaron shook his head. "This is the safest place you could be, here with me. I'm a physician, I know what to do." Even as he said it out loud, his mind was screaming that he was wrong, he didn't know. If he did, the plague wouldn't have spread unchecked through the village. They wouldn't be quarantined. Elizabeth Howe wouldn't be dead.

"If you know what to do, then do it." Cecily stood and threw herself into his arms. "Do it."

Pulling her soft, warm body against the length of his, Aaron buried his face in her hair. She smelled of sweat, damp dirt from the cellar, and lingering hints of

lavender. She smelled alive, and he was going to keep her that way. "Come, my love." He gently released her and smiled. "Let's get you taken care of."

Aaron heated the water and filled the bath himself, dumping liberal amounts of vinegar and rosemary into the steaming tub. He checked to be sure all the windows were shut tight and the curtains drawn, then set some rosemary to burn and cleanse the air.

Satisfied everything was ready, he went and found Cecily sipping tea in the kitchen. "It's time, dearest."

She set down her teacup and gave him a wan smile. "This will be the first time you have seen me without my garments." She lowered her gaze. "Not quite the way I thought it would be."

Aaron knelt in front of her and gathered her hands into his. "It is medicinal, no need to be ashamed."

"Medicinal," she repeated, her voice laced with sadness. "I had hoped for something more."

"One day, it will be." He squeezed her hands in reassurance, then stood and pulled her to her feet. "And that is why we must do this. So there will come a day for me to enjoy your body, and you, mine."

Cecily nodded. "I look forward to that day."

"As do I." He leaned in and kissed her forehead. "Let us not linger here, your water will grow cold."

She followed him upstairs and he left her to undress while he went to retrieve the rest of his things. When he returned, arms laden with supplies, he found her neck-deep in the long copper bathtub.

He paused, his gaze travelling the length of the tub. Her creamy skin shimmered in the coppery glow beneath the water. The sight took his breath away.

"Aaron?"

He startled, so lost in her beauty he'd forgotten himself for a moment. "I apologise, my love. You're just so…exquisite."

Cecily's cheeks flushed a charming shade of pink at his words "Thank you."

He averted his gaze and busied himself laying out his instruments on the bedside table. Once he'd made his preparations, he measured three spoons of buckthorn syrup into a cup and approached the tub. "Here, drink this."

She sniffed the cup, then wrinkled her nose. "What is it?"

"Buckthorn, to empty your bowels, a necessary step in removing toxins from your body." He ignored her gasp and gently held the cup to her lips. "Bottoms up," he smiled.

Though she glared at his bad humour, she obediently drained the medicine in one long swallow.

Aaron returned the cup to the bedside table and picked up a bowl and fleam. "Lay your arm over the edge of the tub, my dear."

"May I have a moment?" Cecily laid her head back and sighed. "Just one more moment to enjoy this."

"I'm afraid we must work quickly, before the buckthorn sends you to the privy." He moved a chair to the side of the bathtub. "Your arm, please."

With a resigned sigh, she sat up and did as he asked. A sharp intake of breath was her only reaction when he made the cut.

"Very good," he nodded his approval as a stream of dark red blood spilled into the bowl. He watched her carefully as the bloodletting continued to be sure she maintained colour in her cheeks. After a good amount of blood had emptied into the bowl, he tied a rag around her arm, then patted her shoulder. "See? Not so bad."

"My dressing gown, please." She stood in all her naked glory, water running in rivulets down her body, and clutched her stomach. "I must use the privy immediately."

Aaron turned to the table as she hurried from the

room. By the time she returned, he'd mixed up a hot mustard poultice. "Lie on the bed, dearest."

Pale and shaky, she sank into the bed with a groan. "That was most unpleasant."

"I know," he soothed, picking up a small jar and spoon. "Syrup of the poppy will make you more comfortable." He poured a spoonful, then slipped it into her mouth. "Excellent, my love, you're doing well."

"We're nearly done, aren't we?" Cecily struggled to keep her eyes open.

"Not quite. There are still many ways to remove toxins from the body, and we must employ them all if we are to ensure your health." He dipped a rag into the poultice he'd made and sighed. "Believe me, if you'd seen poor Mrs. Howe…"

She reached up and touched his arm, trust shining in her eyes. "Do what you must, I'll endure anything not to suffer the plague."

"Listen to me now, this mustard plaster will burn a bit. But we need the skin to blister so the toxins may be drained." His heart twinged at the flash of fear in her eyes. "Are you ready?"

Her face was devoid of all colour now, but she nodded.

Aaron applied a mustard plaster to the bottom of

each foot, secured there by a clean, dry strip of rag tied up and around her ankles.

For the first few seconds, she was still, but the longer the plasters remained in place, the more she squirmed and panted as the poultice seared her skin.

When he saw tears streaming down the sides of her face, he was filled with remorse at her discomfort. "You're so brave, my love. Beautiful and brave."

She stared past him, lost to everything but her pain.

He waited until a good hour had passed, grateful the poppy syrup had finally taken effect. When he unwrapped her feet, he was pleased to find the bottoms covered in large, bulging blisters. He picked up his scalpel and shook his head. "Just look at all these toxins," he breathed in wonderment. "You'd certainly have been deathly ill in no time at all."

Aaron grabbed another bowl and began the tedious process of draining each blister. As he worked, it occurred to him that there were certainly more toxins left. With the bottoms of her feet nearly shredded, that left only one option. His heart ached at the thought, but he had no choice.

When he finished the task at hand, he sat on the edge of the bed and dosed Cecily with more poppy syrup. "My dearest…my love, I'm afraid we must take a more drastic measure."

Cecily moaned, but thankfully, the opium had the desired effect, and she was feeling no pain and offering no resistance.

Before his personal feelings and appreciation of his beloved's beauty changed his mind, he hurried to retrieve his razor.

When he returned, he gathered a handful of her luminous blonde curls and whacked them off with the razor blade. Each swipe of the razor caused him pain, remorse and utter sadness, but he persevered until he couldn't get it any shorter. Then he used the straight edge to shave her head down to the skin.

Afterward, as he cleaned up the mess, he wept.

She's still the same woman, kind, sweet, fiery, and the love of my life. She's the very same.

But he couldn't shake the feeling that he'd changed her.

Cecily stirred, snapping him out of his musings.

He needed to keep working, to flush all the remaining toxins before it was too late. Grabbing another rag, he smeared the hot mustard liberally over it and applied the plaster to the top of her newly shorn head. He knew it would take time to develop the desired blisters, so he bled her other arm while he waited.

When her body writhed in protest a little while later, he dosed her with more poppy syrup.

As she fell back into an uneasy doze, he ran the backs of his fingers down her cheek, marvelling at the smooth, soft skin. He hadn't thought it possible, but his love for her had grown though this experience. He was awed by her trust in him and grateful he had the knowledge and skill to prevent her from contracting such a miserable disease as the plague.

Finally, the edge of a blister peeked out from under the plaster, so he removed rags and set to work.

Aaron was soaked in sweat by the time he'd drained them all, and flummoxed by the amount of toxins he'd released a second time. Surely there should have been less than what had drained from her feet, but there were more.

At a loss for any other options, and with Elizabeth Howe and her pus-filled lymph node still fresh on his mind, he made a decision.

He would cut Cecily's out.

All of them.

Remove the source of the toxins altogether.

He let her rest as he prepared himself, and his beloved, for what was to come.

Without the aid of an assistant to hold her down

while he cut, he improvised by tying her wrists and ankles to the bedposts. It wasn't ideal, but under the circumstances, it would do. He certainly couldn't compromise her modesty this way to anyone else.

He checked the tightness of the bonds, made a few adjustments, then guzzled a restorative glass of brandy to steady his own nerves. This time when he reached for the bottle of poppy syrup, he left the spoon sitting on the side table and tipped the jar to her lips.

She sputtered and coughed, even struggled a bit against the ties, but he finally succeeded in administering the remainder of the opiate.

"There, there, love," he soothed. "This will all be over soon and you'll be safe."

Aaron picked up his scalpel and reached for one of the half-filled bowls.

He closed his eyes for a brief moment and visualised. Six lymph nodes, one on either side of the body at the neck, armpit and groin. Pinch behind the nodule, make a tiny incision, pop it right out. It would certainly be easier than removing one the size of an egg, as Elizabeth's had been.

Aaron opened his eyes. He was ready.

He began at her neck, working quickly so as not to cause her undue pain.

Pinch.

Slice.

Squeeze.

The first of six plopped into his hand, the size of a ripe garden pea, just as it should be. No signs of swelling, toxins or disease. His heart soared.

There was more bleeding than he'd expected, but she hadn't moved a muscle. His instinct was to continue while the poppy syrup worked it's magic and he could staunch the bleeding after.

He dropped the tiny lump into the bowl with a smile and moved to her armpit, then her groin before circling to the left side of the bed.

Within moments, he'd successfully removed the remaining three and set about bandaging the incisions.

So little blood on the left side, he had them dressed in no time. The right side of her body though was a mess, particularly by her neck. Blood soaked the blanket beneath her and dripped onto the floor.

He turned to grab a few more rags and when he turned back, he saw her face and froze.

Her mouth hung open, her cheeks white as snow. Her eyes…half-closed, staring at nothing.

Dread filled his stomach, but he forced himself to move, to touch her face.

Cold.

Slack.

He put his hand on her chest, leaned over and put an ear to her mouth.

Nothing.

No breath on his cheek.

No thumping beneath his hand.

He stood upright and took a step back, his own breath coming in short, painful gasps. "No…no, no, no…"

Aaron watched for as long as he could bear, but she never moved.

He covered his face with his hands and fell to his knees.

He'd failed.

Cecily was dead.

A Name Like Velma Kettering

by Michael D. Davis

There isn't all that much to do when you get to be an old cuss like me, especially when you're in a home, surrounded by people who are either dead, dying, or don't know who the hell they are. The biggest pastime just seems to be television. I guess it's the new babysitter for kids and old folks alike.

I was in the sitting room, tryin' to watch an old western while this senile bastard chewed my ear with the same story I'd heard a thousand times or more, when it happened. John Wayne and Dean Martin went away to be replaced by a blonde woman with furrowed eyebrows. There was a red banner above her head stating in bold letters: **BREAKING NEWS**. The woman said, "This afternoon, at the bottom of The Parker West Lake in Hinchley County, a car has been found."

There were a few audible reactions around the room, one of a man saying, "That's just a few minutes from here."

I only thought, *well, shit…they finally found him.*

The newswoman cut to the car being hauled out of the water; it was still half-submerged, but it all came back to me.

The year was 1966 and I'd been drivin' a hell of a long ways to do a job that would take all of five minutes. I'd come across a little toe jam of a town somewhere in Iowa and thought I'd stop. I'd been drivin' so long, my shoe was losin' its rubber sole from pressin' the pedal. I was also ready to eat roadkill.

There was a small place just on the edge of town with stools in front and booths in back. I sat, a steaming pile of food soon under my nose. As I ate, I looked about the little greasy room. It was mostly empty except for a few paying customers, if this was it at rush hour, I'd hate to see a slow day.

One of the other booths was occupied by a family. Two little kids that were bubbling at the top and playing with their food, a man that snapped at them anytime his children made the slightest noise, and the most beautiful woman I've ever seen. She tried to get the kids in order calmly as her husband ate between swears. Even while wiping the little boy's face, she was exquisite; with short black hair, large blue eyes slyly hiding behind a pair of glasses.

The family and I had finished eating right one after the other. I was coming out the door as they were trying to get all loaded up in an old Mercury. I wasn't two steps out the door when I saw him slap her. The impact of his hand on her face made a sound like a gunshot. She was thrown over backward onto the gravel lot, landing right beside the car. He started to kick rocks at her as she lay there, yelling nasty things. She was as strong as she was beautiful though; I didn't hear one sob or one scream. Then again, maybe she was just used to it.

One of the kids hung their face out the window, bawling their eyes out, crying for their mommy. That put a pretty good stop to everything. He pushed the kids crying head back in the window and stepped over his wife to get in the old Mercury. As he yelled at her from the driver's seat, she slowly picked herself up off the gravel and dragged herself into the car.

When they were finally driving out of the lot, I

made my way to my car. From there, I found a hotel and spent the night.

The next morning, checked out, ready to get back on the road, I saw her. She was alone, going into a grocery store. I figured I could at least get some crackers for the long drive, so I went into the store.

I followed slowly, watching her, then I approached. She was as stunning as the night before. The same glasses now hiding a shiner around one of her gorgeous eyes.

"Hello," I said, holding out my hand.

"Hi," she responded quietly, letting my hand hang in the air.

"I'm Franky August."

"That's nice."

I didn't know how else to do it, so I went for the jugular.

"I saw you and your husband last night...the incident in the parking lot."

She didn't say anything for a while, then she just muttered, "Oh?"

"Yes. Does he do that a lot?"

"That's none of your business."

"What's your name?"

"Velma Glassman." She didn't look me in the eyes

as she spoke.

"That's not your name."

"What?"

"That's his name…Glassman. What's your name?"

"Kettering… Velma Kettering."

"That is an amazing name. A name like Velma Kettering should never be changed, altered, touched. It's the most beautiful name I've ever heard for the most beautiful woman I've ever met."

That's when she finally looked me in the eye. I took a card out of my pocket and showed it to her, saying, "A woman like you, or anyone, should never put up with a husband so awful. If you've had enough, get to the point when you're scared for your life, your children's lives—and trust me, that day will come—you call this number. It's for a bar you've never heard of, in a town you've never been to. A man you'll never meet will answer. Say your beautiful, wonderful name and my name, Franky August. Then all you have to do is wait with the door unlocked, because I'll be there before you can yell for help."

I don't know if she was stunned or confused or what, but she didn't say anything. I gave her the card, said goodbye and started to leave. I didn't get but a few feet before she said my name. I turned back and she said,

"No one's ever said such nice things about me before."

"Every word is true, Velma Kettering. You need me, call."

It was three years later, the summer of '69, that I finally got that call. It took me a day and a half with a whole lot of speeding to get back to that little Iowa town. I kept a watch out for her over the years, so I knew just which house on just which street she was in.

When I pulled up outside, I went straight for the front door and into the house. She'd left it unlocked, just like I said.

I walked through the house quietly. Most the lights were off, but there was enough coming in through the windows I could see what I was doing. I went from room to room finding no one until the back bedroom. Velma lay on the bed naked. Bruises, welts, and scars covered most of her abdomen, back, and breasts. She didn't move until I said her name and touched her head.

"Where is he?" I asked.

"Work."

"Kids?"

"The neighbours."

"Good."

I got her cleaned up then dressed. If I showed up only a day later, I'm sure she would've been dead. When

Mr. Glassman came home from work, I was waiting. He walked in the door, took off his hat, and I slung a tie around his neck. He struggled, he was a big man, but he soon dropped to the floor like a dead deer. An hour or so later, I slapped him awake. He was tied to one of his own kitchen chairs with his own neckties.

"This is how its goin' to go," I said as he struggled in the restraints and chewed on the gag. "I'm goin' to untie your right hand, you are gonna sign a few things, write a few other things. If you do not do what I say, or write the exact words I dictate, I will take this hammer and smash one of your toes."

I think it was at that point he realised he was barefoot.

We started with the letter. I told him to write 'Dear Velma.' He looked at Velma sitting across the room and wrote 'Fuck Off.' He must have thought I was bluffing, I wasn't. I took his hammer and smashed the big toe on his left foot. "We're off to a bad start," I said as he screamed and choked on his gag, "So why don't we do the other big toe just so you know I'm serious." I brought the hammer down a second time, leaving a toe on each foot nothing more than a bloody stain on the floor. He screamed into his gag until his face started to turn a dark shade of blue with his eyes bulging and bloodshot, and snot and spit covering his face. When he quieted down, I said, "Two down, eight to go." He showed his cooperation by writing 'Dear Velma' on the piece of paper.

After the paperwork was done, I let Velma take over for a while. That mostly consisted of her crying, yelling, and a few stout whacks of the hammer to the bastard's ribs.

When she was done, I put the tie back around his neck and made him go to sleep again…permanently this time.

The next step was getting rid of both him and his car, because according to his letter, he was running away with a woman, and he can't do that without his car. The Parker West Lake was Velma's idea. It's a common camping, fishing, recreation spot, but there's a section that's just a tip where hardly no one ventures. It wasn't the most original place to dump a car with a body in the trunk, especially looking at the news today.

I glanced over to the women's little circle of friends, some reading, some knitting. "Hey, Velma," I said, hooking my wrinkled old finger at her, "come look at this."

She sauntered over and said, "Now will you look at that, Franky. They've found a car in the lake."

BAD *Romance*

"That they have." I stood up and held her close. "You know you're as beautiful as the day I first saw you, you're as beautiful as a name like Velma Kettering,"

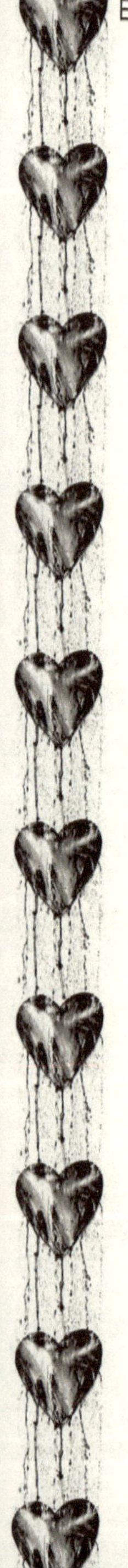

The Power of Love

by Nicola Currie

My assistant, Melanie, enters as I hang up on my CFO—a blustering mansplainer I only keep around to abuse. Laden down with shopping bags from Hermès and Liberty, she still manages to place my coffee order on my desk without spilling it. It's as I told her, she was made to be my assistant.

"Th-these are all they had," she says, biting her lip as she pulls out scarf after beautiful scarf. I scowl.

"Did you not hear me or are you too stupid to understand? I said burgundy. Instead, you get me maroon, aubergine, plum. Invotechna will be our biggest customer by millions when I close the deal this afternoon, and their corporate colour is burgundy. Are you trying to ruin things? Again?"

She starts to tear and whine, like a pathetic little

puppy, as I tell her to get out of my sight. The Prada one will do. It looks burgundy after all, in the right light.

I look through the glass wall of my office and watch Melanie; red-eyed as she unwraps a Mars Bar at her desk covered in paperwork, clearly intent on adding to the two stone she has gained in the last six months or so. I smirk. She's really fallen apart compared to when we first met. It's delicious how things change.

It was Melanie I reported to on my first day as the brightest of that year's crop of graduate trainees. Melanie Baxter was a second year and had already worked herself into a marketing position reporting directly to the CEO. I hated her from the beginning. But it was while she left me waiting in reception, fifteen minutes after she had been due to meet me there, that I met the person who would change my life forever.

I never thought I would go for a tradesman. I mean, really? How would that look to the kinds of professional circles I was aiming for? But Dylan knew how to rock his blue plumber's overalls, with his broad shoulders and cute butt, and when he turned and winked at me as the receptionist tried to figure out what job he had been booked for, I winked back.

The look of shock on his face was thrilling. I could tell he was the kind of guy who winked at women wherever he went, like they were all targets and his eye a chancing shot, knowing that if he scatter-gunned widely enough, he'd hit his mark eventually. But he wasn't used to a woman brazen enough to wink back, to be so bold about what she wanted. He wasn't used to me.

"I'm sorry," the receptionist called over to me, after answering the phone and replacing it. "Ms Baxter will be another ten minutes."

"No problem, I don't mind waiting," I lied. I knew what that bitch was really up to. With a starred first from Cambridge, a master's from Oxford, and a résumé filled with internships of greater distinction than the heights of most people's careers, I was hot property. This wasn't the only company who had headhunted me. I knew my reputation preceded me, that the second year graduates would be gunning for me. Leaving me waiting was a power play, to show me who was boss. The thing is, I would show her. I'd show them all, eventually.

My first opportunity came only seconds later. The receptionist left her desk with an apology, unable to get through to the facilities manager who had booked the services of my overalled Adonis.

"I'm sure we can keep ourselves occupied," he

said, turning to me with a flirtatious smile as she buzzed herself through the security doors and disappeared.

That look of happy shock again as I stood and walked over. When I lay a hand on his arm and knew the power I had over him, it filled me with pleasure.

"What did you have in mind?"

Two minutes later, we were fucking in the visitor toilets next to the reception. He gazed up at me in rapt wonder still as I straddled him and did the work.

"God, you're amazing!"

And I knew it.

He had a good body and a big dick, but it wasn't that that got me off. It was the control, knowing that I wasn't only fucking him, but Melanie too and all the other second years, anyone who thought I would start off here like some obedient little wallflower, happy to fetch coffee at the snap of finger and thumb or nod along to every idiotic opinion. That wasn't me and soon they'd know it.

My satisfaction was complete when, orgasm for the day ticked off my to-do list, I returned to the reception to find Melanie waiting.

"There was a leak in the ladies," I interrupted, when she tried to chastise me for keeping her waiting. "It seemed serendipitous that there was a plumber waiting in reception, so I mentioned it and he insisted on taking a look."

"Just a loose…screw," Dylan said, with a gleam in his eye.

Melanie's sour expression told me that she was one of my kind. She did not like to be kept waiting whatever the reason. Like me, she also couldn't stand the thought of her power moves not paying off. She had to find another way to put me in my place.

There was no doubt she was a beautiful woman—tiny-waisted but big-busted, with sea eyes and sunshine hair, she was corporate Barbie from her heels to her blowjob lips.

She turned to Dylan and smiled. She placed her hand on the shoulder she didn't know I had just bitten as I came.

"Well, aren't we lucky you were here to come to the rescue? Do you have a number we can call you on, in case there are any other problems?"

"Sure," Dylan said, pulling his card from his pocket and handing it over. To me.

As the receptionist returned for Dylan and led him to his real job, Melanie looked at me with burning hatred. We both knew I had won.

I knew I was going to like it here, I thought.

I hadn't planned on calling him. He was a one-time good-time as far as I was concerned and not someone I could ever be serious about. Still, there was a downside to being the best. It could be lonely. As the prettiest new peacock, already standing out amongst my peers, my colleagues didn't exactly warm to me—not that there were many I even wanted to be tepid with, comparatively mediocre bunch that they were. I didn't have any family and never really cared much for friends. They were too much work when your priority was number one, but I had maintained a casual circle of acquaintances for drinks and dinners, for tennis matches and lifts to the airport. However, this was a new city and I knew no one. One Friday evening, a month in, the CEO shut down the building at the ludicrously early time of 5pm and insisted that no one do another ounce of work all weekend. We'd all been working too hard, apparently. That was the kind of ridiculous notion that meant getting rid of him was swift work in the end.

Abruptly forced from my 18-hours-a-day-seven-days-a-week work habit, I struggled to know what to do with myself until I consoled myself with housework around the flat I had, so far, done nothing but sleep in.

As I shoved the laundry I had neglected into the machine, a scrap of cardboard fell to the floor.

Dylan Murray, Elite Plumbing Services

He was something I could do.

An hour later, he was there, looking far more my type in an expensive white shirt, with a quality bottle of wine in his hand. We said little beyond pleasantries.

Hours later, when we were done, I wanted to ask him to leave. It still wasn't quite morning, and I didn't like men to stay the night. It might just have been my exhaustion that meant I let him stay, but there was something different, something nice, about having him resting in my bed, warm against me. And I couldn't stop looking at his eyes, so vivid green, like grass after rain.

You would think warm fuzzy feelings would lead to warm fuzzy dreams, but it was quite the opposite. It started off well, Dylan and I walked together hand-in-hand into an exclusive member's only club. Except we were stopped at the door for inappropriate clothing. I turned to Dylan, and he was dressed in rags, falling apart before my eyes. Next, I walked into my office building. I headed for my desk, but Melanie stopped me in reception, handed me a mop and bucket, pointed me towards the visitor toilet. When my arms were a foot deep in overflowing shit, I woke up in a sweat.

Dylan was already making breakfast, the smell of bacon I did not have in my fridge telling me he had been comfortable enough to take my key, so he could go down to the shop on the corner and then let himself back in. That perturbed me yet I knew it was my fault. I shouldn't have let him stay.

It was difficult to get rid of him, puppy-eager as he was to spend the day with me, but I convinced him I had to work, that I would text him as soon as things eased up. I sighed with relief when I closed the door; but there was something he left behind him. A new colour of loneliness, a shade I'd never seen. I told myself it was the meaningless of an empty day with no work to make me feel productive. I spent the rest of the weekend exercising, running in the park, trampling the vivid green grass to mud.

I had hoped he would eventually lose interest when I didn't answer his texts, but it was little more than a week later when I next saw him. I'd managed to work myself into the way of a promotion already and thought I had it in the bag. I was enjoying a celebratory coffee in one of the smaller, quieter kitchens, having delivered a stellar pitch as to why I was the woman for the job, when Peter Walker interrupted my solitude. Peter was a dinosaur who had worked for the company for twenty years without achieving much. He was pissed at me and I knew it, didn't care. I was surprised he had some game though. Simpletons like him usually wore their rage on their spit-speckled sleeves, without the presence or artistry to channel it. But Peter sauntered over casually and his hard eyes danced with light.

"I've been meaning to thank you," Peter said as he poured himself some coffee.

"Thank me?" I said, surprised, a rare emotion for me. I had garnered kudos from the board by suggesting some cost-saving changes. Suppliers they could change, efficiencies they could make. Job roles they could cut. Peter's had been one of those roles and he'd received notice of his redundancy a week ago.

"Yes! Turns out you can bring about what I couldn't. I have been trying to get promoted for decades but never had any luck. You know company policy is to first consider those at risk of redundancy for any internal vacancies, right? Well, HR just told me. That promotion in the corporate affairs office? It's mine."

FUCK!

As Peter leant towards me and placed a hand on my shoulder, I saw the doorway fill with blue as my eyes swam with angry tears.

"You really have been most helpful," Peter said,

with a smug smile.

"What's going on here?"

It was Dylan in the doorway, I realised, in his blue overalls, tool bag in hand.

"Just catching up over coffee," Peter said, walking away. "We must do it more often, get to know each other. Now that I'll be sticking around."

When he is gone, I turned and sniffed away my tears, like Dylan wasn't even there. I wasn't even slightly interested in dealing with him.

"Are you okay, babe?" he says, hugging me from behind. "It looked like that guy was leering over you. He wasn't bothering you, was he?"

An interesting opportunity, I thought. I screwed up my eyes and restarted my tears.

I turned so I leant against Dylan's chest. I looked up at him with big sad eyes.

"You won't tell anyone, will you?"

"I'll kill him! That's what I'll do!"

He held me as I told him that Peter had been bothering me, touching me. How he had done anything he could to undermine me, to steal the promotion I deserved.

The next morning, Peter came in to collect his things. His eyes were black, his nose taped. He told HR he was leaving with immediate effect. He recommended me when they asked: What about the promotion? By the end of the day, it was mine.

That's when things changed, when I realised for the first time that love didn't have to be a weakness. As long as I could control it, hold it at arm's length, never get lost in it, it could be an asset. It could be a shortcut to power if I played things right. I would have someone who would fight for me as long as I said the right words. Love was a game, I realised, just like business. And I was used to winning.

Dylan wasn't a bad guy, either, so it was surprising what I was able to convince him to do. When I was forced to work with Melanie on the company's most lucrative project to date, a miscalculation led to a significant loss of profit. Several members of the project committee quickly tried to say it was my fault and, sure as shit, Melanie was happy to make a spectacle of my blaming and shaming. But all it took was a few flirty texts from Dylan before there were nudes and threats of sharing them, before she took the blame. I was rightly promoted again, for picking up the pieces and saving what we could. She'd told me to fuck off, on what should have been her last day, as she packed her things and stormed away. But the game wasn't over. I followed her to the lift, told her I wanted her to stay on as my assistant. I still had the photos after all. I saw the trapped look in her eyes and rejoiced. You'll be perfect, I had said, as long as you remember your place.

That was only one of several plays Dylan helped me make over the next few years. It was almost an addiction, not just because of the ever increasing feeling of power, what it felt like to crush someone, who thought they were so much better, beneath me. I liked to see the conflict in his eyes as they revealed the battle between his conscience and his heart. When his heart won and he looked at me? Those were the victories to beat all victories.

It wasn't about him loving me. I knew that didn't matter. Not really. It's not like I really needed him, emotionally, romantically. Not like I loved him. Not really. Not my style. Not ever.

But then I made it. CEO. That was a year ago, when Dylan had started talking about marriage, babies. A CEO and a plumber. How ridiculous. I pictured us, hand in hand, dressed for our wedding, and wanted to laugh so hard I cried.

Besides, the dance of light in Dylan's eyes didn't dazzle me anymore. His gaze was only ever dull now, tired in a way that filled me with old shades of loneliness.

Still, his eyes filled with lightning bolts of pain when I told him we were over.

"Why?" he said, not even angry, only defeated. "I don't understand what you want. I've only ever loved you."

"That's just the point," I said. "I don't want anything from you."

He'd stepped closer and looked at me with a tenderness that somehow frightened me, like it contained a kind of pity and forgiveness that saw through me, like he had known how I was using him all along and loved me anyway.

"Why can't you just let yourself love me?"

I'd always been logical and never liked dealing with people's melodramatic emotions. So I said nothing, but ran from the flat and stayed at a hotel until I was sure he had left.

The smell of him haunted the flat for weeks as I burned joss sticks in every room until all trace of him was gone.

I hear the lift ping and it breaks my concentration. I take a second's break from preparing my presentation to take another joyful glance at Melanie stuffing chocolate into her depressed face. I'm surprised to catch her smirking at me. Who does the cheeky bitch think she is?

As the group exiting the lift comes into view, her smirk breaks out into the kind of grin that makes your cheeks hurt. Police. Three of them. And they knock on my door.

"C-come in," I say, confused. My head spins as they confirm my name, say that they are arresting me.

"What do you mean, embezzlement? I don't know what you're talking about."

"We have your signature, Madam. We know you moved the money offshore."

That's when I realise. Melanie and the papers she always hands me to sign. My pissed off CFO. But Melanie wouldn't have the guts for something like that.

It's not until Melanie follows me, as the police lead me in handcuffs down to the entrance, that I realise, as she smugly watches me from his arms, his hand rubbing her bloated belly.

"How could you do this to me, Dylan?" I scream. "And her? Why her?"

"Because she loves me," Dylan says, no light now when he looks at me. "YOU could have loved me, if you had let yourself, if you weren't so weak."

It's then I burst into tears, but only because it is the perfect storm of defeat, not because of romance. Not because of love. I cry and cry as the police take me away, but I know it is only because I lost the game. I know. It's not because I loved him. It's not.

BLACK HARE PRESS

No Substitute

by Nicole Little

It wasn't Raymond's fault that he'd fallen in love with her. It was one of those things that just happened, he'd explained. His wife didn't quite understand, of course, and if he was honest with himself, he hadn't really expected her to. Callie didn't give Raymond any option but to leave after she'd discovered the pictures on his phone. The same phone she'd maliciously dropped into his mug of coffee at the breakfast table. There was shouting, recriminations, tears, and then she'd had the gall to *laugh* at him as if there was something amusing about his newfound love. He'd packed a bag and walked out; he would sleep on the couch in his office for the time being. It would all be worth it, if he could be with Ailsa.

Raymond Miller wrote code for a living. He was forty-five, his hair was thinning at the crown and his middle-age spread had begun to spread a little further each year. He was married (or at least he *had* been) but he had no children. Work was his progeny. He logged long hours in front of a computer screen and then spent even more time in the lab, where he beta-tested the programs. That was where he'd met Ailsa. He worked alongside her day after day, and as their friendship grew into something more complex, Raymond felt powerless to control it. The flirting was subtle (he was a married man, after all) but before long he was sneaking her into his office after everyone had gone home for the evening; eating dinner at his desk and stealing kisses in the dark. He had to go home to his wife at night, but he made promises to Ailsa; some day.

And that day had finally come. He was free. Free to be with Ailsa.

She was so different to Callie. She listened, *really* listened, to what he had to say. And eventually, when they had taken their relationship to the next level, the quiet, gentle lovemaking was in such stark contrast to being with Callie, who was loud, aggressive and demanding—he had wept on Ailsa's shoulder afterwards.

The short drive to the Ningyo Corp. felt like forever to Raymond. Excitement bubbled in his chest; a foolish grin plastered on his face. It was nearly 9 am. He was running late but Ailsa would be there in the lab, waiting for him. He couldn't wait to tell her the good news. He pulled into the parking lot and snagged a spot close to the entrance. Luck was on his side today. There was a lightness in his step, and in his heart, as he swiped his security pass to enter the building. He hummed a happy tune as he hopped on the elevator and pressed the button for the fifth floor. The doors opened—

There were people everywhere.

Raymond grabbed Tony's arm as he hurried past, tie askew, and a harried look upon his face. "What's going on?"

"Big boss showed up early this morning. He's pulling the plug on the project."

Raymond's face drained of colour. "Wh-why?"

"The higher ups say it's costing too much time and money. It was a long shot anyways, Ray, you know that. They're scrapping the whole thing. Sorry, mate."

"But…but what about…"

Tony was already gone. The question hung in the air, unfinished; unanswered.

Raymond sprinted down the hallway. He collided with Jan from marketing but ploughed ahead without pausing to apologise. He burst into the lab, his breathing ragged. People from the IT department milled about, packing away equipment and coiling cords.

He spotted the lead programmer, sorting through a stack of files. "Lachlan! What's happening?"

"Hey, Raymond! Sorry! We tried calling you earlier to let you know." He gestured to the chaos around him, then shrugged. "I know this project was important to you."

Raymond whipped his head around wildly, ran a hand through his already dishevelled hair. The room was quickly clearing of equipment.

"Where is she?" he demanded hoarsely.

Lachlan shot him a confused look. "Who?"

"Ailsa!!"

"Oh, yeah, right. She's gone, mate. The first thing they did was take the bot to the incinerator. Can't have anyone reverse engineering it and stealing our secrets." He laughed.

Raymond went numb. Choked on a sob. A slow searing pain spread across his chest.

Dear God…the incinerator.

The last thing Raymond saw before he hit the floor was Lachlan slowly feeding a document into the shredder. At the top it read SOURCE CODE - AILSA: Artificially Intelligent Love Substitute Android.

Oh, my darling Ailsa, he thought as his colleagues rushed to his side. *There is no substitute for you.*

And then he thought no more.

BLACK HARE PRESS

Just the Way You Are

by Paula R.C. Readman

The room hummed with music, laughter, and conversation. Being our fourth wedding anniversary, my husband, Patrick, had kindly thrown a valentine's party in honour of our love for each other.

As he stood to take centre stage, he tapped the side of his champagne glass and beamed as he waited for the room to fall silent.

I let out a gasp as a sudden stabbing pain shot up my back. I shifted uncomfortably in my seat and bit the inside of my lip. I sucked in air, determined not to allow tears to fall. The last thing I wanted was gushing insincerities from our guests.

Patrick glared a narrow-lidded warning at me. I steadied my breathing as a shiver ran through me. The look of annoyance slipped from his face, and he replaced it with a perfect imitation of devotion and fondness as his strong features prepared to make an announcement. He tapped the side of his glass again, and the room fell silent.

My husband raised his glass and gestured towards me. Everyone turned in my direction, their painted smiles not quite reaching their empty eyes as they feigned their hypocrisy by cooing at me in harmony.

I blinked, hating the focus to be on me. I was in a room full of fools. They were there to worship their idol; my husband, Patrick. 'Love' he called it, but he was a master of manipulation.

Patrick's perfect kissable lips parted as he ran his tongue around them; something I saw as unnerving, which others didn't see in his otherwise charming smile.

"Firstly, I want to thank you all for coming," he said, drinking in their admiration. "It means so much to us, you all being part of this special occasion. Four years ago, I became the luckiest man on earth when my beautiful fiancée became my darling wife."

My stomach heaved. If I had not been seated, I might have fainted.

"As you all know," Patrick continued, his brilliant smile not reflected in his eyes. "It has been a difficult few years for Sandy, but there's a light at the end of a dark tunnel. So please raise your glasses on this happy occasion and wish my beautiful wife a pain-free future."

"To Sandy," they cried before downing their drinks.

I took no pleasure in my husband's devotion. His kind of loving had taken its toll on me. Patrick had not allowed me any input into the party's arrangements, nor had he protested when Sally had side-lined me to a corner of the room.

I studied the physiotherapist, Sally as she took the seat next to him. She tried to get his attention, but he was in deep conversation with the man seated on his opposite side. Sally nervously pushed her long blond hair over her shoulder before turning to speak to the woman seated next to her. As she turned, she looked in my direction. A fleeting smile crossed her face as she gave a nervous nod to me.

I wanted to reassure her, but I couldn't acknowledge her. She had what my husband liked—a natural beauty. The symmetry of her flawless face would fascinate him. Her long elegant nose gave a sense of balance to her high cheekbones, large intelligent eyes, arched eyebrows and all-important cupid-bow lips.

I watched our guests busily indulging in the endless supply of expensive food and drinks without sparing a thought for me. Patrick had selected our guests with care. No, I can't say 'our.' They were *his* friends. He used the oldest trick in the book to manipulate his control over me. I saw no friendly faces among his worshippers. Their black eyes saw only the fucking wheelchair as they talked over the top of my head.

Oh yes, my chair was a luxurious thing. No expense spared. My husband wanted me to look my best at all times. After all, I'm the reflection of his love, his beautiful perfect wife.

The lightweight wheelchair was a marvel of modern engineering. Thanks to my darling husband severing my Achilles' tendons, I was unable walk.

The chair, at a press of a button, lifted me into a standing position. It allowed me to make eye contact, if someone took the trouble to speak to me. On the rare occasion I did use the facility, I came face to face with looks of discomfort in the eyes of our guests. It became clear to me that most people preferred not to talk to the disabled elephant in the room.

Of course, the elasticated facemask—another wonderful gift from my ever-loving husband—didn't help to put our guests at ease. The bright pink mask had slits for eyes and two tiny holes of my nostrils and a hole for my mouth. It also covered my neck, making it difficult to do anything other than stare straight ahead.

He explained that the mask enhanced blood circulation, promoted metabolism to improve my facial veins after my latest round of surgery.

"It's to increase the elasticity of her skin and rebuild the collagen," he said, while gripping my shoulder.

Under the mask, no one could see the pain on my face as my husband's perfectly manicured nails dug into my shoulders.

I wanted to scream at them. To tell them what I really thought of their shallow little lives and their over-botoxed faces. No one knew the real reason why I was in this chair. I doubted that they cared about the endless pain I endured for the sake of my husband's idea of what an ideal woman should look like.

Every cut, every incision, Patrick made into my once perfect body had been for his improvements. Every slice cut deeper into my love for him.

I watched him as he stood out of earshot, all smiles but not for me. Sally's beauty was astounding. Her white lace dress sheathed her perfect silhouette as the late afternoon sunshine poured through the French windows behind her. She giggled and covered her pink lipstick mouth with her slender hand and lowered her eyes. My husband, with a roguish grin, leant into her.

I knew what would come next. I had seen it so many times before and knew it would all end in tears as my husband won over his contributor.

Playfully, he took her hand in his. With a sweep of her other hand, she brushed her golden locks away from her delicate ear so she could hear what he was saying. He tilted her head so he could stare into her eyes. She smiled and brushed something off his collar.

I wanted to warn her, to tell her not to play his game.

Patrick would, little by little, strip away her self-belief, robbing her of her confidence. She would want to please him, to win his smiles and reassurances that she was beautiful in his eyes.

"Are you alright, my dear?" My mum said as she blocked my view and interrupted my thoughts.

Between the dancing bodies, I watched as Patrick and Sally slipped out through the French windows into the garden.

I sighed, knowing where he was taking her.

"Sandy, my dear, you'll feel much better once the bandages are off," Mum said though her smile didn't disguise her real feelings.

I tried to plead with Mum, but she could not read my mind. I wanted to tell her to stop him, that I could not take anymore, but since he had wired my jaws together, I had lost all hope.

"Shall I help you with that straw?" Mum said, lifting the beaker of liquidised food. "You really must eat something."

I tried to push it away, but gave in. I had no choice, but to drink, not wishing to upset Mum. She forced the straw between my lips. As I sucked up the liquidised chicken dinner, Mum smiled. It saddened me, because Mum believed she was helping me.

Hit by a wall of exhaustion, I knew he had drugged me again. Every day, I wanted to believe that I would be much stronger tomorrow.

The sounds of their voices emphasised my loss of control as I slipped into unconsciousness. Mum's one of concern. My husband's sickly sweet as he reassured her everything was okay.

"She's just a little tired. A major operation, but she's strong and healthy, Martha."

"I don't understand why she needs so many operations, Patrick. She was beautiful the way she was."

"I just want Sandy to be happy," he said, patting my shoulder.

"You know best," Mum said, though it sounded as though she was trying to convince herself. "You're her doctor…"

As a teenager, I believed in Mr Right. I longed for him to come, sweep me up in his arms, and carry me off to bed. Wisdom had made me wise to Patrick. When he swept me up in his arms, it was to carry me through to his operating table after he had selected another donor for his ultimate creation.

I wasn't beautiful in the classic sense of beauty. No flowing locks, hourglass figure, blue eyes, or porcelain skin, but beauty was in the eye of the beholder, so I believed. Once I was a confident, independent woman, having my own career, home and fast car until I met Patrick.

Charming, golden-haired Patrick leant against the bar in the hotel I had booked into for a work's conference. As I walked towards him, he stood out from the other men. Under a blue cotton shirt and light-stone chino trousers, I saw well-defined muscles that rippled as he moved. He made direct eye contact with me as I pulled out a barstool.

"Hello beautiful lady, let me buy you a drink?" he said.

I nodded to the barman, who returned a smile and said, "Doctor Jameson is a regular here, Miss Lockwood."

"Doctor Jameson?" I repeated to the tanned, good-looking man.

He gave a sweeping bow and took my hand, kissing the back of it. I glanced nervously around, but no one, not even the barman, seemed to notice his old-fashioned gesture.

Soon we were chatting like old friends. He told me he had spotted me in the airport lounge as I waited to board the plane to Madeira. Of course, I was flattered to think he thought I was the most beautiful creature he had ever seen.

Not long after we were married, Patrick's comments changed. First, it was little things like changing my hairstyle. He had seen a style, which he thought would suit me so much better.

"Sandy," he said softly, with the right pitch that made my knees weaken, that I would be willing to crawl over broken glass just to please him. He gave a thin-lipped smile, only I saw it as playful.

"You would look so much better if I took just a little off your waistline. Your eyes would really shine, if your cheeks were just a shade higher."

Not long after that, I found myself waking in a brightly lit room, with no memory of how I got there. I sensed, more than I knew, I was naked. Then I became aware of movement in the room.

I tried to cry out, but for some reason I couldn't speak. I closed my eyes against the glare as confusion flooded my mind. I thought I heard Patrick murmuring something reassuring. I tried to move my mouth, to ask him for help but no sound came. Something touched my arm and I tried to twist it away, but found my wrists were pinned. A stabbing pain shot up my arm as everything faded to darkness. I drifted away in a mixture of antiseptic smells and a metallic odour that I couldn't name.

I woke on my stomach, unable to open my eyes because of the pain. It wrapped itself around my body and I felt nauseous. Why was I in so much pain? What had happened to me?

I tried to turn over, as it was unnatural for me to sleep on my stomach, but I couldn't move. I struggled to summon help, but my voice came out as a whimper. I bit back the pain and forced myself to focus on the room.

Next to the bed, I saw a metal trolley. The smell from it caused me to gag. I pulled back. A pain shot across my back and down my legs. As I lifted my head, I saw a row of bloodied surgical instruments, a blood-spattered mask and apron.

I found myself muttering, "Everything in its place," as the light faded.

For days, I slipped in and out of consciousness. When I finally came to, Patrick informed me that I had a nasty reaction to some medication I had been taking. I knew I hadn't been on anything.

Anger grew in me. Now unable to speak or walk, I had lost my job and independence. Soon my friends stopped coming to see me too. What else could I do, but admit defeat?

I feared sleeping most. I never knew quite what I would find on waking. Gingerly, I lifted the bed sheet to find another part of my body swaddled in bandages. Soon I feared that I would not be able to recognise myself.

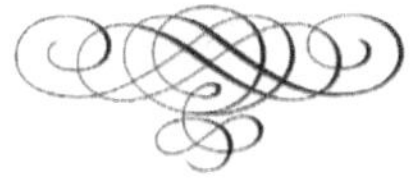

The silence told me the party was over. At first, I couldn't open my eyes. The drug Patrick had slipped into my food was stronger than the one he normally used. I rubbed the gunk from my lashes as I forced my eyes apart and blinked.

As the room came into focus, I realised I was in an antechamber off to one side of my husband's playroom. I forced myself to take a few deep breaths as panic overtook me. Then, to my relief, I noticed that the air lacked the thick acrid smell of the antiseptic. What could Patrick possibly be planning to change on me this time?

I kept my nausea under control by focusing on getting away. I twisted my head trying to see what surrounded me and managed to cause the room to swirl before me. Once everything came back into focus, I stretched my arm over the side of the bed and reached as far as I could. My fingers searched the air around me until finally they contacted with something familiar.

"Thank god, he's so predictable."

My relief was short lived. I could only just reach it with my nails. My middle finger caught the rubber of the armrest and for once, I found myself thanking my husband's vanity. Any sensible woman would not wear their gel fingernails so long as to be unpractical, but they were useful when needing to escape a hellhole.

I inched the folded-up wheelchair towards me, thankful that the brakes were not on. Once I could get a firm grip, I jerked it as hard as I could. Each time the tyres squeaked, I held my breath and listened before giving it another tug.

My head ached, and my throat dry. I was desperate for a drink but focused on getting off the bed.

My husband's vanity allowed me one exception to his manipulation, an excellent physiotherapist, who seemed to have a crush on Patrick. When he first introduced her to me, Sally stared up at him with large come-to-bed eyes while hanging on to his every word.

"Hello, Mrs Jameson. Your husband has told me so much about you."

I sat in the corner of the room, unresponsive.

For days, Patrick watched her massaging my back, legs and shoulders. I knew he wasn't concerned about my welfare, more the fact he wanted to keep me supple and toned. On the day she dismissed Patrick from the room, I began to see her in a different light.

Patrick kissed the top of my head as his fingers gripped my shoulder to remind me that he was in control. After the door closed behind him, I wrote one word on my notepad 'cameras'.

Sally nodded and covered my hand as she tore the page from my notepad and wrote on it 'I know, act natural' before slipping it into her pocket.

The look on Sally's face told me all I needed to know.

After five weeks, with Sally's help, I had regained strength in my upper body and the tops of my legs.

Caution screamed at me, as I used the wheelchair for support. I pushed the button on the armrest, and with a satisfying swoosh, it rose up into a standing position next to the bed.

I had only one opportunity to catch Patrick off guard. I heard him moving around in the other room and knew that he was preparing his operating table.

An image of him flashed through my mind; the smell and the sticky squelching of blood under his feet as he sliced into me. I could feel the pull of my flesh as it yielded to his touch.

With care, I pulled myself up into a sitting position and dragged my legs one at a time over the edge of the bed.

We knew it would be the most difficult part for me,

but we had practised. I needed to be in a standing position to deal with Patrick, and to do that I needed to control my feet.

After manipulating my legs to get my feet into a position where they would drop into the right spot on the footrests, I felt my energy levels plummet. I grasped the arms of the chair and worked the controls, lifting the seat level with the bed. I inched myself into the seat before allowing my legs to drop.

Panic rose in my gut; I was taking too long. My means to escape would die at my husband's hands like all the rest.

I pressed the button, and the chair shuddered into life. Ghost-like, it moved soundlessly forward, and I slipped out of the room and into my dressing room. Another button on the chair's control panel opened a narrow drawer on my dressing table.

I tilted the chair forward just enough to allow me to reach in. Sally had concealed a small scalpel as promised. It took me three attempts to hold the handle in a comfortable position that allowed me to control the chair.

I inched out of the room and felt my chest ease at the sight of an empty corridor. I nudged the control forward, and with a spurt of energy, the chair carried on to the end.

At Patrick's playroom door, I listened.

I wasn't sure whether I could hear him. I took a deep breath and pressed the button on my chair. As I did so, I manoeuvred the scalpel into my hand, knowing at any moment Patrick could disarm both my chair and me.

As I inched towards the door, I heard a scream. The long, anguished cry that brought tears to my eyes.

"Please… Someone help me!"

"Come on, don't be silly, Sally. Isn't this what you wanted, just the two of us together."

"Don't touch me."

I knew what his game was; with a sharpie pen, he would begin to mark out the changes he would make to Sally's flesh.

"Stay away from me!" Terror rose in her voice.

My freedom was fading. I threw the switch on my chair, which opened doors, and rammed the door at the same time.

As the door crashed open, Patrick swung round. I careered into him. On making contact, the scalpel slipped with surprising ease into him.

My husband stepped back, puzzlement marring his handsome face. He shook his head as a spray of warm blood hit me.

Wordlessly, Patrick looked down at the river of red and pressed his fist against his gut. The shock in his eyes gave me satisfaction after years of pain.

"Why, Sandy," he said, reaching out to steady himself.

I charged him again, like a knight on a horse, gripping the slippery blade as tightly as I could. Once again, I hit my target hard. He staggered back, hitting the table before falling to the floor with a deep groan.

On the operating table, Sally shrieked and struggled against the restraints. She lifted her head in an effort see what was happening.

I was not sure what I saw in her face, relief or fear.

"Hush, I'll need your help to get you out of here," I said.

"Thank you," she mouthed back, her fight gone.

I lowered the chair and dropped the armrest, with ease I'm able to lean over Patrick's handsome face.

"Help me, Sandy, please," he whispered.

The room stank of the metallic odour of blood mixed with the antiseptic smell. I smiled, knowing for once it was not mine—not that Patrick could see my smile under the mask that he made me wear.

"Let me show you, my darling husband, just how much I love you. In the same way you showed me your devotion."

Without a sharpie, I sliced off his nose. Patrick snorted blood as I sliced at his kissable lips before cutting into his eyes.

My Fair Minstrel

by Peter J. Foote

Knock, knock.

Queen Vilineva stops writing, places her gilded quill upon her desk, and turns towards her chamber door, cringing as she places her hand over the stitches on her chest. In the nearby mirror, she ensures her posture has the correct regal bearing, that and no ink or candle wax mars her pristine white gown, and no sign of pain shows on her pale face. Tucking a dangling piece of hair back beneath her scarlet ribbon, she says, "Enter." She allows her shoulders to relax as her trusted advisor Roderick shuffles into her chamber.

Leather sandals slap against the tiles floor, the

familiar stuttering footsteps of her advisor and confidant make her glad. Muscles unused for decades tug her face into a smile, and she can't help but trace her jawline with her ivory fingertips.

"It warms my heart to see you smile, my Queen, I feared that my old bones would be dust before it happened. The minstrel has done us all a great service, my queen." Roderick bows deep, his old and twisted body creaking as the cuffs of his robes brush the floor.

Dear faithful Roderick, where would I be without you? I fear that I will soon find out. Now that I'm whole once again, with a beating heart, your reason for continuing on has left, I hope you can enjoy some peace in your final days. Thinking of those who have passed through her life, these long and lonely centuries, brings the contents of the letter she's writing front of mind, and her smile fades.

"The arraignments?"

"All is as you commanded, my queen. Your stone masons have finished carving the sarcophagus's lid and your court await you in the gardens. The sun is about to rise and bodes to be a wonderful day." Advisor Roderick nods toward the stained glass windows along the chamber wall and the glow growing within the colourful pieces light the room.

BAD *Romance*

The queen's gaze follows that of her advisors, and her smile returns. "I'll be down in a moment, Roderick, I'm almost done here." Queen Vilineva taps the parchment on her desk.

Hand to heart, Roderick bows again and shuffles from the queen's chambers leaving the door open.

Mimicking her advisor's gesture, Vilineva feels a stickiness against her fingers and looks down. Blood has seeped through the stitches and marred her gown again and stained her fingertips. With fingertips wet with her own blood, Queen Vilineva picks up her letter and rereads what she has already written.

My dearest Minstrel,

You arrived in my life and court with nothing but your lyre and a beaming smile of confidence. You swore to me that your love and music could reach the darkest recesses of my shrivelled and dead heart. You said that you could return life into this hollow shell I call a body. I remember your lilting voice reverberating through my throne room as clear as a diamond and sweet as a rose. How, on bended knee, you pledged your music would return me to a mortal life, part of me dared to believe you could do it, that belief sustained me.

When you left my chambers, I would hear you stalk the hallways of the castle your dropped song sheets streaming from your grasp like autumn leaves. Scratching on pieces of parchment as if your existence depended upon it, drops of thick black ink trailing behind you, as if you were bleeding your art—perhaps you were.

I watched you strumming your lyre from my terrace your, beaming face pointed at the sun. Composing songs of love and sacrifice, your brow knitted in concentration as you practiced and performed, the rose bushes in the garden your audience. Your voice was so beautiful as your callused fingers flittered along the strings, only to pause in frustration when your muse fled and inspiration dissolved. You never gave up on me.

Placing the letter upon her desk, Queen Vilineva retrieves her quill, drips it into the inkpot, and after a moment's pause, concludes her letter.

Satisfied, Vilineva lies her quill down, blows upon the ink to hasten its drying, and rolls the blood-spotted parchment. Taking the scarlet ribbon from her head, allowing her white hair to flow freely over her shoulders, Queen Vilineva binds the parchment in a bow. With the letter grasped tight, she walks from her chambers to say goodbye to the minstrel.

Her slippered feet glide over the flagstones of the garden path. Members of her court bow as she passes, each wearing a rose from the garden pinned to their breast as a tribute to the minstrel.

Vilineva stops in front of the open tomb in the centre of the garden. The carved stone cover a perfect likeness of her loving minstrel right down to the carved rose over his breast. Queen Vilineva feels the warmth her first sunrise in centuries upon her skin. As she places the rolled letter into the bloody hollow where the minstrel's heart used to be, Vilineva recalls the final words of her letter.

Fear not my fair minstrel, your efforts paid off in full. Your music and love has touched my cold dead soul, and I smiled, cried, and laughed for the first time in centuries. It was then I knew that your heart and the magic it contained within it would grant me, your queen, a second life among the living. I will remember your sacrifice every time I feel your heart beat within my breast.

Your loving V.

As the masons secure the lid of the sarcophagus, Queen Vilineva turns toward the sun and smiles.

Buster

by Gregg Cunningham

I turned the handle with my good hand and walked inside the shop, spying the young, sobbing girl behind the counter looking my way. Her lower lip was quivering as the bell above the door tingled, and she quickly put away her hanky forcing a smile.

"Hi, how you going darlin'?" I said, smiling while she dabbed her eyes with a tissue and slid aside da paperwork that she was reading.

"I'm looking for a buddy, lady," I continued. "A mate, someone to share ma day wit, and I don't really care what dey look like."

She tilted her head with a grimace of doubt. "Really, you don't care what type of dog you want?" "No, sista', just as long as they is a good listener, and make me happy," I replied.

"Are you sure? I mean most folks have a breed in mind before they wander in and bring the family to choose. Have you had a dog before, Sir? They can be quite a…" She trailed off looking at my stump.

"A handful?" I smiled, lifting ma good hand. "Yeh, I've had a dog before I joined up, and I live alone now since…" My voice trailed away. I swallowed, wiped my dry lips, and tried again. "I just want me a mate to throw Frisbee wit, and walk in the park. As I said, I don't care what they look like, ugliest mutt in the pound is fine by me."

"That's great!" Relief blossomed in her flushed cheeks, "Really awesome. We don't get many people in here with that attitude. Hang on..." She ducked under the desk and produced the obligatory paperwork. "I just need to see some identification, please."

"Sure." I nodded, then pulled out me military ID and handed my credentials to her. She stared at ma stump with a hint of obvious shock, which she quickly concealed behind a smile.

"Were you injured during the war?" she asked, studying my details.

"This?" I raised my stump. "Yeh, lucky to get out alive, apparently!"

She smiled again, slightly embarrassed.

"Oh, well, Chris, I have just the mate you're after. He looks like he's been through the wars too." She gasped at actually saying that out loud. "He's…smart as hell, and so loyal, friendly…and he's toilet trained. He'll be so happy to finally be out of here." She sniffed, checking my military I.D again.

"I can't tell you how many people have been put off by his appearance, but once you get to know him, he is a real charmer. He's been here forever; they found him on the streets months ago, wandering aimlessly, no collar, charred fur. We're not sure how he lost his eye." She wiped the tears forming under her glasses.

"This is actually his last day." She pointed to the paperwork on her counter. "I was just filling the paperwork, to you know...try and save him from the needle again."

I nodded sympathetically, smiling as I juggled my wallet with stumped remains of my left hand and returned my identification card.

"Well, lucky for him dat I came along then."

"It sure is, and I think you both will be well matched; he loves playing Frisbee." She disappeared behind de counter again, returning with a blue dog collar and lead.

"I'll just go and get him. He'll be so happy to meet

you."

She almost skipped from that counter as I stood and watched. It seemed like years since I had been in that very same dog pound; the last time it had been with ma ivory skinned goddess, Maggie, the love of my life.

"Here he is, say hello to Buster!" She beamed, talking to me like I was a child.

Buster's tail wagged frantically as he paced back and forth, his paws clicking on the tiles.

"Oh look, he's so happy to see you."

She used that baby talk again as I approached that big old dog and held out ma stumpy hand. His tail stopped wagging instantly. Buster whimpered and backed off as I smiled, sneering back, baring my teeth.

"Hi, Busta," I growled softly in his ear, petting his nose with my stump. "Who's a good dog?" My smile turning into a curled sneer.

"Remember me, remember dis?" I lifted my stump, "...remember Maggie?"

He whined at the sound of her name, looking up to the beaming girl for some support.

"Oh, Buster, what's wrong, honey? This man is going to take you home, don't you want that?" Her baby talk faded as Buster's bladder relaxed, and he emptied the contents onto the floor.

"Buster!" She gasped.

"He's never done that before." Busta sat down in his own steaming piss as I sneered at him, shaking my head.

"Actually," I began, starting to feel a bit sick. "I don't think I'll bother today, that dog looks a bit...mangy!"

Her mouth dropped open as I slowly made for the door.

I shrugged at her. "I guess he'll just have to be...you know, put out to pasture!"

My fingers snatched the door handle and grated my teeth. My head buzzed. I was so damn angry with that dog, but what da hell made me think I could handle this?

It had been Maggie's idea to get a dog from the pound. She said it was for protection while I was posted overseas, ya know, and a nice bit of company, but da overseas postings were killing our relationship. And because I was so in love wit de woman, I agreed; she was my life.

We saw Busta, sitting in his cage all proud and regal like, an dat was dat.

So, Busta had joined the family, and because

Maggie loved him so much, my consent was no big deal. Maggie ruled the roost, no doubting that, and Busta knew that too. We was one big happy family, going out on long dog walks down the coast, watching him play with de other dogs.

I had a few tours here and there before I left for Kandahar the following year, but our huge Irish hound of a lodger had made himself at home by then, but not before I made some house rules. I at least had to pretend to myself that ma opinions mattered.

First, no bloody dog in de house at night. Fair enough rule, and Busta seemed fine with that. I made him space in da garage, and Maggie made him a huge blanket for them colder nights. The next rule, no barking at night, this had been tougher to enforce, mainly because Maggie took offence to me slapping Busta', calling me nasty. Reluctantly, I agreed to no physical punishment, but told her she was digging her own grave. I didn't want to upset my ivory princess. Me and Busta was tight no matter. He was always by my side. A good loyal dog who would protect us at all costs.

I could trust Busta with Maggie's life.

When I left, tings were good. Busta slept outside, and da neighbours were happy, and Maggie and I had our whole future ahead of us.

She told me she was pregnant over the phone while I was away, and I reluctantly agreed for her to be able to bring Busta inside for protection while I was gone. Truth was, I couldn't wait to get back to see dem both.

Six months later, de problems started.

You see, ma tour had been cut short—an IED put a halt on my operational duties, taking ma left hand and de sight in ma left eye. PTSD they said, and sent me home. Just like that. Honourable discharge, topped off with a shitload of drugs to take.

Sure, I was pissed, who wouldn't be? My world would never be de same again, and I had no fucking say in da matter.

When I got home, Busta was now a full-time house lodger, taking up residence on our entire bed with Maggie squished to the edge of da quilt. I kicked up shit about that arrangement, but Maggie insisted.

I said it was unhealthy, but she just reminded me how Busta made her feel safe. I said I should be da one to make her feel safe, but she said I should take da time to recover and not be worrying about him. So, he would lay by da end of our bed, tail wagging, while I cursed his stinkin' furry ass.

I'll admit it now, I did instigate Busta's barking at night with a few swift kicks from under the blanket to his ribs.

Why?

Because he didn't belong der, that's why, de stupid mutt.

Before long, he was back in de garage, howling at da moon in defiance.

One up for persistence in Busta's book.

I soon put a stop to that, those god-awful howls echoed in ma nightmares man, taking me back to de night of the attack; the horror of the aftermath, and de stray dogs that surrounded my mate's bodies as they lay on the street, smouldering amongst our burning armoured personnel carrier.

A few good slaps to Busta's nose wit ma stump subdued the nightmares…for a while, at least. I kept telling Maggie he was no good, he seemed jealous of me being with her, but she had taken his side, telling me I was de one who was jealous.

Me!

Things didn't improve, and Maggie suggested I sleep in da spare room while I settled in and adjusted to civilian life again. I didn't settle, though.

Those drugs made me angry. I'd snap at de slightest ting, and Busta took de brunt of it. It was da nightmares that Maggie feared. She was afraid of what I might do as a result of those damn drugs I was taking.

She was right to be afraid. I would hear her talking to her mother on de phone at night, telling her how hard it was with me being home, but I would be too pissed to care. I loved that woman, she was my goddess, but I just wanted de pain gone, all them images gone from my head as they mocked me constantly. The only way to drive them out was to drive her away, and welcome in the bottle.

Man, I didn't know at de time how bad de drugs completely messed me up back den, but I think Busta knew. That dopey fucker would stare at me from de toilet entrance as I took my daily dosage, knocking back a dozen or so prescription pain killers and suppressants with good old Captain Morgan to wash em down with.

I took them all, Paxil, Pexeva, Prozac, Sarafem, Zoloft de whole shebang, but still that 'black dog' from the past followed me relentlessly. Busta didn't make tings any easier; he served as my very own shaggy reminder of just how shitty my life had become. He never left Maggie's side in the beginning—wherever she went, he went. Her very own chaperone. When she cried, she hugged him…the fucking dog!

Whenever he got near me, all he got was a crack on da head with my stump.

My stump, hell, I was sick of the sight of that damn thing. All that stump did was remind me about Kandahar...shit, what a cluster-fuck! Truth is, ma life had been ripped from my chest right alongside that damn armoured personal carrier the night my friends died. So I done what any tortured soul would do; I turned to my new friends, Jack and Jim.

I hit them two bottles hard, almost as hard as I would hit Busta when he tried taking over da sofa, that whining flea bag. Who da hell gets an Irish wolfhound as a house pet anyway? It was like living in a stable and having a damn horse as a roommate.

But I started to wonder why he was no longer by Maggie's side all de time, and soon after a while, a few weeks perhaps, I realised that damn mutt was hovering around me now. All he would do was look at me with those big dopey eyes when they both came back from their long morning walks. Every day would be a longer walk than the last.

Or I'd find him sulking by the sofa when I came home from de drug store, with Maggie locking herself away behind de bedroom door out of de way. She said she needed time to adjust to me being back in de house, and that Busta was just yearning for attention.

I'd hear her talking on de phone and sobbing all

night, while Busta seemed determined to keep me awake every damn night. When she did take Busta out, they would be gone most of de day, which was fine by me. And when they got back, he would come sit by me and nuzzle my face, putting his big sloppy tongue all over my damn face.

Every time! Damn dog.

When I did see Maggie, she seemed distant to us both. There was little love left in her eyes for either of us—I saw that clear as da rum sloshing at de bottom of my bottle.

I wanted to tell her how I was feeling, but I felt safer just hugging the bottle. Then she just stopped taking Busta on his walks, and left da two of us alone while she went god knows where to cry all day. That goddamned dog whined for days by that door, waiting for her to return.

When she did, it happened. The last shreds of my life torn from ma chest, like a hungry dog tearing da last bite at me heart.

Maggie said that she was moving out to be with her mother for de last few weeks of pregnancy, and she left me with that damn dog, saying der was no room for him at her mother's.

She insisted her exit would do me good, give me

space to adjust and find myself again. All it did was make me angrier.

Wit Maggie gone, Busta became ma outlet. Having something to blame and take that anger out on helped me, but not Busta. He would sit by ma feet and wait for his daily walk with his eyes staring. The same walk Maggie would make wit him to the park every morning, where they would pass the trees, and da traffic, and take in the fresh air.

Yeh, right. He'd get his walk when I was ready. He would crap when I was ready to go for my refills. Until den, he would just have to hold it in, and if he didn't, well, then it was say hello to Mr Stumpy.

Da first few times he shat on my carpet, I beat that dog so hard, he bared his teeth briefly den whimpered into da corner. Seeing that just brought back more memories of my buddies lying in da street back there, with der guts spattered on der uniforms...and da stray dogs.

Oh, them fucking stray street dogs, sniffing around ma dying buddies as I lay pinned under ma burning rig. All I could do was throw rocks at them mongrels while they chewed on the sloppy innards of ma mate, spilling from between the fingers of his dying grasp. It was them screams, them awful pitiful screams, as der bloody snouts rummaged deep inside his torn rib cage for more...

But, as I stared blankly into ma horrors, Busta would just sit der, under the tv, watching me from afar with his sad knowing eyes. Sometimes he would amble up and nudge me, most times he'd get slapped and return to his spot on the carpet. We'd stare at each other, neither gazing away.

"What do you know, dog?" I would growl at him.

One thing he knew for certain was that I was da boss. He knew whose balls hung lower. I made sure of that.

I eventually took him for his goddamn walks along de cliffs and fed him that stinking dog meat when I remembered—or when I could be bothered—but truth is, I just couldn't take de pain anymore. Busta, like everything else around me, seemed so fucking unimportant. I was just so numb, so fucking numb.

I lost track of everything, ma life collapsed, and I just wanted them nightmares to end. But they didn't, how could they, when Busta followed me around like one of my Kandahar demons? He just kept on staring.

Big old dopey Busta. Looking sorry for me!

Time drifted by without sense or meaning, and Maggie never returned.

Fuck her. Fuck her and her goddamn dog. She was dead to me. Ma Ivory queen had become a wicked witch. But I still loved her.

"What are you looking at, fuckwit?" That was the last thing I remember saying to Busta before the fire.

The fire, what can I say about that mess?

Well, I was in da house alone, Busta was doing his usual whining under da table, as de thunder cracked above, so I took him outside and chained him to the kennel where I cursed him as the rain soaked into my clothes.

Busta stared up at me with them sad eyes, whining in the downpour. I remember staring back through de bottom of a bottle and uttering those magical words— "What are you looking at, fuckwit?"—before leaving the soaked mutt chained der, his tail tucked under his shaking hind legs, as a bout of fresh lightning crackled above.

I staggered back inside through de mud and made myself something to eat.

I remember having another night in with the boys, Jack and Jim, and a new buddy we liked to call Fireball. Man, did we party, and why not, I had just become a father!

Not that I'd get to see da little rugrat any time soon.

Maggie said I really needed help before that could ever happen. She said it was too painful for her to visit and watch me spiral out of control. What da hell would she know about pain? I wrote that book on fucking pain, man, and she dumped me like last month's dirty nappies.

Now, here's the ting; when you're pissed, you think it's okay to put your garlic bread in the microwave. Only most folk take der TV dinner out of da oven foil wrap and don't slump on der couch in a drunken stupor while the dial counts down from 15 minutes.

Well, not dis drunken fucktard, man. I must'a hit that couch and passed out while that mutt barked away outside.

I woke, panicked, to da sounds of mortar shells striking de walls and machine gun fire echoing in ma head. I rolled to the floor in a dizzying daze, ducking out of the enemy fire and shouting out ma orders to ma men. That was de last I remember—being back on the Kandahar streets again, pinned under that burning vehicle and watching the chaos unfold as those damn dogs barked and fed and fought.

Smoke choked me as flames engulfed the kitchen, setting de couch alight. Broken glass crunched under my back, and da smell of burnt garlic wafted through burning plastic from de kitchen. Jamaican Rum soaked ma shirt as I lay der, clutching the bottle in a daze, de burning room spinning as I gave up, laughing helplessly at the total injustice of my life, and still that bloody dog howled hysterically outside. Fuck you, Busta!

When I came round, choking in da swirling darkness, I saw one of them devil dogs staring back at me through de smoke, its bloody snout hovering above ma face like de whore of Babylon herself, eager to delve into my organs and gorge on ma flesh as I burned on the ground. Snarling teeth snapped by my face in a feeding frenzy, turning to me spilled guts. I raised de gnawed bloody stump to protect ma face from the rabid beast that clamped its snarling jaws down hard and began chewing.

Dull pain shot through ma drunken body as I swung da bottle against that street dog's head, then I blacked out.

This time, when I came to, I was outside the blazing house. Da puncture wounds on ma stump were deep, down to de bone, and de paramedics said I was lucky to have been dragged from that fire. I asked in my drunken state if they had seen de street dogs that attacked me, but they ignored my questions. My stump looked like a badly chewed stick now with large ugly punctures all the way down to ma elbow.

Maggie cried when she visited de ward, telling me her Buster was lost in the fire. That, and de news that she couldn't take any more of my bullshit and wanted a divorce.

Simple as that.

Christ, she never even brought our baby along. Said it wasn't da right time.

I said fine, and defiantly turned away, knowing she shed tears for Busta but not for me.

Busta.

I knew what that dog had done. I knew he had saved me from the fire, but I wasn't telling her anything, man.

After all I had done to that dog, he had stayed loyal by my side.

Unlike Maggie.

So, that shit was five months ago, and I haven't seen Maggie since that night in the hospital. Or my kid, for that matter. I'm still double dosing the medication, though. The nightmares continue to haunt me, but de pills keep da screaming voices at bay…most of da time anyway…and I keep away from de fucking crowded areas. I can get through most days without a drink.

I reckon the park is the best place to hide away,

man. It's just a short walk from ma flat, so I go der most days, or whenever I feel that black dog bite. Depression sure does ride you like a bitch sometimes. Talking of bitches, at least Maggie isn't around to tell me to get over it. I miss ma white Goddess like crazy, but she has told me I need to do better if I want to be part of her life again. Fuck knows what me doing better entails.

I keep away from her, as asked. I keep away from de drink, as asked. And I pay her the child support from ma compensation, as asked.

I give ma ivory queen everything she asks for.

So how come I knew about Busta' in da pound, you ask? Yeh, I know, I'm getting to that, man. It's no secret. I see them guys walking the pound dogs for exercise down the park most days, and I just happened to get chatting to a handler who was bitching about the strays they had to put down every month. I asked if he had seen a big fuck off Irish wolfhound on his travels. He'd laughed—not only had he seen him, they'd caught the one-eyed dopey fuck da same night they pulled me from that fire. Now he faced the needle any day, unless they found a home for him.

This was a turn for the better, and ma brain started plotting ma return into my ivory queen's life. All I needed to do was go down de pound and pick da walking flea circus up, den turn up on her doorstep with her hairy baby. Den *boom*, happy families, once again.

But, as I saw Busta in front of me, I looked at my chewed-up stump and got to thinking about all the fucking misery he had caused me and my family, and that dreaded black dog chomped on my thoughts once more.

Seeing Busta wagging his tail without a care in the world just flipped the trigger. I just wanted to smack that whining snout of his as hard as I could. Instead, I walked away, and left de mutt for the needle.

"You heartless bastard!" The girl sobbed. "You fucked up heartless bastard." She dropped to her knee, ignoring the hot piss on the floor, and wrapped her arms around Busta's shaggy coat.

"You know what...you don't deserve a dog like Buster, anyway." She sniffed as Busta whined, licking her face nervously.

"What the hell did this dog ever do to you, mister?"

I turned and stared at them both huddled on the floor.

"What da hell did that dog ever do to me!" I

replied. ma blood boiled, and ma temples throbbed wit the accusation.

"WHAT DA HELL DID THAT FUCKING MUTT EVER DO TO ME?" I shouted, spittle and fury flying from ma mouth, man, as I lifted ma stump and pointed it at them. The girl winced at my pain as Buster shrank away.

I was ready for the kill, I wanted vengeance so bad.

Then I stopped.

I stopped and thought about her question. What *had* Busta ever done to me?

Nothing.

Busta' had done nothing to me. Not a single fucking thing, except be there to take ma drunken fury each night, and still save my sorry life by dragging me from the fire by the very stump I used to beat him with. He was de one who tried to protect me from the black dog that circled me every day.

It hit me like lightning, god's truth. He was the only loyal friend I had, and I beat him for it. My cheeks flushed with guilt as I lowered ma stump. Den I just stood there as they both stared back at me.

"Nothing," I mumbled, lowering my gaze, "Man, he ain't done nothing to me, ever…except be there for me!"

The room pulsed in and out of focus. I felt sick, grabbing onto de counter with the dog treats and collars. All dis time I had been fighting de monsters in my head when it was me who had been the biggest fucking monster of them all.

No, that wasn't true. When I thought about it, I reckon Maggie was de real monster in dis whole shit fest. She left me when I needed her most. Spat me out like a piece of chewed gum.

Her fault. It was her fault. All of it!

I spun away from Busta and da weeping girl and threw up on de counter. I couldn't help it, any of it. Maggie had just dumped me on de side of the road like the fire-damaged microwave on the grass verge.

"I'll fucking kill her," I muttered as da demon's revenge swam in ma head.

Something wet nudged my stump, breaking the maddening thoughts. Busta was looking up at me, his ears back and his tail tucked under his belly. His whining was low, almost pitiful, as he licked at what remained of my nightmares.

"Oh shit, fella..." I choked as I understood de pity in Busta's one remaining dopey eye.

"Oh shit, Buster...what have I done!"

It was da first time that I had really seen Buster

through sober eyes since returning from over East, and these eyes of mine filled up with utter shame.

"Hey, boy." It was all I could manage as ma voice broke through another gasping choke.

I watched as his tail slowly lifted, his eye meeting mine, and I saw the fear lifting slightly from his gaze as he cautiously began to walk around me, sniffing at my scent.

The alcohol was gone now, I had been a clean a while, and he could tell.

"You should leave now, Sir," the girl said with fear in her eyes, probably slightly pissed that I had thrown up on her counter.

"Please, Mr Eubanks, just leave." The order was now a plead.

"I'm taking Buster home with me," I replied, and before she could protest, I had his lead in my hand and was walking him to the door.

"Let's get you home eh, Buster."

The girl stepped forward to block our path, den stopped after sizing me up and decided against tackling the six-foot-tall angry Caribbean fella staring at her through his wild bulging eyes.

"I'll call the police..." she began, but I was already walking from da shop.

"You know where I live, sista'," I replied, leading Buster outside. I doubted da police would be hunting the scary nigga' who stole his own dog back from the dog pound.

It was a new address, but not hard to find, seen as our bank account was still in joint names. I had thought about just keeping Busta at my place and hiding him from Maggie, but that was just fucked up. Buster was her dog, and she seemed genuinely upset when she thought he was lost in the fire.

So, I made the long scenic walk to her place, throwing Buster sticks as we walked through da field, finally stopping outside her garden gate. Buster never strayed from my side, and I never once needed to pull on his leash. I noticed him gaze up every few lampposts as if he was making sure I wasn't turning back into da old me, the angry me, and I got the sense of finality with our reunion, as if he understood what was happening to me. He was going home. Home to Maggie, and he looked as content as I felt.

And who knew, maybe dis would bring Maggie and me back together again. I actually smiled at that idea, and da possibility of seeing our child. Rekindle our love for each other.

I rang the doorbell to her new flat and waited, and a hopeful smile spread on my face, feeling good for da first time in ages. I stood back from the large wooden door, patting Buster on the head with my stump as he looked up and managed a panting smile back. I felt full of hope and promise. It had been too long since I had seen ma ivory queen.

After a moment, the door cracked open, and a white pasty face dude appeared in the opening. He looked at me, his pale face giving me da once over, then he lowered his gaze to Buster.

"Buster!" he cried and opened the door wide to greet the mutt.

"Hey, thanks mate. Are you from the pound? We've been looking for him for an age!" he lied.

"Who is it, honey?" Maggie called from da next room, as Buster backed off and began growling.

"It's Buster, honey! They found Buster!" He laughed, and Maggie stepped into da hall.

"What? are you serious?"

I wasn't sure what I was seeing at first; Maggie hurrying to da door with our baby in her arms.

Ma eyes wouldn't process de scene properly. Maggie saw Buster first, den followed his long lead to me. That's when I saw the colour drain from her face too.

"Chris!" she stumbled as Buster growled, baring his teeth at da pasty white guy bending down to pet him.

"Maggie...what da fuck...who's this?" was all I could manage as I stared at de guy, and den over to the ivory baby in her arms.

"What the fuck is going on?" I asked, the smile sliding from my face as fast as de song now spinning on da decks in ma head.

"One of these kids is not like the others..."

I looked down at the kid's white face, and then to Maggie's heavily made up pasty face...and den to his! Buster was straining on da leash now, his teeth snapping as da scared guy began backing off.

"Jeff, get inside," Maggie was mumbling, but all I was hearing was da same tune beat building in my head.

"One of these kids is not like the others..." Around and around, bouncing from wall to wall, ma head spinning, ma anger bubbling.

"What da fuck, Maggie! Are you fucking dis guy?"

"One of these kids is not the same..." Around and around.

Ma eyes bulged, seeing stars, as Buster began barking and snapping at dis man, his lead pulling tight as he rose up on his back legs, snapping and jerking to be let free as if he knew all along what had been going on behind my back. Snapping and twisting, jerking and pulling.

"Chris…you don't understand. Jeff was there for me while you were gone…"

Buster was pulling hard on the leash, twisting and whining to be let free, pleading with me to seek justice for da both of us as we stood der face to face with our deceiving partners. Jeff was the reason for the long walks. And buster hated him for it. He knew what Jeff was doing to Maggie and me.

He barked to be let free, barked at me to let go of his leash.

So, I did.

I let him free.

And then I watched as he bounded up the stairs to the doorway.

I heard de screams as Buster's large teeth tore into Jeff's flesh, tearing out chunks from his leg muscle as they all crashed and struggled on da floor. Maggie screamed, pleading for Buster to stop, pleading for me to help her as Buster savaged them both. But I just stood at that doorway and closed my eyes as that Jeff wailed in horrendous gurgling torment. I kept my eyes closed, but still watching on in my mind as legs kicked and arms flailed, one big bloody twister party, wriggling and writhing on da bloody floormat—left leg here, right ear here, intestines here!

Crashing wall units fell to da floor as Maggie's blood splattered up da floral wallpaper and spurted to de ceiling. Buster barked and snarled and lunged again and again as Jeff's twitching leg kicked at de open door, and it slowly closed on da bloodbath before me.

The screaming finally faded, and da wailing ebbed to just a sob as the struggle faded to just the odd knock from a shoe heel on Maggie's wooden flooring.

Then there was silence.

I stood der for a moment, waiting. And after a while, the door slowly creaked open again…and it was Kandahar all over again.

Buster was noisily feeding on the imposter and the cheat of the man who had been fucking ma ivory queen behind ma back. The very same woman who had promised to love me through sickness and health.

Busters snout was deep inside the dead man's chest, his teeth tearing at de frothing organs spilling from his wounds. When Buster looked up, I saw him stare at me, as if that dog knew about revenge.

I got your back buddy, he said, den licked his

bloody face and stuck his snout inside de shawl by Maggie's side.

I sighed, breathing in the fresh air outside, den stepped forward, careful not to stand in the puddles of oozing crimson spilling from Jeff's throat, and made my way over to Maggie's twitching body.

I pushed Buster aside, patting his head as he panted happily, then I stared down at ma ivory queen for a moment, the baby blanket draped over the wriggling child. Busta sat proudly by the crying baby as I bent ma knees to squat by her legs, and hesitated before I slowly pulled back de bloody baby shawl by her side.

Tears welled in ma eyes as I saw de little white face of the baby boy Maggie had hidden from me all dis time.

"Hello, son!" I smiled, lifting up his tiny helpless body and cradling him to ma chest as Buster licked his snout and sat by my side.

"Good dog!" I whispered, stepping outside and closing the door behind me.

Our Love Cannot Be Broken

by Shawn M. Klimek

Oh darling, wipe away your tears,
Now that the truth is spoken.
The weight you've carried all these years…
The silent pain, the secret fears,
Were all in vain, since it appears,
Our love cannot be broken!

Though tears look sweet on any bride,
Your rosy cheeks should smile now!
I'm not the least alarmed you lied
About your youth! Who doesn't hide
Some awkward truth because of pride?
I've done that for a while now!

These pearly whites you so adore,
For instance, are just dentures!
But that's not what you love me for!
True love is blind! And what is more,
What petty kind of love takes score
Of censored sins with censures?

If I were brazen, self-obsessed,
Perverted or immodest,
By now you'd know that, when undressed,
I have no bum, a concave chest,
My manhood's some genetic jest,
And where my skin looks oddest!

We both have all our lives to share
And love to see us through it!
With love like ours, why should we care
If one of us, once, on a dare,
Hijacked a bus of kids somewhere,
And blithely set fire to it?

BAD *Romance*

So what if all my friends are thugs,
And parole officer is missing?
"*So what!*" says a love like ours, and shrugs!
So what if I spend our dough on drugs?
While we can depend on heartfelt hugs
And (once this sore heals) kissing!

Now, there you go with those tears again!
And trembling like a loose rivet!
Don't worry a cluck, my little hen.
I'm not like those foul, fickle men
Who throw in the towel before counting ten,
Whatever it is, I forgive it.

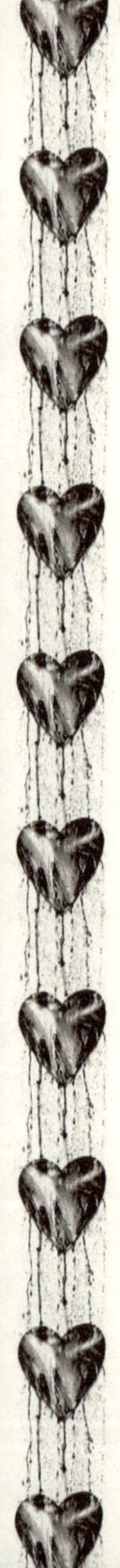

A Solution

by Stephanie Scissom

I stared out my screen door at the man on the tractor and wondered when it'd all changed. When we married 32 years ago, I'd been so madly in love, and I was sure he'd felt the same. We'd had everything going for us. Steven was a hard-working farmer and I was an LPN at the local hospital. Everyone had thought we were a perfect couple—everyone except my father.

My father was a practical man, and like Steven, he made his living with his hands in the dirt, digging ginseng and other plants in McMinnville, Tennessee— the nursery capital of the world. They should've had a lot in common, but my father took an instant chill to Steven, and it persisted until Dad died in 1994. Seconds before he'd walked me down the aisle, he'd grasped my hands and said, "Addy, you don't have to do this. It's not too late."

I'd laughed and kissed his cheek, dismissing it as wedding jitters, but I wondered now what he'd seen, and what I hadn't.

Maybe it started with the miscarriages—my absolute, utter failure to give Steven the son he so wanted. He'd stayed beside me during the first one, holding my hand as we both grieved. By the third, I grieved alone while he drowned his sorrows at the bar.

The devil wears black and he goes by Jack, the saying went, and I believed it. Steven was a bitter, hateful drunk. The words he'd spew first shredded my heart, then scarred it and made it tough as gristle. It should've mattered more when I found out about his first affair, but all I felt was relief when I heard his truck rumble out of the drive after he fed the cows. We were both tied to the land and the sprawling house we'd built together. I'd invested too much time and money in this place to be forced to sell it in a divorce.

So, I worked nights at the hospital while Steven did God knows what in town, and spent my days sleeping or tending flowers in the small greenhouse my father had built for me while Steven worked the fields.

In early 2019, I fell asleep at the wheel on my way home from work and wrecked, shattering my pelvis and damaging my spinal cord. A doctor I worked with regularly had tears in her eyes when she told me I'd probably never walk again, but my husband's face was stone.

One night after my third surgery, I told Steven I didn't know how much more pain I could endure. He merely looked at me, then pointed at the gun cabinet and said, "There's you a solution."

Then came the soliciting call from the insurance company, where I learned that the life insurance policy Steven had carried on me for years was much bigger than he'd led me to believe. I knew it existed, but I thought ours were the same, enough to cover our mortgage if something happened. When the lady asked if I wanted to match coverages, I accepted, citing my recent disability and had it drafted from our savings account, where I knew Steven never checked.

Two months later, after a morning spent in my greenhouse, I rolled myself inside the house and found Steven sitting at the table, red-eyed and hungover from the night before, clutching a coffee cup in his hands. I glanced at the beige streak of make-up on the shoulder of his white t-shirt and rolled my eyes. He followed my gaze, sneered, and drained the rest of his coffee.

"It ain't like a broken old hag like you can satisfy

me," he said as I rolled to the kitchen to make another pot.

When I returned, he said, "Look at yourself. I couldn't live one day like that. You're pathetic."

He took a pistol from the cabinet, loaded it, and laid it on the table. I ignored it and poured him a fresh cup of coffee.

"Why don't you do us both a favour and end this?" he asked.

"I think I will," I murmured.

He looked at me in surprise, then sipped his coffee. When I said nothing else, he finished the cup and stood to go outside. As he walked by me, he brushed a kiss on top of my head and said, "Good girl."

I took the cup to the sink and carefully cleaned both it and the pot and put them away. I hadn't heard the tractor start, so I glanced outside through the screen door. Steven stood beside it, staring back at the house. He looked a bit queasy. Then he jumped on the tractor. I quietly shut the door and went to get the gun.

I carried it to the bedroom, cleaned it with my shirt tail, and placed it in the top drawer of his nightstand. Then I took a couple of sleeping pills and lay down to nap.

When I awoke, it was nearly dark. I made my way

to the kitchen and opened the door. Steven lay slumped over the wheel of his tractor, in the same spot I'd left him.

I thought about my father and the wolfsbane he'd planted in my greenhouse. He'd stared at the pretty purple blooms and said, "Now, don't ever touch these with your bare hands. It doesn't take much of this to kill a full-grown man."

I knew the aconite in wolfsbane would make it look like a heart attack. The only symptom that would show in a standard autopsy was asphyxia. It took a special machine to detect aconite, and that would be even harder if decomposition had started.

I made myself a sandwich and rehearsed what I was going to say to the 911 operator.

 BLACK HARE PRESS

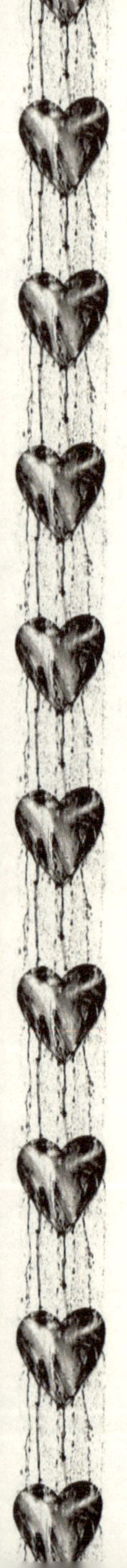

The Way We Carve Love in Our Eyes

by Terry Miller

Nancy Woodward loved Ian Carver, at least, that's what she always said. Ian loved Nancy, there was no question about that one. He'd given up a decent paying job to move so she could be closer to her family. It was the least he could do since she had moved to be with him during her college years. But college was over now, and he wanted to make her happy no matter the cost to himself. After all, he planned to continue his education as well, and it happened to be much cheaper at the community college near her hometown of Pennington, IL.

That was two years ago. Now, he didn't know where she was half of the time. They had one car between them, and many times she'd drive him to work so she could have the car to hang out with this or that *friend*. She worked too, and when he had the car, he was always there on time and excited to see her. But when he would call her to pick him up, he would often wait up to half an hour for her to get there. That's when he really began to get suspicious. Being the lovesick puppy he was, though, he forced himself to push all of it to the back of his mind.

One night, after she returned home from *visiting a friend* on Ian's night off, it happened. He confronted her, but she merely replied that she had no idea what to say. Then she broke down in tears, hands covering her face, and the haunting words escaped her quivering lips, "I'm not happy!" His whole world crashed down around him in the matter of a second. His suspicions were confirmed. She admitted that she had feelings for another man. *Classic.*

That little trip down memory lane brings us to the current situation. Ian sat at a small drop-leaf table in the corner staring at Nancy sleeping soundly in the bed, burger grease dripping from his goatee. He wiped it with his arm sleeve and took a drink of soda. The basement reeked of piss and shit, but his stomach had become acclimatised to the odour. He figured it was time to change the sheets and give Nancy a bath.

"Hey, hey, Nance, wake up!" He shook her shoulder. She opened her eyes, but didn't look at him. She just stared at the wall.

"What do you want, asshole?"

"Come on. It doesn't have to be this way. I just want you to see how much I love you."

"You love me? *You fucking love me?!* Is that why you have me down here chained to this disgusting bed?!"

Ian took a deep breath, exhaled, and looked at the floor. "Look, just give it time. You'll see." He put on some disposable gloves. "Now lift yourself up when I tell you to so I can get this sheet out from under you." She was quiet, but she obliged. It was always better to listen than fight.

The sheets were changed but the smell still lingered, soaked into the mattress. The handcuffs were tight around Nancy's wrists and Ian refused to loosen them even the slightest bit. She had small wrists, being so petite. She twisted and wiggled, but it only served to dig the metal into her skin. There was no escape. She knew it. After countless days in her prison, she accepted that she would likely die there. Ian wasn't right. Something had snapped in him and it was all her fault. Maybe she deserved all of this, just like he said when it began. Who knew how far he'd devolve and what he'd do to her as a result? She had seen too many crime shows to want to entertain the idea, but her head refused to let her think of anything else.

The basement door opened, and Ian descended the stairs in an apparent foul mood. He dragged over a chair from the table and sat at the foot of the bed staring at Nancy. She moved her eyes to meet his, there was something unsettlingly in his stare, *different*.

"You know something, Nance? You're the most beautiful girl I've ever seen. Maybe that's the problem. You're *too* beautiful. Guys can't help themselves." His eyes were bloodshot, he was either drunk or had been crying.

"Don't be ridiculous, Ian." She didn't know what to say to the remark. All she really wanted to say was *fuck you*!

He laughed and wiped his nose with the back of his hand. "No, I'm serious. Maybe if you didn't look like you do, there wouldn't be so many opportunities; you wouldn't have cheated. I mean, I've really thought about it. Like, all day."

"Ok, whatever then." She was clearly agitated. His facial expression revealed that he was on the way there as well.

"No. I mean it. Perhaps if…if you were more average looking, you'd still love me." His voice shook.

Nancy almost felt sorry for him. It was clear he was broken. He had done so much for her, but could she really help the way she felt? Was it really a matter of fault and not just the regular course of things?

"Nance, please, just listen. I have an idea, but first we have to eat. I'm starving. After we eat, I'll explain it all to you. Will you eat with me? I'll feed you."

The thought of his fingers near her mouth disgusted her. Maybe she should just bite them off. She knew better. She agreed.

"Good. I picked up tacos," he happily announced.

Nancy finished off half of her soda. She was sleepy. She slept.

Ian began to carry out his plan. It would be easier for her to accept if he *showed* her than if he just told her. Visuals had always served him better, anyway. The knife was sharp. His hands felt the smooth skin of her face for what would be the last time. The blade traced her left cheekbone, cutting deeper as it descended. The blood that trickled down assured him this was the right thing to do; it was the colour of roses, of love. He shaved a couple of layers from her forehead, the knife carving the shape of a heart in the dead center. She, too, would see this was an act of love.

He continued with his masterpiece until he was satisfied. Only he wasn't satisfied. It was hardly fair. She would live with all of these scars while he had none. Standing in front of a mirror, he began to disfigure his own face. She would see that they were the perfect match, just like he had always said. He cut until the pain was too much and he fell unconscious to the floor.

Hours passed before Ian came to. He heard groaning coming from the next room where Nancy remained handcuffed to the bed. Struggling to stand, he pulled himself up at the sink and slowly moved into the room. She mumbled incoherently, obviously still under the influence of the drugs from her drink. He had done a job on her, but he didn't look too well, either. *This would do it. It had to.*

About another hour passed before she caught her bearings. The pain settled in. As her eyes focused on Ian, she knew what he had done. She couldn't feel her face with her hands, couldn't see herself in a mirror, but with the pain and burning sensations, she knew. They would both be scarred for life.

"Now we're perfect, Nance! Just like I told you I thought we always were. I just needed you to see it." He smiled, dried blood at the corners of his mouth.

For weeks they stayed in that basement. Before executing his plan, Ian stocked the fridge and pantry well enough for a few months. They talked. Nancy even began to smile again.

The following Valentine's Day, Ian and Nancy stood on the corner of Fifth Street and Vine. A couple passed, the woman with tears in her eyes while the man bore an arrogant grin. Nancy glanced at Ian. He nodded. The couple turned the corner, and Ian and Nancy followed.

The basement was damp and cold, the room still stank of piss. The couple lay handcuffed to the bed, sleeping. Ian and Nancy finished off some tacos at the drop-leaf table, then Nancy sharpened the knives.

BLACK HARE PRESS

Clichés and Truth

by Virginia Carraway Stark

I lay awake, watching his chest rise and fall. I reached a tentative hand out and I could feel his warm breath on my fingertips, but I didn't quite dare stroke his face, even though my fingers longed for nothing more than the feel of his skin against mine.

I closed my eyes when I heard his breathing change. He moaned. I could hear him open his eyes in the darkness. You don't believe me? That's fine. *He* thinks I'm crazy too. But that's the truth; I could hear the minute sound of his eyes pull open against the soft line of mucus that had formed in the hours he had been sleeping. We were facing each other, curled up together like two little beans. I had let my hand fall so that it was close to his hand, so close to his…it would be easy, the easiest thing ever, for him to reach over and touch it, take it in his…not even a kiss, just a touch.

I consciously breathed deeply, restfully, giving out the impression of trusting love, not a care in the world. I knew that I looked adorbs when I slept; he used to take pictures of me when I slept. It wasn't a creepy thing; he took pictures of me all the time. He *used* to take pictures of me all the time. He didn't anymore. He didn't notice much that I did anymore, and when he did, it was never the right thing.

My heart was still his and I couldn't help myself. I knew he wouldn't touch my fingers, but all I could do was lie there and pray that he *would* touch them. Instead, he grumbled and kicked out at my feet that were on his side of the bed. I slowly pulled them away from the invisible boundary that cut the bed in two.

I opened my eyes again after his breathing returned to normal after a few ragged snores. The moonlight came through the window and made it easy for me to pick out the auburn colour of his hair; it stuck up, unruly in the moonlight as it was in the sunlight. I tried with all my hurting heart to hate the back of his head, but I couldn't; I wanted to cry instead. I loved him.

I had come to him damaged, and he had told me that he was okay with my baggage. It had taken two years for me to feel safe enough to unpack my spiritual suitcases after we moved in together. He had his work schedule changed, and then his mother had died, so, there were reasons for why he had seemed different. Good reasons. It had taken awhile for me to clue in that one of those very good reasons was that he had lied to me when he said he was okay with my baggage. I'd shown him my wounds, my flaws, and all my dirty laundry, and he had decided that he didn't like what he had seen.

It was the worst thing that could happen. A nightmare. We had fallen in love with each other; it hurt us both on a physical level to be apart from each other when we had first met. Burning tears were silently working their way down my cheeks. I hated these nights of lying in the dark and crying silently, hoping he wouldn't wake up and ask me why I was crying because I wouldn't have the self control not to tell him, and then we'd end up fighting about it.

He always had a good excuse for his actions. He'd be furious if I blamed him for how he acted in his sleep, but wasn't that the most telling? How close someone wanted to lay beside you in bed? We had entangled our legs at the start, and our arms. We would wake up, one of us would start to kiss the other…sometimes I'd wake up already in the act of passion. It was some of the best love making I had ever had. Even with the tears on my cheeks, I smiled at the memory of his lips, how they'd craved my lips, how he'd craved me!

I got out of bed. He used to always wake up when I got up, but he didn't now. I sat on the couch in the dark. I couldn't stand being so close to him, but so far away. That was such a cliché. Clichés are just clichés because they're true. That's what my mother had always told me, and it turns out she was right.

I hadn't thought I'd ever feel like I could love anyone the way I loved Clayton. I'd loved before. Philip had been my love before, but it hadn't been like this at all. He'd been vicious to me. Cruel. He'd hurt me and he'd humiliated me in front of his friends. He'd even gone so far as to make me do things with… I stopped my mind mid-thought. It was exactly those sorts of alleyways of the mind that had gotten out of hand, had been confessed, and had led to Clayton despising me. I saw it on him. I disgusted him.

There had to be a way to *make* him love me. Make him forget about the things I had told him and force him to remember that I'd once been the most precious thing in the world to him. After all, nothing had changed. I hadn't changed. All that had changed was what Clayton knew about me.

As quietly as possible, I started cleaning the house. It was something I frequently did when I was stressed out. I had done it all throughout the trial after Phillip's death. It was the only thing that helped. I got down on my hands and knees, still in the red lingerie I'd put on for bed the night before, and I went from smelling like Shalimar to smelling like Pinesol and bleach, my blonde hair tied back in a messy bun and yellow gloves up to my elbows.

I dumped out the mop water outdoors so the glugging of the toilet wouldn't wake Clayton up. It was coming back into the house that I saw the yellowed-orange bleach marks on my stomach from bleach splatters. I cursed under my breathe, found a red Sharpie marker, and took my tight-fitting nightie off. I was standing in my thong, my C cups pertly watching me colour over the bleached spots, when I heard Clayton's shuffling slippers. I didn't have time to get back into my nightie, so I pretended not to hear him coming.

He looked at me groggily. "Audrey, what the hell are you doing? It's three in the morning and the house smells like you were cleaning? What did you do? Get rid of a crime scene?"

"Is that supposed to be funny?" I asked, my eyes narrowing.

He froze. "Yes, actually, it was. Thanks a lot for making it very not funny. Can I use the bathroom? I've gotta use the toilet."

"Oh, well, don't let me stop you." I seethed. How dare he? How dare he bring up crime scenes? I had clenched the sharpie in my fingers and my fingers were now stained red.

"You are, could I have a bit of privacy?"

"Since when? We used to shower together. We used to follow each other around while we went to the washroom all the time."

"Oh my god, I just have to piss. Seriously, Audrey, do I have to go outside?"

I twirled on my heel; my hair flew out of its messy bun and fell in a cascade down my back. I knew I looked amazing with my naked breasts and my high, nearly naked butt, and yet when I peeked behind me, he wasn't trying to sneak a peek at me. He had turned his back and was doing what he said; using the toilet.

I squirmed back into my repaired nightie and sat on the couch, attempting to look relaxed and as though I had been unphased by our encounter. I grabbed a book

I hadn't started reading yet and opened it up halfway through so I could pretend to be engrossed in it. He walked by me, giving a sigh and rubbing the back of his neck the way he did when he wanted to say something and yet wanted nothing more than for neither one of us to say anything.

I had cleaned when I got nervous before I had killed Philip. It was a good way to keep him from getting angry; but that crime scene comment had surprised me and cut me to the quick. Clayton had known I had been accused of murder, and that it had been reduced to manslaughter and then eventually dismissed. How could he not know? It had made news headlines and we were from the same city. He'd been non-judgemental about it. He'd surprised me by how much he'd trusted me. He had surprised me so much that I'd opened up and told him everything. I think if there had been a way, he would have gotten rid of me.

The next day, I didn't see him until dinner. He brought home a pizza and forgot that I didn't like peppers. I didn't want to remind him that he'd forgotten, so I choked them down and spent the rest of the evening feeling bloated and sick. They'd always made me feel ill, and Clayton had been the one to tell me that I was probably allergic to them and should avoid them entirely. Then he brought home pizza covered in them…because he just didn't care anymore.

I tried to imagine telling him it was over. I could find someone else. I didn't need him. I could go find someone, anyone, else and never ever tell them any of the things I had told him…but I would know that Clayton was out there, and that he knew about it and was judging me. That he had judged me. He'd probably tell people about me. Maybe he *had* told people about me.

I had slumped over while we were on opposite ends of the couch. He was on Facebook, I was pretending to read my book from the night before. I'd slept all day, and tonight wasn't looking promising. I studied him surreptitiously. He could be telling people right now. I compared how things were between us. It had always been a little off balance on the trust side of things. Clayton had all of my passwords for my banking and Facebook because I only had a few and I had needed him to log in when I was busy. He never left his passwords the same and I didn't know any of his words. He even had my fuel card in his wallet because then I earned double the points, and hey, it came out of the house budget anyway, right?

I didn't know the password to his phone, he knew the password to mine. He knew all my dirty icky secrets, and the worst he'd told me was that he had once thought about stealing a five out of his mom's purse but then hadn't. He smiled at something on the screen, typed, thought and then smiled more broadly and laughed a bit, then typed some more.

I poked him gently with my foot. "What's so funny?"

He looked up, smile vanishing. "Nothing, just something from work. You had to be there."

"You used to explain those things…" I started.

He slammed his computer shut. "God! You're always so negative! Can't I just enjoy myself and smile at a joke with someone who isn't you without you ruining it? You have serious mental issues, you know that?"

I didn't say anything, I bit the inside of my lip until blood welled up but no one could see it. He took his laptop into the bedroom and slammed the door.

I had tried being honest. That had been my first mistake. I had killed someone—someone who had ruined my life and told me many times every day that he would kill me one day soon—yes, that was true. I had done it when he was attacking me; Philip had nearly killed me and not the other way around. I had fallen unconscious, covered in both of our blood, not sure which of us had been victorious. In fact, I had been pretty sure that I had failed and was dying. I had woken up in the hospital and under arrest. Fortunately, it was pretty clear I hadn't used unreasonable force.

I had a head trauma. That was true. I had post traumatic stress syndrome and vivid nightmares and flashbacks. That was true. I had injuries. That was all true. Maybe I wasn't right in the head, but he had said he was okay with that. He had said he loved me, scars and all, and that as far as he was concerned, everything that had happened just showed I was a fighter. That I was strong.

I sat there, a CD was playing a sorrowful Coldplay song wistfully in the background. I couldn't bear it. I hurt too much. I had to do something to stop the pain. I pulled back my hand and smacked myself as hard as I could across the face. I was so numb and hurt at the same time, it felt like I was losing my mind having him close the door on me like that. The smack helped somehow. I did it again. I felt like I could think a little again. Besides, wasn't this all I deserved? Wasn't that what Philip had shown me? What Clayton was showing me by shutting me out? I slapped myself again and again. It hurt my hand, I was hitting my face so hard.

The door to the bedroom flew open, slamming into

the wall it was thrown with such force.

"What are you doing now? Stop that! Stop that! I'll call the hospital."

I smacked myself again and raised my hand to do it again. He grabbed my arm, "I said stop it! You're scaring me."

"Why can't you love me?" I screamed.

"Because! Because of this sort of crazy shit! I can't handle this anymore! I'm taking you to the hospital, I think you're out of your mind. I'll make sure you get help, but you aren't my problem. I didn't sign on for this."

"Oh yes, you did! What the hell did you think you signed on for? Huh? Did you think that after what happened to me, I would just shake it off and be fine?"

"I didn't know what happened to you!"

"No, and it would have been better if you had never known. But you opened the door and told me it was safe and then you rejected me. You left me after I told you everything!"

I freed my hand and this time that smack landed on his face instead of mine. I freed myself from his hands and pushed him, I didn't mean to push him so hard, but he fell to the floor, falling back and hitting his head against the television stand when he did.

He rubbed his head and looked at his fingers, they came away bloody. "Look what you did to me." He held up his fingers with the faint smudges of blood.

I had to struggle not to laugh. He thought that was bad? Poor baby.

"Oh, did something *real* happen to you? How upsetting."

"Just because awful things happened to you doesn't mean they have to happen to everyone. Forget the hospital. I'm calling the police."

He pulled his cellphone out of the pocket of his hoodie with shaking hands. I grabbed the phone from him.

"Give me the passkey for your phone. I'll dial 911 for you," I offered.

"You don't need the passkey. Just dial it. It will put you through."

"No, I need the passkey. I won't dial it without the passkey." He started to get up. A surge of anger like I had never felt before surged through me; he wouldn't tell me the passkey for his phone so I could call 911 for him? What was he hiding?

I shoved him back down, he was off balance with his arms holding him up, so it wasn't hard. His head connected with the tv stand harder than I intended, and he blacked out but came back after only a moment.

"Audrey, did you call the ambulance?" he asked, his voice quiet, almost childlike.

I felt my heart melt in my anger. "No, you didn't give me the passkey."

"Six, one, four, two."

I punched in the numbers and went right to his messages. I'd call 911, but first I had to see if my fears were true. Maybe he would have deleted any messages anyway, or maybe I was worried about nothing.

She's mental, I think she was staring at me when I was sleeping last night.

What are you going to do? From what you said, she really is mental…like…really mental

IDK, I need to get rid of her, get her locked up and then move to a new address or something

You could move in with me <3

I'm soooo tempted today, she's more nuts every day. I don't even know if any of the things she said that guy did to her are true. Sometimes I think they are fantasies she had or worse, things she wanted to do then blamed him for, you know?

Yuck, so gross

I walked out of the room and into the bathroom, walking quickly. *I'm not going to cry. I'm not going to cry.* I dropped the phone in the toilet. No 911 calls. No calls to whoever the girl was he was talking to.

Clayton was on his knees in the other room. I had picked up a clawed back hammer from the kitchen drawer on my way back. I couldn't live with him. I couldn't live without him. But I could kill him. No one was going to find his body when I was done with him.

Already an idea was forming. I'd call his work; tell them that he'd gone hunting and hadn't come home. I could take his truck out to the middle of nowhere and leave it there…

Meanwhile, Clayton could become part of my mother's stew recipe. Is that a bit of a cliché? He'd always be part of me. Another cliché, a moment of the lips, a lifetime on the hips! I brought the claw of the hammer down. It had to be fast. No more noise, no risk the neighbours would report any screams. I'd braise the meat with the vegetables and give the bones to the dog. Good thing Clayton loved his Pitbull so much, that thing destroyed bones!

I don't think he was in pain long. Not like me. The pain lasts forever. He said it would be okay. He said he'd love me forever. He said a lot of things, and they were all lies. A hammer to the head isn't much compared to the sort of thing he'd put me through.

A Good Heart

by Wendy Roberts

Jena smiles when she sees another text from Braydon. The warm butterflies in her stomach threaten to erupt until she reads that he's working late and won't be able to make it to dinner tonight.

Something stabs at her heart, and something makes her glances out of the coffee shop window at the dark-haired man across the street.

There's a huge smile on his face as he greets another blonde that isn't her, and she sees red. Gripping her phone so tight that she might crack the screen, she watches Braydon and the blonde sit at *their* favourite table.

She is the one that should be smiling at him, holding his hand, laughing at his stupid jokes. Not this Karen persona, whose smile is far too fake.

With a huff, Jena storms out of the small coffee, determined to make him see that she's the girl for him and no one else will do.

She's half a mind to face him right now, but instead, she wipes at the tears and replies: okay, maybe tomorrow.

She won't let it get her down; she'll just have to try another approach.

That night is the longest wait she has ever endured, but there's a sense of relief when she hears footsteps and laughter from upstairs. His voice is like a calming balm to her nerves as she listens to them walk through the house. Jena grips the knife a little bit tighter and mumbles a prayer for a few more hours so they can be together as planned.

Her chance finally comes when the house goes silent sometime later. Quietly, she creeps out of the basement and up to the bedroom where the couple lie together. She's nearly at the bed when she notices one side of the bed is empty.

Panic washes over her, and she freezes, unsure of what to do when two arms wrap around her and drag her to the hallway where she fills her lungs with his scent in hopes it'll calm her down.

"What are you doing here, Jena?" Braydon holds

her tight to keep her from running away.

The tears build up as she takes another shaky breath and mutters, "I just wanted us to be together. You said you would leave her so we could be together, and I'm helping. I'm just helping."

Braydon brushes her hair from her face and turns her around. "I know I did. There's nothing I want more. I told you that."

She nods, remembering last week in the hotel room. The whole weekend was spent with him, bonding over dinner dates, and shared interests.

Her vision blurs as she breaks down in tears and slumps into his arms. Unable to keep quiet any longer, he lights suddenly go on and his wife glances from Braydon to her, gaping at them as she shakes her head and reaches for the phone.

"Give me the knife," Braydon says, grabbing Jena's hand so she'll relinquish her weapon. "It'll be okay, just give me the knife."

Jena sobs when Braydon's wife turns to speak with someone on the phone. "Please, please, I love you. I'll do anything for you. Please."

Braydon wipes the tears from her eyes. "I know, sweetheart, and I love you. We have such a good time together."

There's a finality in his tone that Jena can't comprehend and another sharp pain shoots through her chest; one that twists and tears her up from the inside as she looks down at the sight of her knife sticking out of her, just as her legs seem to give out and he lowers her slowly to the floor as she tries to make sense of what is happening.

"But...but..." she stutters, all feeling quickly leaving her body, and she looks up to his wife, her arms crossed.

"I've told you, I don't mind you playing with these girls, but you've got to watch out for the obsessive ones."

Braydon shrugs. "But those are the most fun."

He silently pleads with his wife to forgive him, using that cocky half-smile he knows she loves.

"And you stabbed her in the heart. Do you know how much a good heart would have gone for on the market?"

He shrugs. "The other parts are still good."

Kacey gives him a long look as she taps a finger on her elbow. "I'll get the tarp from the basement, you're mopping up this mess."

Braydon laughs. "Yes, ma'am," he mutters as he stands to kiss her.

The Ham That Broke the Camel's Back

by Wondra Vanian

Theirs was one of those sweet romances townsfolk swooned over for decades. Dawn and Eddie's mothers were best friends, so they knew each other from the womb. They were best friends through elementary school, hated each other in middle school, and fell in love in high school. Everyone knew they were made for each other.

Well, nearly everyone. More than twenty years into

their marriage, with their children grown and gone, Dawn was starting to have serious doubts.

"Here we go," she said, forcing the old mask of a happy wife in place as she entered the living room carrying a plate of finger foods. Unfortunately, placing it on the coffee table meant crossing in front of the television. It blared some inconsequential ball game that the men present couldn't stand to be parted from for the ten seconds it took Dawn to set the plate down and turn away. Several grumbled loudly at the interruption.

No one thanked her for the snacks.

Not that she expected them to. She was starting to feel as appreciated as that damned coffee table.

Smothering a disappointed sigh, Dawn returned to the kitchen, where she went about gathering cans of cold beer from the fridge for Frank and his friends. No one had asked for one but that was what a good wife did, right? Her task was interrupted by a bellow from the living room.

"Hey, Dawnie!"

She hadn't minded the nickname when they were fourteen. That was a long time ago, though. Now, she loathed it.

Smothering a groan of annoyance but allowing herself an eyeroll—it wasn't as though they could see her, after all—Dawn turned, shut the fridge door a lot more gently than she wanted to, and returned to the living room. Her smile was painful.

"Yes, dear?"

"Yes, dear," Larry, her husband's oldest friend, mocked unkindly. He'd never forgotten that time Dawn turned him down. In the fifth grade. Eddie gave him a playful punch on the shoulder, as if that made the insult okay. The buffoons he called friends chuckled without looking away from the television.

Dawn only realised that she'd made the mistake of getting too close when Eddie grabbed the back of her tee-shirt and hauled her onto his lap. The motion pulled her shirt tight across her chest. Larry took the opportunity to stare blatantly at her breasts.

"Come on," she said, feigning a laugh, "lemme go."

She batted his hands away playfully while her brain screamed, *Get your hands off me, you drunken lout!* It just made Frank squeeze her harder while his friends guffawed loudly.

Cringing inwardly, Dawn gently pushed her husband away. "I left the beers in the kitchen," she told him, hoping it would be enough enticement to release her.

It was.

"Go on, get," Eddie said. He smacked her ass for good measure.

"'bout damn time," one of the others complained. He squeezed a fist around the can he held, crumpling it. She looked away before she could watch him toss it aside but heard it hit the table.

Back in the kitchen, Dawn leaned against the wall. All the sloppy kisses and groping was cute when they were kids. Even when they had their own kids, Dawn's friends were jealous of Eddie's attentions. "At least he notices you," they'd say, using the opportunity to launch into complaints about all the ways their partners failed to show affection.

Affection? More like habit.

That was what it was on her side, anyway.

Her temper was getting away from her. It happened more and more often those days. Dawn balled her hands at her sides and tried to focus on breathing, like her shrink taught her. In with the good, Dr. Trent always said, out with the bad. The tentative sense of calm inspired by her breathing exercises lasted only until a "What the hell?" erupted from the living room.

In with the good, out with the bad.

In with the—

"Dawnie!"

She choked back the angry words that rose to her tongue with some difficulty. It was harder to control her fists, which beat against her legs in frustration. She'd have to come up with a new excuse to explain away the bruises when Eddie saw them…

"Dawn!"

Grabbing the beers from the fridge (but not bothering to shut it gently,) Dawn returned to the living room. Her smile was more of a grimace, not that any of the men noticed.

"Dammit, woman! Didn't you hear me calling you?"

There it was. Eddie had crossed the thin line between happy drunk and angry drunk. Seemed like it happened faster every time.

Dawn replied with, "I was just getting these." She held up the six-pack for his inspection. Eddie grunted as Larry reached across him to snatch the cans from Dawn's grip. He narrowed bleary eyes at her and held up a hand.

"What the hell is this?" he demanded. The neatly cut sandwich half fell open as Eddie waved it at her. A piece of lettuce fell onto the floor that Dawn had only just steam-cleaned the week before.

It was damned near impossible to keep that phony smile in place.

"Is there a problem with your sandwich, dear?" Only an idiot could have missed the hateful inflection placed on the word.

None of the men so much as batted an eye.

Idiots.

"Is this ham?" Eddie said angrily. "You know I hate ham!"

Dawn didn't point out the fact that Eddie had liked ham well that morning, when he'd asked her to make sure there was a plate of ham sandwiches available for the game. Or the fact that, after their *entire lives* together, she knew which damned sandwich meats he liked.

"I'm sorry," she said, the lie coming too easily to her lips. Had she always lied so easily, or was that new? Dawn didn't even know anymore. "I'll make something else."

She retrieved the platter of sandwiches and turned to leave.

"Don't forget this!"

As she walked toward the kitchen, something hit her back. Eddie and his friends laughed heartily. Looking down, Dawn saw part of a sandwich, laying in pieces at her feet. She reached up to touch her back and found the rest of the sandwich stuck to her shirt with mustard.

Something inside Dawn snapped. She could hear her husband cracking some joke, some inane quip that made his friends howl. It became a kind of dull roar in her ears, like loud wind on a stormy day beating at windows that, desperately in need of double-glazing, couldn't quite keep the noise out. Dawn couldn't make out their words but, to be fair, she didn't try.

She'd stopped caring.

For the first time in their marriage, maybe in her whole damned life, Dawn didn't care about being the good wife. Didn't care about what she should do, or what was right. Didn't even give a damn about the room full of people watching. She just acted.

Walking into the kitchen, Dawn found the knife she'd used to cut the sandwiches on the counter, next to the scarred, wooden cutting board. Absently, she noticed the ghost of mustard smeared across its blade. She stared at that yellow stain as she picked it up and returned to the living room once more.

When the roar in her head finally abated, Dawn found herself staring down at her husband. He was quieter than he'd ever been. Death does that to a guy.

She glanced around at his friends. They stared back in mute horror, backed against the walls. One clung to the hand of the man nearest him. Larry peered, wide eyed, at Dawn from behind a recliner.

"Everyone else okay with ham?" she asked in a voice so detached it didn't feel like her own.

The men nodded in unison.

Dawn said, "Good," grabbed a beer off the table and popped it open as she left the room. This time, the smile she wore was 100% genuine.

Wolf Heart

by Zoey Xolton

Zarya strode past the long line of waiting Others outside of Club X and up to the bouncer with all the authority of a queen. Before she even made the door, the red rope was pulled aside, and she stepped from the cool night and into the heat of the club. Her keen wolf ears picked up the whispers that followed in her wake.

What's she doing here? one said.

Last I heard, the Alpha had her on house arrest in the bayou... answered another.

She's trouble.

Zarya only smiled at the curiosity and unease of her subjects. Confidence, and her natural werewolf allure, rolled off her in tangible waves as she entered the fray of tangled, dancing bodies. Neon green, vibrant pink, and hot blue lighting strobed in pulsating patterns across the floor, casting the patrons of Club X into distorted forms, their shadows stretching across the establishment. The revellers jumped and gyrated, supernatural bodies close, grinding as the rhythmic tribal fusion sung through them, awakening their inner monsters.

With what appeared to be a casual, nonchalant gaze, Zarya noted that the club was particularly packed tonight, boasting a great variety of Others. There were vampires, fae, witches, shifters and bold half-breeds, and of course, there were werewolves—her kindred. Flicking her dark hair over her shoulders, she sat down at the bar, one leg crossed over the other. "Riley!" she called over the din, a smile on her face.

A chiselled and roguishly good-looking shifter sauntered over behind the bar.

"Hey, hey, hey, it's the queen!" he said, putting on the charm. "Long time no see, pretty lady. What can I get you?"

Zarya leaned forward in a conspiratorial manner. "I'm here on serious business," she teased. "I'm going to need a Heartbreaker, with an extra shot of O neg."

Riley whistled. "Heavy," he said, impressed.

"I didn't say business couldn't be fun," she returned.

Riley grinned, reaching for an array of liqueurs from under the bar. "So, are the rumours true?"

Zarya cocked a manicured brow.

"Come on, throw me a bone. It's gone around like wildfire…"

"A lady never kisses and tells, Riley."

The bartender rolled his eyes. "Fine, keep your secrets, Queenie. Drink is on the house."

"Thank you, dear Riley." Raising her multi-layered drink, she took a deep slug through the straw and turned on her stool to survey the crowd. She *had* been on a house arrest of sorts for the past three months, that part of the rumour held at least some truth. However, the vicious rumours about *why* she had been, didn't even come close.

She'd lost the Alpha's baby and had been on *bed rest* at Matthias' command. Rumour would have the French Quarter believe she'd strayed and slept with the Alpha of the Rocky Mountains Pack, or that she'd disappeared with a Mundane, a mortal. *No, the truth wasn't as titillating as lies, nor as convenient,* she mused. *There are always going to be those who will discredit my position as Queen of the Appalachian Mountain Pack.*

Born and raised in the Carpathian Mountains, she

was a Romanian princess, the daughter of one of the most feared werewolves in all of Europe. Most Others revered her out of fear, some respected her for her noble, ancient lineage, while a minority despised her as an imposter; a foreigner trespassing on their turf; an outsider who had claimed one of the most eligible, and strong Alphas in North America for her own.

Several pairs of eyes watched her, none of them making any effort to mask or conceal their interest. They thought they were predators, and she their prey. *Bold*, she thought, *or stupid*. She was spoken for, and it was known, however, there were always those willing to challenge an Alpha for his prize and territory. *Ugh! Like I'm some kind of commodity.* As a pure-blood, she knew that wasn't an image she could easily change.

Despite stalking the streets in a killer pair of heeled boots and a slinky, red dress, with nothing more than her instincts to guide her and the strength of at least twenty mortal men, few saw her as a beast in her own right; as anything more than a First Class meal ticket to a castle, title, and the power that came with claiming the daughter of one of the Ancients. Tradition and blood were everything to the wolves, and queens were always highly sought-after commodities.

None of it mattered at the moment, though—at

least not for tonight. She had one thing on her mind; a personal mission to consolidate the packs' strength and her union with Matthias. A witch—a true voodoo queen of the French Quarter and a direct descendant of Marie LaVeau—had read the bones and given her the answer to her heartbreak. The loss of her first child had been crushing, and even now a part of her longed to retreat to the mountains and mourn. But the pack needed an heir, and she wanted a baby.

Sipping from her drink again, she assessed her options. She wasn't completely cold hearted. If she was going to do this, she was going to make her choice count. A few young bloods ogled her; she could practically scent their lust in the air. They were useless and too easy. Besides, with time—perhaps a couple of hundred years—they may become half-way descent wolves. They were obnoxious and full of self-importance, but they were mere babes themselves; they just lacked guidance.

No, she thought. *I'm after a bigger, badder wolf tonight.* In the booths, at the back of the club, a golden pair of eyes glinted in the darkness, catching her attention. Unless threatened, it was unusual to display one's true eyes. He wanted her to notice him. Zarya recognised him instantly as a rogue wolf, a loner, a traitor—cast out of the Canadian Shield Pack, he'd crossed the border, seeking asylum in the United States. His reputation preceded him, and he bore a great triple scar across the left side of his face, where his Alpha had marked him before exiling him.

He's lucky he wasn't killed for trying to rape their queen! she thought. Sculling the last of her Heartbreaker, she slid off her stool and into the throng, her gaze locked onto his as she made a b-line for his booth. She danced as she walked, enjoying the music as she went. His lust was almost sickening as he leered over her. *It's a means to an end*, she reminded herself. *Just a means to an end*. She could stomach him, for a little while.

"Hi, stranger," she said, sliding onto the plush seat beside him.

Arrick smirked.

"What brings you to New Orleans? Looking for a Valentine?" she teased.

"I hear the night life is good here," he began. "Ah, Valentine's Day, is it that insipid Hallmark holiday again?"

Zarya laughed, gesturing to the holographic hearts suspended from the ceiling. "Ah, kinda."

"I think the question you should be asking yourself,

Queen, is why you are here—alone? Where is your Alpha, your guardians?"

Zarya straightened her posture in a mockery of indignation, raising her brows. "Excuse me, wolf royalty or not, I am a modern woman, and I can do as I please. I can go wherever I want, whenever I want. I am beholden to no man."

"Is that so?"

"It is."

"Seems foolish, if you ask me," he said. "Modern or not, you are what you are, and you are alone."

"Maybe I like danger," Zarya said suggestively, biting her lip. "Besides, who have I to fear? You? Are you dangerous, Arrick?"

Arrick leaned back against the curved cushions, a look of absolute self-surety plastered upon his face. "Would you like to find out, pretty girl?"

Zarya smiled, though she felt nothing but latent rage building within her. *What a pig!* "I think it's going to take a few more drinks, and perhaps a dance, before I'm likely to accept any such invitation."

"Yes," he conceded. "The lowering of one's inhibitions always leads to ruin."

Zarya scoffed. "So, you think you can ruin me, *Lone Wolf?*"

"In ways you didn't think possible."

"Colour me intrigued! I'll tell you what. You go fetch me the strongest drink on the menu, and then we can see about making this a Valentine's Day to remember."

"As the lady wishes," he leered before leaving the table and sauntering off through the crowd.

Ugh. Gross. It was true. All things worth having come with a price, yet she felt dirty just playing the part that was necessary to pay it. Already tongues were wagging across the club. Lovers on the dance floor whispered into each other's ears, while patrons at the bar kept glancing back at her. She was adding fuel to the fire of the rumour mill, but that didn't matter. None of it did. Words could never hurt her.

Adjusting the thigh-split in her dress to expose more skin, she arranged herself artfully across the seat. Her long, curled hair spilled over her shoulders, teasing down her décolletage, to rest across her breasts, drawing maximum attention to her ample cleavage. *This is in the bag,* she told herself. *Just play the part, and we can all move forward with our lives. Well—almost all of us.*

Arrick hesitated for just a second as he approached their shared booth. She knew he was questioning his actions, determining if she was worth the repercussions;

if she was worth potentially incurring the wrath of Matthias.

Patting the space beside her, she leaned forward to accept her drink. As she took the tall glass, her fingers alighted upon his, and his mind was made up. He sat down beside her, and she slid nearer. "So, have you decided?" she asked. "Will you be my Valentine?"

Arrick's lower lip hung low as he drank her in.

Zarya laughed and took a sip of her drink. "Should I take that as a 'yes'?"

Arrick's rough, masculine hand came to rest upon her thigh, his fingers sliding back and forth as he rubbed nearer to her crotch.

She cringed internally but maintained her facade. "Drink with me," she said, leaning into him. "Then dance with me," she whispered. "And after that, we can take our party outside…"

Arrick leaned forward and forced her head to the side, then proceeded to lasciviously drag his tongue from the confluence of her shoulder and throat, up her neck. He inhaled deeply as he clutched a fistful of her hair. "Sounds like a plan," he said into her ear, his lips hot against her skin.

It took all her fortitude not to tear herself away and punch him in the face. He was beyond brazen. His ego was a beast of its own. She thought of her beautiful Matthias, and her insides squirmed. *I'm doing this for us.*

Raising her glass, he mirrored her. She sculled the whole glass, gulp after gulp, in one go, then slammed the glass on the table. She raised a fist in victory, tossing her hair back. "Wooo! Yeah! That's how you do it!"

Arrick finished his drink, clearly impressed.

Slipping off the edge of the seat, she wiggled to straighten her dress, drawing his attention to her body once more. "Dance with me," she beckoned, curling her fingers as she walked backwards, disappearing as she was enveloped by the mass of dancing Others. Three songs later, and he was shoving her through the rear exist of Club X and into the dingy, poorly lit alleyway beyond.

He pinned her against a graffiti covered wall, arms above her head. He forced her legs apart with his knee, his tongue ravaging her mouth as his free hand slipped beneath her dress. His fingers toyed with her, rubbing her through the fabric of her satin G-string. She could feel his lust, hard against her, as he enjoyed the tease. Domination was everything to him, that much was clear.

Just as he unbuckled himself and unzipped his fly, she moved, slipping out of his grasp with ease. She traded places with him, slamming Arrick into the grimy wall, her golden werewolf eyes afire.

"Let *me* play," she said, her voice thick with put-on desire. The lone wolf's expression shifted from surprise to deviant delight in a heartbeat. Trailing her fingers down his chest, she ripped his shirt open in one swift motion. Her eyes locked on his. Her fingers continued on their path until they found the waistband of his jeans, and they eased them from his hips, letting the denim fall around his ankles.

"Do you want me?" she purred.

"I want to break you, pretty girl," he replied, pulling her mouth to his. She kissed him with equal amounts of passion and revulsion, as her left hand grasped at his groin. He groaned into her mouth and she pulled away ever so slightly. Cupping his face, she pressed her forehead to his before meeting his gaze with a frightening intensity.

"And what if I want to break you?" she growled.

In the next second, her left hand was crushing his throat, lifting him a foot up off the ground. He gagged, choking, his legs dangling as her right hand smashed through his rib cage and ripped his still beating heart from his chest. His wide eyes stared blankly as she dropped his meaningless corpse to the asphalt.

Licking her lips, she grinned at the pulsating organ clenched in her fist. "Yon lavi pou yon lavi," she said aloud, thrice; *a life for a life*, in old Creole, as the Voodoo Queen had instructed her. Then, eyes glowing under the full moon, she devoured the traitor's heart, licking her fingers clean of his thick, crimson essence.

Taking a deep breath, satisfied with the outcome of her mission, she adjusted herself and left the alleyway and the dead werewolf behind. Mattias awaited her return to the mountains, and they had a baby to make.

BAD *Romance*

Author Biographies

BLACK HARE PRESS

A.L. PARADISO

Author of *Romance on Wheels*

A.L. Paradiso was born in Europe, English is his second language, following Italian—then Latin, Pig Latin, French and assorted computer languages. In college he took a dislike to writing of any kind and swore never to try that again. Well, some years later, influenced by Babylon 5's creator and his own pressure to write about two traumatic events, he turned to creative writing. As of 2018, he has shared 126 published stories with others online, in four anthologies and two literary journals. We suppose he's one of those who just can't keep a job!

Amazon: www.tinyurl.com/Paradiso-dragons
Books2Read: books2read.com/ap/RWjj5e/AL-Paradiso

ANGELA ZIMMERMAN

Author of *The Anniversary Dinner*

Angela Zimmerman is a writer living in the Southern United States. She has been published in Unnerving Magazine and Coffin Bell. You can find her personal writings at Conjure and Coffee.

Website: conjureandcoffee.com

ARCHIT JOSHI

Author of *Up in the Tree House*

Archit Joshi is a published author who loves writing character-driven stories. He also works as a content writer, and is eager to add more and more writing styles to his arsenal. His fiction has found a home in many reputable anthologies and online magazines, with works ranging from short stories to drabbles (100-word stories) to 10-word micro-fiction. Many of the anthologies he's featured in have reached bestseller status in Australia, France and other regions. These include 'Sea Of Secrets' (Dragon Soul Press), 'Blaze' (Clarendon House Publishing) and 'Worlds' (Black Hare Press). Archit hated coloring within the lines as a child.

C.L. WILLIAMS

Author of *Foreword*

C.L. Williams is an international best-selling author currently living in central Virginia. He has written eight poetry books, four novellas, one novel, and a contributor to a multitude of anthologies and magazines. His most recent anthology appearance ANGELS: Dark Drabbles #2 from Black Hare Press became a number one in hot new releases. C.L. Williams is currently working on his second novel and a new poetry book.

Facebook: writer434
Twitter: @writer_434

CHRIS BANNOR

Author of *The Call*

Chris Bannor is a science fiction and fantasy writer who lives in Southern California. Chris learned her love of genre stories from her mother at an early age and has never veered far from that path. She also enjoys musical theater and road trips with her family but is a general homebody otherwise.

Facebook: chrisbannorauthor
Website: ChrisBannor.com

CINDAR HARRELL

Author of *Red Fallen Snow*

Cindar Harrell loves fairy tales, especially ones with a dark twist. Her writing is often fairy tale inspired, but she also loves mystery and horror. Her stories can be found in various anthologies from publishers such as Black Hare Press, Iron Faerie Publishing, Dragon Soul Press, Blood Song Books, Soteira Press, Fantasia Divinity and more. Traveling is a passion for her as it inspires her imagination to run wild, especially in places that have a mystic presence in the air. She regularly moonlights as another human, but no matter who she is, she is always writing. Her novella inspired by The Snow Queen is set to release in 2020 as well as her debut novel, Lithium, and short story collection, Perchance to Dream.

Facebook: CindarHarrell

D.M. BURDETT

Author of *Mr Right*

D.M. Burdett initially roamed as an army brat, but now lives in Australia where she spends her days avoiding drop bears and killer spiders. She has published a Sci-Fi series, has short stories in various anthologies, and has published two children's series. She is currently working on the first book in a dystopian series.

Website: www.dmburdett.com
Facebook: DMBurdett

DAVID BOWMORE

Author of *Second Date*

David Bowmore has lived here, there and everywhere, but now lives in Yorkshire with his wonderful wife and a small white poodle. He has worn many hats in his time; head chef, teacher and landscape gardener. His first collection of short stories 'The Magic of Deben Market' is available from Clarendon House.

Website: davidbowmore.co.uk
Facebook: davidbowmoreauthor

DAWN DEBRAAL

Author of *Roasted*

Dawn DeBraal lives in rural Wisconsin with her husband Red, two rat terriers, and a cat. She has discovered that her love of telling a good story can be written. Published stories with Palm-sized press, Spillwords, Mercurial Stories, Potato Soup Journal, Edify Fiction, Zimbell House Publishing, Clarendon House Publishing, Blood Song Books, Black Hare Press, Fantasia Divinity, Cafelit, Reanimated Writers, Guilty Pleasures, Unholy Trinity, The World of Myth, Dastaan World, Vamp Cat, Runcible Spoon, Dark Christmas, Siren's Call, Iron Horse Publishing, Falling Star Magazine 2019 Pushcart Nominee.

Amazon: amazon.com/Dawn-DeBraal/e/B07STL8DLX

EDDIE D. MOORE

Author of *Eternity*

Eddie D. Moore travels hundreds of hours a year, and he fills that time by listening to audiobooks. When he isn't playing with his grandchildren, he writes his own stories. You can find a list of his publications on his blog or by visiting his Amazon Author Page. While you're there, be sure to pick up a copy of his mini-anthology Misfits & Oddities.

Website: eddiedmoore.wordpress.com
Amazon: amazon.com/author/eddiedmoore

G. ALLEN WILBANKS

Author of *The Best Part*

G. Allen Wilbanks is a member of the Horror Writers Association (HWA) and has published over 100 short stories in various magazines and on-line venues. He is the author of two short story collections, and the novel, When Darkness Comes.

Website: www.gallenwilbanks.com
Blog: DeepDarkThoughts.com

GREGG CUNNINGHAM

Author of *Buster*

Gregg Cunningham has had several short stories publishing by Zombie Pirate Publishing in anthology books such as Relationship add Vice, Full Metal Horror, Phuket Tattoo, World War four, Flash Fiction Addiction and Grievous Bodily Harm. Most recently, his work has been accepted into Black Hare Press Dark Drabbles series including Monsters/Angels/Worlds/Unravel/Beyond and Apocalypse, with his latest (and best) short story included in their Deep Space anthology.

Website: cortlandsdogs.wordpress.com
Twitter: @GGGcunningham

HARI NAVARRO

Author of *Tuesday Night Special*

Hari Navarro has, for many years now, been locked in his neighbours cellar. He survives due to an intravenous feed of puréed extreme horror and Absinthe infused sticky-spiced unicorn wings. His anguished cries for help can be found via 365 Tomorrows, Breachzine, AntipodeanSF, Horror Without Borders, Black Hare Press and HellBound books. Hari was the Winner of the Australasian Horror Writers' Association [AHWA] Flash Fiction Award 2018 and has, also, succeeded in being a New Zealander who now lives in Northern Italy with no cats.

Amazon: amazon.com/Hari-Navarro
Tumblr: harinavarro.tumblr.com/

J.M. AMES

Author of *Beneath the Blue Irises*

JM Ames is an award-winning multi-genre speculative fiction author native to Southern California. He has multiple short story publications dating back to 2016. One thing holds true throughout all of his stories - you can Expect the Unexpected. When not working his day job or enjoying his fatherly adventures, he writes short stories and novels, including an upcoming series. You can follow him on a variety of platforms, details on his website.

Website: jm-ames.com/contact-jm/

J.W. GARRETT

Author of *One Perfect Love*

J.W. Garrett has been writing in one form or another since she was a teenager. She currently lives in Florida with her family but loves the mountains of Virginia where she was born. Her writings include YA fantasy as well as short stories. Since completing Remeon's Quest-Earth Year 1930, the prequel in her YA fantasy series, Realms of Chaos, she has been hard at work on the next in the series, scheduled to release August 2020. When she's not hanging out with her characters, her favourite activities are reading, running and spending time with family.

Website: www.jwgarrett.com
BHC Press: www.bhcpress.com/Author_JW_Garrett.html

JASMINE JARVIS

Author of *If I Can't Be Loved...*

Jasmine Jarvis is a teller of tales and scribbler of scribbles. She lives in Brisbane, Australia with her husband Michael, their two children, Tilly and Mish; Ripley, their German Shepherd, and indoor fat cat, Dwight K. Shrute.

JODI JENSEN

Author of *Cecily's Cure*

Jodi Jensen, author of time travel romances and speculative fiction short stories, grew up moving from California, to Massachusetts, and a few other places in between, before finally settling in Utah at the ripe old age of nine. The nomadic life fed her sense of adventure as a child and the wanderlust continues to this day. With a passion for old cemeteries, historical buildings and sweeping sagas of days gone by, it was only natural she'd dream of time traveling to all the places that sparked her imagination.

Twitter: @WritesJodi
Facebook: jodijensenwrites

JOEL R. HUNT

Author of *Love Potion*

Joel R. Hunt is a writer from the UK who dabbles in the darker aspects of life, particularly through horror, science fiction and the supernatural. He has been published in a number of short story anthologies, and hopes to have released his first single author collection in early 2020.

Twitter: @JoelRHunt1
Reddit: JRHEvilInc

MICHAEL D. DAVIS

Author of *A Name Like Velma Kettering*

Michael D. Davis was born and raised in a small town in the heart of Iowa. Having written over thirty short stories, ranging in genre from comedy to horror from flash fiction to novella he continues in his accursed pursuit of a career in the written word.

MICHELE FREEMAN

Author of *Heartbreaker*

Award-winning author Michele Freeman writes horror and dark fiction. She loves crochet, chocolate, and zombies. She lives in Texas with her Viking husband and their adorable fur babies.

Website: www.authormichelefreeman.com

NICOLA CURRIE

Author of *The Power of Love*

Nicola Currie is from Cambridge, UK where she works in educational publishing. She has published poetry in literary magazines, including Mslexia and Sarasvati, and short stories in various anthologies. She has also completed her first novel, which was longlisted for the Bath Children's Novel Award.

Website: writeitandweep.home.blog

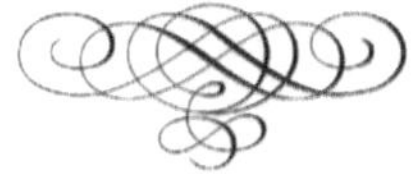

NICOLE LITTLE

Author of *No Substitute*

Nicole Little is an award winning short story writer living in St. John's, Newfoundland, Canada. Her publishing credits include Sweet Sixteen (Kit Sora: The Artobiography, 2019), The Market and Last One Standing (Dystopia from the Rock, 2019); Far Out and On a Wing and a Prayer (Flights from the Rock, 2019). Her short story Doxxed placed favorably in the Writers Alliance of Newfoundland and Labrador's "A Nightmare on Water Street: Scary Story Reading". In her spare time, Nicole can be found with either a pen in her hand or her nose in a book. She is married with two daughters.

PAULA R.C. READMAN

Author of *Just the Way You Are*

Paula R. C. Readman learnt 'How to Write' from books which her husband purchased from eBay. After 250 purchases, he finally told her 'just to get on with the writing'. Since 2010, she's had 34 stories published.

Blog: paulareadman1.wordpress.com

PETER J. FOOTE

Author of *My Fair Minstrel*

Peter J. Foote is a bestselling speculative fiction writer from Nova Scotia. Outside of writing, he runs a used bookstore specialising in fantasy & sci-fi, cosplays, and alternates between red wine and coffee as the mood demands. His short stories can be found in both print and in ebook form, with his story "Sea Monkeys" winning the inaugural "Engen Books/Kit Sora, Flash Fiction/Flash Photography" contest in March of 2018. As the founder of the group "Genre Writers of Atlantic Canada", Peter believes that the writing community is stronger when it works together.

Twitter: @PeterJFoote1
Website: peterjfooteauthor.wordpress.com

BAD *Romance*

RAVEN CORINN CARLUK

Author of *Belladonna*

Raven Corinn Carluk writes dark fantasy, paranormal romance, and anything else that catches her interest. She's authored five novels, where she explores themes of love and acceptance. Her shorter pieces, usually from her darker side, can be found in Black Hare Press anthologies, at Detritus Online, and through Alban Lake Publishers.

Twitter: @ravencorinn
Website: RavenCorinnCarluk.Com

SHAWN M. KLIMEK

Author of *Our Love Cannot Be Broken*

Shawn M. Klimek is the middle child of seven creative siblings, a globetrotting, U.S. military spouse, an internationally best-selling short-story writer, award-winning poet, and butler to a Maltese. More than one hundred of his stories and poems have been published in digital magazines or anthologies, including BHP's Deep Space, Eerie Christmas and every book so far in the Dark Drabbles series.

Website: jotinthedark.blogspot.com
Facebook: shawnmklimekauthor

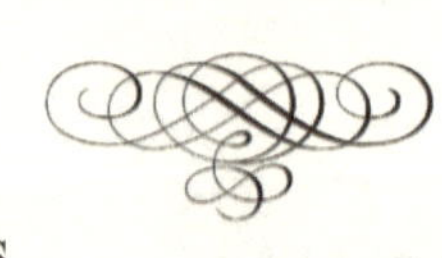

SHELLY JARVIS

Author of *Hillbilly Necromancer: a Love Story*

Shelly Jarvis is a speculative fiction author from West Virginia, US. She found a life-long love of sci-fi and fantasy in the 3rd grade when she found Madeleine L'Engle's "A Wrinkle in Time." Shelly is an avid reader, a Whovian, the ideal viewer of dog rescue videos, and undoubtedly Ravenclaw. She currently has three YA sci-fi books available for purchase on Amazon.

Website: www.ShellyJarvis.com

STACEY JAINE MCINTOSH

Author of *Stay*

Stacey Jaine McIntosh was born in Perth, Western Australia where she still resides with her husband and their four children.
Although her first love has always been writing, she once toyed with being a Cartographer and subsequently holds a Diploma in Spatial Information Services. Since 2011, she has had a vast number of stories and a few poems published online as well as in various anthologies. Stacey is also the author of Solstice, Morrighan, Lost and Le Fay and she is currently working on several other projects simultaneously. When not with her family or writing she enjoys reading, photography, genealogy, history, Arthurian myths and witchcraft.

Website: www.staceyjainemcintosh.com

STEPHANIE SCISSOM

Author of *A Solution*

Stephanie hails from Altamont, TN. She works nights in a tire factory and plots murder by day. She's currently working on a twisted apocalyptic trilogy starring Lucifer and his tortured wife.

Facebook: stephaniescissom2019

STEPHEN HERCZEG

Author of *Cold Love*

Stephen Herczeg is an IT Geek based in Canberra Australia. He has been writing for over twenty years and has completed a couple of dodgy novels, sixteen feature length screenplays and numerous short stories and scripts. His horror work has featured in Sproutlings, Hells Bells, Below the Stairs, Trickster's Treats #1 and #2, Shades of Santa, Behind the Mask, Beyond the Infinite; The Body Horror Book, Anemone Enemy, Petrified Punks and Beginnings. He has also had numerous Sherlock Holmes stories published through the Belanger Books - Sherlock Holmes anthologies.

Amazon: amazon.com/-/e/B07916SQQS
Facebook: stephenherczegauthor

TERRY MILLER

Author of *The Way We Carve Love in Our Eyes*

Terry Miller lives in Portsmouth, Ohio. His work has been featured in Sanitarium Magazine, Devolution Z, Jitter, Rhysling Anthology 2017, Poetry Quarterly, Sirens Call Ezine, The Horror Tree's Trembling With Fear, SpillWords, Organic Ink Vol. I, Curses & Cauldrons Anthology from Blood Song Books, Forest of Fear from Blood Song Books, the Dark Drabble Anthology Series from Black Hare Press, 100 Word Zombie Bites from Reanimated Writers Press, Scary Snippets, Guilty Pleasures & Other Dark Delights, 100 Word Horrors 3, and O Unholy Night In Deathlehem from Grinning Skull Press.

Facebook: tmiller2015
Amazon: amazon.com/author/millerterryl

VIRGINIA CARRAWAY STARK

Author of *Clichés and Truth*

Virginia Carraway Stark has a diverse portfolio and has many publications. Over the years she has developed this into a wide range of products from screenplays to novels to articles to blogging to travel journalism. She has been published by many presses from grassroots to Simon and Schuster. She has been an honourable mention at Cannes Film Festival for her screenplay, "Blind Eye" and was nominated for an Aurora Award. She also placed in the final top three screenplay shorts as well as numerous other awards for her anthologies, novels, blogs and other projects.

VONNIE WINSLOW CRIST

Author of *City of the Hungry Coyote*

Vonnie Winslow Crist is author of The Enchanted Dagger, Owl Light, The Greener Forest, Murder on Marawa Prime, and other award-winning books. Her fiction is included in "Amazing Stories," "Cast of Wonders," "Outposts of Beyond," Killing It Softly 2, Defending the Future - Dogs of War, Midnight Masquerade, Chaos of Hard Clay, and elsewhere. A cloverhand who has found so many four-leafed clovers she keeps them in jars, Vonnie strives to celebrate the power of myth in her writing.

Website: www.vonniewinslowcrist.com

WENDY ROBERTS

Author of *A Good Heart*

Writing short stories and novels started as a past time for Wendy Roberts and has now become a fully fledged passion. She posts short stories on her website and can be found most days on Twitter.

Website: flippinscribbler.com
Twitter: @_WARoberts

WONDRA VANIAN

Author of *The Ham That Broke the Camel's Back*

Wondra Vanian is an American living in the United Kingdom with her Welsh husband and their army of fur babies. A writer first, Wondra is also an avid gamer, photographer, cinephile, and blogger. She has music in her blood, sleeps with the lights on, and has been known to dance naked in the moonlight. Wondra was a multiple Top-Ten finisher in the 2017 and 2018 Preditors and Editors Reader's Poll, including the Best Author category. Her story, "Halloween Night," was named a Notable Contender for the Bristol Short Story Prize in 2015.

Website: www.wondravanian.com

ZOEY XOLTON

Author of *Wolf Heart*

Zoey Xolton is an Australian Speculative Fiction writer, primarily of Dark Fantasy, Paranormal Romance and Horror. She is also a proud mother of two and is married to her soul mate. Outside of her family, writing is her greatest passion. She is especially fond of short fiction and is working on releasing her own themed collections in future.

Website: www.zoeyxolton.com

BAD *Romance*

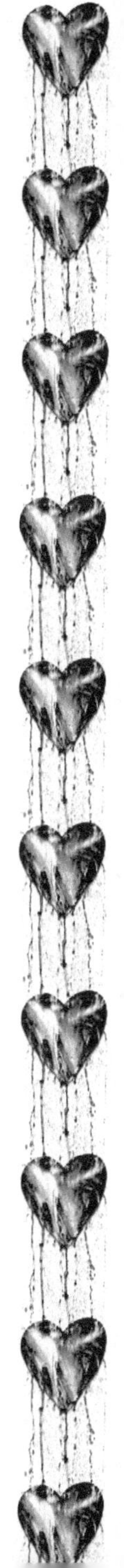

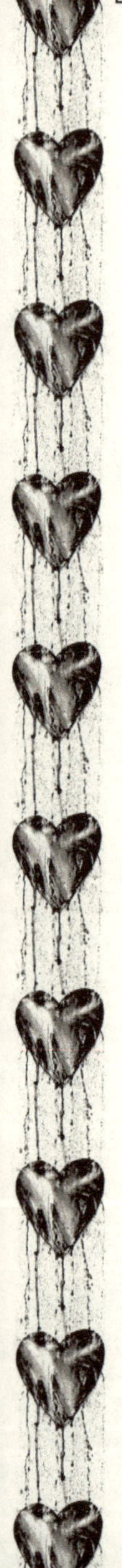

BLACK HARE PRESS

Acknowledgements

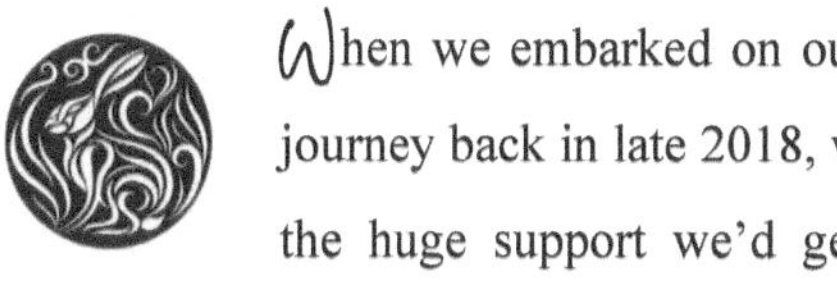

When we embarked on our Black Hare Press journey back in late 2018, we never envisioned the huge support we'd get from the writing community. We have been truly humbled by the number of submissions we've received (around 3,000 over our first eight publications!) and have loved reading every single one.

So, thank you to everyone who crafted tales just for us—from the tiny tales in our Dark Drabbles series to these un-romantic tales you have read here in Bad Romance—we thank you from the bottom of our hearts.

To our families and friends, collaborators, random strangers who took pity on us, and everyone who has helped us on the way: we couldn't have done it without you.

And to you, our discerning reader, we and these talented writers did it all for you. We hope you enjoyed these tales, and if you did, don't forget to leave a review.

Thank you all—see you next time.

Love & kisses
Ben & Dean

www.blackharepress.com

Publications

9 781925 809459